DARKNESS
FALLS

Also in the Immortal Beloved trilogy

Immortal Beloved

About the Author

Cate Tiernan was born in New Orleans, LA. She loves the idea of magick, and tries to write worlds that she would prefer to live in. She currently lives in North Carolina with her husband, four children, and a bunch of pets.

DARKNESS
FALLS
Cate Tiernan

HODDER &
STOUGHTON

First published in America in 2012 by Little, Brown and Company
A division of Hachette Book Group, Inc.

First published in Great Britain in 2012 by Hodder & Stoughton
An Hachette UK company

1

A CIP catalogue record for this title is available from the British Library

Hardbackback ISBN 978 1 444 70700 7
Trade Paperback ISBN 978 1 444 70707 6
Ebook ISBN 978 1 848 94991 1

Printed and bound by Clays Ltd, St Ives plc

Hodder & Stoughton policy is to use papers that are natural, renewable
and recyclable products and made from wood grown in sustainable forests.
The logging and manufacturing processes are expected to conform
to the environmental regulations of the country of origin.

Hodder & Stoughton Ltd
338 Euston Road
London NW1 3BH

www.hodder.co.uk

With love to my advance readers,
Nina and Piera—thanks for your help.

CHAPTER 1

want you." Reyn's voice, low and insistent, seemed to come at me from all angles. And no wonder, because he was looming over me obnoxiously as I filled a big glass jar with basmati rice from the twenty-five-pound sack we keep in the pantry.

Look at me: "we." I'm all about the "we-ness," as if I belonged here at River's Edge, rehab central for wayward immortals. Sort of a twelve-step program. Which in my case had more like a hundred and eleventy steps. I'd been a Riverite only two months and had no idea how long it would take to undo 450-plus years of bad behavior. At least several more weeks, for sure. Probably more like seven or eight years. Or longer. Ugh.

I shifted closer to the big wooden kitchen worktable and hoped I wouldn't spill rice everywhere, because God knows that would be a pain in the ass to clean up.

"You want me, too." I could practically hear his fists clenching and unclenching.

"No, I don't. Go away." Welcome to the freak-show circus of Nastasya's romantic exploits. It isn't for the faint of heart. Or the faint of stomach. Is that a phrase?

Nastasya: C'est moi. One of your friendly neighborhood immortals. Except for the friendly part. If I'm being honest. A couple months ago, I'd realized I'd good-timed myself into a wretched place of depraved indifference, and I'd sought help from River, an immortal I'd met back in 1929. Now I was here in rural Massachusetts, learning how to be one with nature, magick, peace, love, harmony, etc. Or at least trying not to feel like throwing myself headfirst into a wood chipper.

There were other immortals here: four teachers and currently eight students. Such as me. And Reyn, Viking wonderboy. For example.

Reyn: the thorn in my side, nightmare of my past, destroyer of my family, constant irritant of my *now*, and oh yeah, the hottest, hottest, most beautiful, stunning guy I had seen in 450 years. The one whose image haunted my brain as I shivered in my cold, narrow bed. The one whose fevered kisses I had relived over and over as I lay exhausted and unable to sleep.

What fevered kisses, you ask? Well, about ten days ago we'd had a mutual sudden brain attack and given in to the inexplicable, overwhelming chemistry that had been building between us since my arrival. This had been closely followed by the soul-destroying realizations that his family had killed everyone in my family, and my family had basically killed a lot of his family. That was our shared heritage. And we were on fire for each other. Fun, eh? I mean, when I hear about couples struggling because they're different religions or one's a vegan or something, I think they just need to get some perspective.

Anyway, since our make-out session/horrible realizations, Reyn had continued to pursue me with winter raider persistence and ruthlessness. And yet night after night, he—who has kicked down hundreds of doors, battered his way through hundreds of doors, set fire to hundreds of doors—had not brought himself to knock on mine.

Not that I wanted him to, or would know what to do if he did.

Are you dizzy from being flung into my world like this? I feel the same way every morning when I open my eyes to find I'm still me, still here.

Outside, the late December sunlight, as thin and gray as dishwater, had faded rapidly to a darkness seen nowadays only in rural areas. Which I was in.

"Why are you avoiding this?" In general, Reyn kept his emotions under very tight control. But I knew what he could be like—for the first hundred years of my existence, Reyn and his clan had terrorized my homeland of Iceland, as well as Russia and northern Scandinavia, earning himself the title Butcher of Winter. I hadn't known it was him back then, of course. Just that the raiders were bloodthirsty savages responsible for looting, pillaging, raping, and burning dozens of villages to the ground.

Now the Butthead of Winter slept two rooms away from me! He did farm chores and set the table for dinner and a bunch of other homey things! It was positively creepy. And of course meltingly attractive. But I still found it impossible to believe that his current "civilized" status couldn't just be ripped away like wet tissue paper, revealing the marauder I knew was still inside.

I filled up the glass jar, carefully tipped the bag back onto the worktable, and screwed the lid on the jar. A handful of snarky, sarcastic retorts hovered on my lips, and just two months ago, I would have been flinging them at him the way James Bond's car spews nails. But I was trying to *grow*. To *change*. As nauseatingly clichéd as that

was and as wretchedly painful and difficult as it was prov-
ing to be—still, I was here. And as long as I was here, I
had to keep trying.

What a revolting notion.

"I prefer to avoid things," I said truthfully while I tried
to come up with something stronger.

"You can't avoid *this*. You can't avoid *me*."

He was so close that I could sense the heat of his body
through his flannel shirt. I knew beneath that shirt lay
hard, smooth, tan skin, skin that I had touched and kissed.
I felt an almost irresistible longing to press my face against
his chest, to let my fingers trace the eternal burn scar I
knew was there. The burn that matched the one I had on
the back of my neck. The one I'd kept hidden for more
than four centuries.

"I could if you left me alone," I pointed out irritably.

He was quiet for a moment, and I felt his golden eyes
raking my face. "I'm not going to leave you alone." Promise? Threat? You decide!

I was saved from having to come up with a more worthy defense by the sound of voices coming toward the
kitchen from the dining room.

This house, River's Edge, had once been a Quaker
meetinghouse. The downstairs had a couple offices, a
small workroom, a front parlor, a large, plain dining room,
and this, a somewhat inadequate kitchen that had last

been updated in the 1930s. Before this, my most recent living situation had been an expensive, much-in-demand flat in London with amazing views of Big Ben and the Thames. I'd had a doorman, maid service, and a catering kitchen right downstairs. But my life here was...better.

Like I said, everyone here is immortal, and a fun bunch we are, too. Actually, not really. Considering we were all here because our lives were grievously flawed in many unique ways. There is in fact a River, of River's Edge. She's the oldest person I've ever met—born in 718, in Genoa, Italy, back when it still had a king of its own. Even among immortals, we were like, *Whoa.* She owns this place, rehabs immortals who are wrestling with their darker inclinations, and is pretty much the only person in the world that I even halfway trust.

I myself am 459 years old, though I have the looks (and apparently the maturity) of a seventeen-year-old. Reyn is 470. He looks like a very hot twenty.

The swinging door pushed open and Anne, Brynne, and River came in, talking and laughing, their cheeks pink from the cold air outside. They were carrying bags of groceries, which they set down on various counters. We produced most of our own food, actually, but River still bought the occasional items from the one grocery store in town, Pitson's.

"And I said, is that a *mustache?*" Anne said, and the

others almost collapsed with laughter. "And if she could have killed me, she would." River leaned against the kitchen counter and wiped tears out of her eyes.

Reyn muttered something and left through the outside kitchen door, going out into the black, freezing night without a jacket. Not that I cared. At all.

"Oh goddess, I haven't laughed like that in…" River trailed off, as if trying to remember. I'm guessing she was thinking since before Nell (another student here, who tried to kill me, BTW) went schizo and had to be loaded up with magickal tranquilizers and carted away. Just a guess.

"Is he okay?" Brynne asked, gesturing at the door. She'd been here a couple of years, I think, and of all the students was the one I was closest to. *Close* being a relative term. "Did we interrupt something?" Her brown eyes widened with sudden interest and speculation. The night she had cracked, Nell had shrieked that she had seen Reyn and me kissing. I'd hoped people would chalk it up to the hysterical ravings of a nutcase, but there had been too many meaningful glances since then to really lie to myself effectively.

"No," I said, scowling. I took the burlap sack of rice back into the pantry, then put the glass jar on the shelf.

"Well," said Anne, apparently deciding to let the Reyn thing go, "the big news is that my sister is coming to visit!" Anne was one of our teachers and looked around twenty, with a dark, sleek pageboy and round blue eyes, but I knew she was 304. Despite being 150 years younger than I was, she seemed light-years ahead in knowledge, wisdom, magick — okay, everything.

"You have a sister?" For some reason I was still surprised when I met immortals who had siblings. I mean, of course many did. But in general I felt that most immortals were more solitary creatures — like, after seventy, eighty years, anyone would get sick of their family, no matter how nice. Three hundred years was a long time to keep doing everyone's birthday parties, you know?

"Several. And two brothers," said Anne. "But Amy is nearest to me in age. I haven't seen her in almost three years."

Immortal sisters who were close. I hadn't run into too many of those. I was starting to feel like I had spent the last four centuries living with a kind of tunnel vision, a varied but narrow existence, choosing not to see, not to *know* so many things.

Finally, Anne and Brynne went out to set the long table for dinner. River unpacked the groceries, handing me a few things to put in the fridge.

"Everything okay?" River asked.

"In that sentence, does *okay* mean tortured, confused, sleepless, and worried?" I asked. "If so, then yes, I'm dandy."

River smiled. She's had a thousand years to develop the patience to deal with the likes of me.

"Am I the worst person you've ever had here?" I don't know what made me ask that question. Just—one can make a lot of bad decisions in 450 years. A *lot*.

River looked surprised. "Worst in what way?" Then she shook her head. "Never mind. No matter how you define 'worst,' you aren't it. By a long shot."

I was dying to ask who had been worse, and how, but there was no way she would tell me. Then it occurred to me that of course Reyn, for one, was worse than me, probably worse than most immortals who had come here aching to be made whole. Reyn had slaughtered entire towns, enslaved countless people, plundered and pillaged and whatnot. I mean, I'm a total loser in many ways, but you can't pin anything like that on me.

And yet Reyn was the one I wanted. Above all others. Karma had pretty much drop-kicked me into an unending universe of irony.

"So, Anne has a sister, huh?" I said, lamely changing the subject.

"Yes. She's very nice. You'll like her."

"I know why I don't have siblings," I said, skirting by that thought quickly, "but I feel like I haven't really met many other immortals who have siblings, either." I didn't weigh in on whether I would like Anne's sister or not. I don't really like most people. I can tolerate them pretty well, but like? Much harder.

"I think you'll find that immortals who are less than about four hundred years old might have siblings," River said, washing her hands at the farmhouse sink. "And those older than about four hundred rarely do."

"Why?" I asked. "You have brothers still, right?"

"Four of them," said River. She turned to me, her almost unlined face looking thoughtful. She brushed a strand of silver hair off her forehead and shrugged. "It's kind of unusual for someone my age."

"Why?" I asked again. Some weird immortal genetic thing?

"In the olden days," she said slowly, "immortals made it a habit to kill other immortals around them, to take their power."

My eyes widened. "What?"

"You know how we make Tähti magick, magick that doesn't destroy other things?" she said. I nodded. "And you know how to make Terävä magick, where instead of channeling your own power, you just take power from something else, destroying it in the process."

I nodded. The whole good-versus-evil thing. Check. Starting to get a handle on it.

"You can get that power from plants, animals, crystals…people." Her lips pressed together. "You can take someone else's power and use it for your own. But it kills them, of course. Or worse."

It should have occurred to me that such a thing could happen. It seemed stupid and embarrassingly naive not to have made that leap. But I hadn't.

River saw the surprise on my face. "You know we can be killed," she said gently.

A pain twisted inside me, a pain so familiar, so long a part of my life that it seemed natural to feel its sharp rasp with every breath. Yes, I knew. My parents had been killed in front of me. I'd seen my two brothers and two sisters also killed, beheaded. I'd walked across a carpet soaked with their blood. So, no siblings. I tried to swallow and felt a knot in my throat.

"If an immortal kills another immortal, they can take that person's life force, add it to their own power," River went on. "And then also—that's one less person who might try to kill *them*."

My breath was coming shallowly now, my quick descent into my family memory seeming to dull everything she was saying. "I see," I said, my voice thin. "So that's pretty much what Reyn's father was trying to do when he killed my family. While Reyn kept watch in the hall."

River was very solemn, and she let one hand glide along my cheek. "Yes."

CHAPTER 2

iver had bought this property, with its several buildings and about sixty acres of land, in about 1904, I think. Like most immortals, she'd been one person, then pretended to die, then came back as her own long-lost daughter to claim the property again. All immortals have a bunch of different names, histories, passports, and so on. We tend to have networks of excellent forgers, hoarding the best ones the way some people hoard their favorite clothes designer or hairstylist. But I sure do miss the days before picture IDs and social security numbers. It's so much more complicated nowa-

days to drift from country to country, incarnation to incarnation.

My bedroom, like all the others, was on the second floor. Each room is pretty sparse, with a bed, a sink, a few other items. I'd just finished throwing some clean laundry into my tiny wardrobe when I heard the dinner bell chime. Like animals responding to a feed call, all of us on this hallway left our rooms and headed downstairs. I said hi to fellow students Rachel, who was originally from Mexico and was, I think, about 320 years old, and Daisuke, from Japan, who was 245. Jess, who was only 173 but looked much, much older, nodded stiffly at Reyn, who was closing his door. I tried not to think about Reyn sleeping in there, lying on his bed —

In the large, plainly furnished dining room, the long table was set for twelve. An oak sideboard held steaming serving bowls, and a large gilded mirror reflected it on the other wall. As I lined up behind Charles, another student, I caught a glimpse of myself. Before coming here, I'd been stuck in a nineties goth vibe, with spiky black hair, heavy eye makeup, and a junkie's skeletal pallor. With yet more irony, I now looked totally different from anything I had looked like for the last three hundred years — because I looked only like myself. My hair is its natural whitish-blondish color, common among my clan in Iceland. Both my gaunt face and too-skinny body had filled out and now looked healthier. With no contacts in, my eyes were their original dark, almost black color. Would I ever not be surprised about looking like myself?

I took a plate and went down the line. Another change in my life had been my diet. At first the simple food, mostly from our own gardens, had made me feel like I was choking. There's only so much fiber a girl can get down. Now I was more used to it—used to picking it, digging it, preparing it, and eating it, whenever it was my turn to do any of those things. I would still give a lot for some champagne and a molten chocolate cake, but I no longer screamed silently when confronted with kale.

"Hello, all," said a voice, and I looked up to see Solis (teacher) coming in from the kitchen. I'd heard he was originally from England, but like most of us he had an unplaceable neutral accent. Brynne had told me he was around 413, but he looked maybe in his mid-to-late twenties. Asher, down at the end of the table, was the fourth teacher and also River's partner—I didn't think they were married. He was originally Greek and was one of the older-looking people here—which meant that at 636, he looked like he was in his early thirties. The three of them, plus River, did their best to teach us about herbs and crystals, oils and essences, spellcraft and magick-making, stars, runes, sigils, metals, plants, animals, etc. Basically, every single freaking thing in the entire world. Because it was all connected, somehow—to us, to magick, to power. I'd been taking lessons for about five weeks, and my head already felt close to exploding. And I was still in, like, magickal preschool. I had a long slog ahead of me. I hated thinking about it.

"Solis!" said Brynne, waving her fork at him. As usual, she was wearing a colorful combination of head wrap, scarf, sweater, overalls, and work boots. The fact that she was lovely in a tall, slender, teenage-model kind of way somehow helped it all work. She was 204, the daughter (one of eleven children!) of an American former slave owner and a former slave.

I sat down at the table, stepping carefully over the long bench so I wouldn't whack Lorenz with one of my high-top Converses. I hated these benches. Chairs. Chairs would be the way to go here. River should set up an "ideas" box somewhere so we could all make helpful suggestions. I could come up with a significant number, actually.

"You're back!" said Anne, kissing Solis first on one cheek, then the other.

Solis smiled, looking more like a California surfer dude than ever. His dark blond hair curled around his head in an untidy halo, and somehow he always had just the right amount of scruffy beard—not too long or too short.

There was a chorus of hellos and welcomes, and River kissed him, too.

I kept my head down and started plowing through—Jesus, what *was* this? Squash casserole? Who would *think* of something like squash *casserole*? And *why*?

"Nastasya?" Solis's voice made me look up, my mouth full of mush that I couldn't bring myself to commit to, in the belief that my stomach would hate me forever and start rejecting even good food.

"Mmm," I managed, then gave an almighty swallow. I'm sorry, stomach. "Hi."

"How are you?"

Gosh, what a loaded question. When last he saw me, everyone had just heard Nell shriek that she'd seen Reyn and me making out.

Nell had loved Reyn. For years. Desperately. And he, being an oblivious moron, hadn't noticed. And then Reyn and I sort of—exploded. And it made Nell crazy. Or, cra-*zier*. I had to believe she'd already had one arm in the straitjacket before I even got to River's Edge.

Anyway, Solis had accompanied Nell to what I assumed was some kind of asylum for immortals who were completely bananas. Now he was back. And his being back made that whole disturbing, mortifying tableau spring to vivid life again.

"I'm fine," I managed, then drank some water. Did I know enough magick to turn it into wine, I wondered. Or, better, gin? Probably not.

"Good," he said easily, and unfolded his napkin.

"Solis," Charles said. It was hard for Charles to look solemn, with his bright red hair, green eyes, freckles, and round, cheerful face, but he was doing a good imitation. "How is Nell?"

Yep, just put it out there, Chuck. Go on. We *face* things here. We aren't *afraid* of *emotion*—

"She's not good," said Solis, pouring himself some water. "Pretty raving mad, actually. But in Louisette's capable hands, and with the healers there, I think she'll be okay. One day."

Charles shook his head—it was a shame, such a nice girl—and then went back to his meal.

"My aunt Louisette has been able to create deep healing in people who were far more troubled than Nell," said River. "Nell knows that we'll be sending her our good thoughts and wishes."

I couldn't help glancing at Reyn quickly. His face was still, his jaw set, as he pushed food around on his plate without eating it. I wondered if he felt responsible in any way, because he hadn't noticed that Nell was pining for him. I didn't know.

"Oh, everyone, I'm sure you've realized this," River went on, "but tomorrow is New Year's Eve. It seems incredible that this year is almost over! We'll be having a special circle tomorrow night, as we do each year. I hope you'll all be there—I would love for us to welcome the new year together."

There went my plans to head down to New York and get plastered in Times Square.

Not really. It was an amazing notion for me, but I actually had no desire to leave here, go drinking with strangers, be around lights and noise and chaos. Lights, noise, and chaos had been my companions of choice for the last century—they were probably feeling pretty left out.

Or maybe they hadn't noticed I was gone. Maybe my pals Innocencio, Boz, Katy, Cicely, and Stratton were still giving them plenty of playtime. I'd hung out with the same friends for so long that I hadn't noticed how useless we were all getting. I hadn't noticed Innocencio learning magick, working on developing the power that all immortals have, in varying degrees. Then one night Incy had used his magick to break the spine of a cabbie who'd been rude to us. Actually *broke his spine*, paralyzing him for life. And even though he was a regular person and "the rest of his life" wouldn't be that long, comparatively, still his world was destroyed in an instant, on a whim. And that had been a real eye-opening moment for me. To put it mildly.

I sighed and pushed my plate away, wishing I had a cheesecake stashed in my room. Individual minifridges. Another valid suggestion for River.

After dinner I checked the chore chart and amazingly had no classes, no chores, nothing to do tonight. It happened once or twice a week. Whoopee! So I headed upstairs, took a hot bath, and then curled up on my narrow bed with a book about Irish herbal cures. I know, I couldn't help it: I would always be a madcap, frivolous party girl.

Soon I was deep into the wonder and delight of eyebright, feverfew, cowslips, and dandelions. Of course I'd been born long before there was any kind of chemical medicine, and plants had been the prime component of every household's remedies, along with dried deer blood, spiderwebs, etc. But the addition of magickal intent changed these plants' properties and uses. So. Much. To. Learn.

It was riveting stuff, and I'd drifted off only two or three times before I gave up and let my eyes stay closed. I wasn't totally asleep—I still sensed the bright reading light through my eyelids, still felt semiaware of my small room and the black night outside. But I was drifting, dreaming, and then I found myself waking up in a forest. Hundreds of years ago, forests were everywhere, and to get from point A to point Anywhere Else almost always entailed going through a forest. I'm not a huge fan. The occasional tree, sure. A very small grove that I can see through to the other side, fine. But not forests. They're dark, seem unending, are incredibly easy to get lost or confused in, and are full of noises and fluttering things and sticks cracking behind you. In my experience, they're best avoided.

But here I was. I felt like me but could also somehow see myself, the way you can in dreams. I appeared to be pre-River, with black hair, heavy eye makeup, superskinny and pale. That had been normal for me for years. Now, in hindsight, I thought I looked like Edward Scissorhands but without the handy blades. I was immediately aware of feeling anxious and lost, making my way through the trees, pushing through thick underbrush that slowed me down. My face and arms were scratched and stinging. The ground was thickly covered with years of fallen leaves, and it felt like walking on the moon.

I was upset, getting more upset, searching for something. I didn't know what. I just knew I had to find this thing somehow and that I would know when I found it and that time was running out. I hated being in this forest and tried to go faster, which only meant that I got more scratched. I'd long ago lost any hope of finding my way back to where I'd come from. I'd even given up on ever trying to find my way out but instead pressed on, looking, looking, feeling more tense and afraid with every step.

The light was fading, time was passing, and dread filled me as night fell. I was close to tears, hysteria—I desper-

ately wanted a fire, a friend, help. But I couldn't stop—
something bad would happen to me if I stopped. Then—
over to my left! It looked like—it was—a fire! I turned
quickly and headed toward the light, the comforting scent
of woodsmoke finding its way to me through the trees. I
heard a voice. Was it…singing? It was singing. I pushed
my way through some stabbing holly branches and then I
was in a tiny clearing, and there was a fire flickering wildly
inside a circle of rocks.

"Nas." My head jerked at the voice. I looked over to
see Innocencio, my best friend for a hundred years, stepping out of the darkness of the woods.

"Incy! What are you doing here?"

He smiled, looking unearthly beautiful. His eyes were
so dark that I saw tiny fires reflected in them. I stared at
him, feeling alarmed even as I held my hands out to the
fire's warmth.

"I've been waiting for you, darling," Incy said in a voice
as sweet and seductive as wine. "Come, sit down, be
warm." He gestured to a big fallen log at the edge of the
clearing. I didn't want to—everything in me was screaming, *Run!* But my feet took me over to the log and I sat
on it. I didn't want to be here, didn't want to be with him,
but then again, the fire was so comforting, so cozy.

"You've been gone too long, Nasty," Incy said. "I've
missed you so much. We all have." Still smiling, he gestured

around, and I scanned the place for my old gang. No one was there except me and Incy, and I started to ask why.

Then I saw. The fire...there was a skull in the fire, the flames blackening and devouring bits of its peeling flesh. My mouth opened in a horrified gasp. The fire was *full* of bones, *made* of bones. I knew in a split second that this was Boz and Katy—maybe Stratton and Cicely, too. Incy had killed them all and was burning their bodies. I jumped to my feet, only to have Incy smile at me again; he had me. There was no escape. Suddenly the wretched, acrid stench of burning hair and flesh filled my nose and mouth, gagging me, making me retch. I couldn't breathe. I tried to scream, but no sound came out. I tried to run, but my feet were literally rooted to the ground—thick, dark, vining roots covered my feet, locking me into place, and started to climb my legs.

Knock knock.

I gagged again and in the next instant bolted straight up and opened my eyes. I was gasping, wild-eyed, covered with icy sweat—in my room at River's Edge.

Knock knock.

My hands were clenched into claws, my breathing ragged. I tried to collect myself. I felt Reyn's energy outside my door, and within a second I was on my feet.

I took some gulping breaths, trying to calm down. "What do you want?" I asked through the door, trying to make my voice normal. I felt like I'd just jumped off a bridge, and I leaned against the door, shaking. I glanced at my bedside clock—it was almost ten. Most people would be in their rooms by now and many of them already asleep. Our days started ungodly early.

"Open the door," came Reyn's low voice.

"Why?"

"Just open it." He already sounded exasperated. I was getting better.

I wasn't afraid of *him*, and to convince myself of this I opened my door and stood with my arms crossed. And it was right about then that I had the blessedly normal insight that I hadn't combed or untangled my hair after my bath and then had fallen asleep on it wet. It was probably sticking out on one side of my head in a snarled clump. Coupled with the no makeup, the pillow creases on one cheek, and the feminine, come-hither getup of fuzzy socks, long johns, scarf, and cardigan, I was pretty sure I had never presented a more compelling picture.

Reyn titled his head slightly, looking at me. "Are you okay?" he asked. "You look—"

"Is that why you woke me up?" I said. "To comment on my *appearance*?" It was such a relief to be doing this, sparring pointlessly with the Viking god. As opposed to, say, seeing your former best friend burning all of your other friends in the forest.

"Come with me," Reyn said. "I want to show you something."

Frankly, I had expected something more original. "Really?" I asked. "That's it? That's what you came up with?"

He frowned and of course looked even better. Reyn wasn't a pretty boy; his features were angular, his jawline sharp, his mouth hard. His nose was a little crooked and had a bump in it from being broken who knows how many times. And he had dressed up to impress me the same way I had for him: jeans that still had bits of hay stuck to them, his beat-up work boots, a flannel shirt so frayed that the collar was about to fall off.

I wanted to eat him alive.

Forget I said that. Delayed shock.

"I'm serious," he said, looking about as serious as someone could look. "There's something you should see. In the barn."

My eyes widened. "Are you *kidding*?"

He sighed impatiently. "This isn't a trick. I thought you'd like to see this. It happens to be in the barn."

The barn was where we'd had our first, searing kiss, where his mouth and hands had woken up nerve endings that I'd thought were long dead. Every time I remembered it, his hard muscles, his urgency, I had to suppress an audible whimper.

The barn was also where we'd had the sickening realization of our shared history: his father, the clan leader of rapacious raiders, had stormed my father's castle. They'd killed everyone except me—I'd been hidden beneath my mother's dead body. But my mother had flayed Reyn's brother with magick, and my older brother had hacked his brother's head off. Later, when his father and some others tried to use my mother's amulet, they'd been incinerated. Reyn had stood there as they turned to ashes in front of him, next to him.

Anne had told me he'd been working on his anti-marauder goal for almost three hundred years. I suspected there had been more involved than writing *I will not sack villages* one hundred times on a chalkboard.

And he and I had made out like crazed high schoolers.

See my comment re: karma, above.

He sighed again: I was such a pain. Then he said, "Please."

Oh, he was going to fight dirty.

I gave a heavy, obvious sigh myself and pulled jeans on over my long johns. I didn't bother trying the laces on my sneakers, and tucked my scarf tighter around my neck as I followed Reyn down the quiet hall. I was actually thrilled to get out of my room for a while, imagining that I could still smell the slightest hint of charred skin.

Outside the air was damp and cold, turning my nose

to ice. I hated how dark it got here. Ever since I could get to a city, I'd lived in cities. Thirty feet away from the house we were encased in velvet darkness that felt like a suffocating shroud. I edged closer to Reyn, somehow knowing that despite everything he would absolutely protect me from trolls or land sharks or deadly best friends or other things that went *ka-chonk* in the night. When we reached the barn, I practically leaped through the door into the relative warmth of the hay-scented air.

It was dim and quiet inside, with only the occasional *whuff*ing of a horse. There were ten stalls, though only six were occupied by River's horses. Grooming the horses and mucking out the stables were some of my least favorite chores. For various reasons.

At the end of the barn, Reyn stopped. The stall door was open, and he gestured to me to go inside. I hesitated — was this just a straightforward plan to throw me down into some hay? I hated the fact that I felt a split second of intense longing so strong that my fingers tingled, that I felt unsure of what my response would be.

Then I heard tiny noises.

One eyebrow raised, I poked my head around the stall door...and saw River sitting in the hay. She looked up at me, smiled, and put a finger to her lips.

Curled up in the hay, one of the farm dogs, Molly, growled slightly. River said something soothing to her.

I saw one, two—six tiny squirming things nuzzling up to Molly. Puppies. I knelt next to River. I'm not a dog person. Or a cat person. Or a pet person. Pets take care, require you to think about something other than yourself, and I'd quit doing that ages ago.

Still. Even I was hardwired to melt a little when confronted by fat puppies, eyes and ears closed, tiny muzzles covered with fine fuzz.

"Molly did such a good job," said River, stroking the dog's head. Molly closed her eyes; the bulk of her work was over.

"Good-looking dogs," said Reyn. I'd almost forgotten he was there.

"Yes," said River. "We mated her with another German pointer. But—I can't explain this one." She pointed to the smallest puppy, struggling to get out from under a larger, more vigorous sibling. River gently extracted it and arranged it at the end of the milk bar, where it wouldn't be smushed.

Five of the puppies looked like miniature Mollys—solid brown heads, light gray bodies with just a hint of the liver-colored spots they'd develop later. But the little one seemed to be from a completely different litter. Possibly another species. It was thin and long-legged instead of cute and chunky, and maybe half the size of the biggest puppy. It was almost solid white except for large red blotches in an uneven pattern, as if someone had spilled a glass of wine on it.

"It's the runt," said Reyn. "Anything wrong with it? Cleft palate?"

"Not that I can see," said River. "Poor little girl. Looks like everyone else got the groceries in the womb." She stroked a light finger down the puppy's side. "Isn't it a miracle?" she murmured. "I'm always awed, always in wonder at the miracle of life." She seemed dreamy, almost wistful, an unexpected change from her usual brisk good humor.

Then she seemed to come back to herself and rose with smooth grace. "Such a good job, Molly," she said again, and Molly's tail thumped twice. "I'll be back to check on you in a bit. Get some rest." *Thump.*

I stood up and the three of us headed back out into the cold. River stayed in the kitchen to fix some broth for Molly, and Reyn and I headed back upstairs. Seeing the puppies had put me in a strange mood—I almost wished I hadn't seen them.

"I always had battle dogs." Reyn's voice was quiet as we climbed the stairs. "Half wolf, or mastiffs. Kept them hungry, so they'd always be ready to attack. Send a pack of those ahead of me, then sweep in and clean up what's left."

He was deliberately reminding me of his savage beginnings, and anger heated my blood. I opened my mouth to say something biting, full of disdain—but then I stopped. Why would he say that? Was he trying to show me how far he had come?

"Do you miss it?" I asked. "Battle? War? Conquest?" I wasn't being snide. For once.

We paused outside my door. The hall was barely lit by a few small nightlights low to the ground. It was still, silent—I could feel the quiet patterns of people sleeping.

The barest hints of emotions passed over Reyn's face, with its high cheekbones and almond-shaped eyes the color of old gold. I wondered if he would lie to me.

He looked away, as if ashamed. "Yes." He spoke so quietly that I had to lean closer to hear him. "It's what I was taught. It's what I do well." He didn't look at me.

My high horse of judgment lowered a notch.

"How long has it been?" I asked.

A quick glance, meeting my eyes, and then just as quickly slanting away. "Since I gave up leadership over my clan, three hundred and eight years. No marauding, raiding since then. But war? Battle? World War Two."

My surprise must have shown on my face because Reyn turned away again and a flush stained his cheeks. "Anyway. I thought you'd like to see the puppies."

"Do I really seem like a puppy kind of gal to you?" Having changed so much over the past couple months, I had no idea how I came off to people now.

Reyn rubbed a hand over the day's stubble on his chin. "No," he said finally. "No. Not puppies, not bunnies, not babies. But—you don't have to give that up, you know."

Okay, time for me to leave this conversation. I reached for my doorknob. Reyn's hard, warm hand stopped me. "Most of us are reluctant to have that," he said, his voice low in the half-lit hallway. "Reluctant to have lovers, children, horses. Homes. Because we've lost so many. But to give all that up means time has beaten you down—that time has *won*. I think...I might be ready to battle time again. Might be strong enough to take a chance."

Reyn was a man of few, terse words. That had been almost a whole paragraph. And it had been so self-revealing. Had he been drinking? I couldn't detect it.

My brain processed thoughts rapidly, skirting around all the possible meanings of his words. I was terrified of what he might be saying.

"So...you're going to get a puppy, then?" I asked, choosing the least scary interpretation.

He looked tired. Meeting his eyes was almost physically painful, but I refused to be the one who blinked first. His hand came up, and I kept myself from flinching. With one finger he traced a line down my face from temple to chin, the same way River had touched the runt puppy.

"Good night," he said.

CHAPTER 3

he people in the town of West Lowing (population 5,031) think that River's Edge is a small, family-run organic farm. Which is even true, to a point. The fact that we're all immortals and most of us are trying to get over meaningless lives of dark endlessness, or endless darkness, is something we don't advertise to outsiders. In fact, we hide it. But if someone were to drop by, they would just see regular-looking people weeding gardens, tilling fields, feeding chickens, chopping wood, and mucking stables.

You would think all that wholesome outdoor living

would be enough for anyone, but some of us (mostly me) were required to have jobs out in the real world as well. Asher had explained the whole reasoning behind it, but my mind had blanked after a few key words like *job* and *minimum wage*. After he suggested something like shelving books at the local library, I had started to cry inside.

Much to everyone's surprise, however, I'd been gainfully employed for almost six weeks at MacIntyre's Drugs on Main Street in West Lowing. The "downtown" part of Main Street was four blocks long and included five empty, abandoned stores, a shut-down gas station, a feed store, a grocery, a diner, a hot-dog shop (literally nothing but hot dogs), and in West Lowing's nod to international cuisine, a combo falafel/Chinese food joint.

So...stocking shelves at a CVS in Manhattan would be bad enough. I was stocking shelves at MacIntyre's Drugs in freaking West Lowing, Massachusetts. And to improve this rosy picture, my boss was an angry, bitter old guy. He was hateful to me and constantly screamed at my coworker, his daughter. I couldn't even think about what he might be like to her at home.

But it was all part of my rehab: learning to work and play well with others.

When I pushed through the front door of the store one minute before my shift started, Meriwether MacIntyre was already cleaning the front counter with spray and a rag.

"Are you still on Christmas break?" I asked, walking past her to hang up my coat.

"Yeah. Two more days," she said. Meriwether was a senior in the town's only high school. She was at least five inches taller than me, maybe five foot eight, and was one of the most colorless people I'd ever met. Her hair, skin, and eyes were all basically the same pale shade of ash brown, and her whole persona was that of an abused rabbit. I blamed her horrible dad.

Old Mac, as I called him, glared balefully at me as I skipped to the time clock and punched my card in with fifteen seconds to spare. I gave him a blithe smile and headed out front, where Meriwether and I had been trying to yank the store into at least the twentieth century, if not the twenty-first.

"Okay, so, we've got a couple of bins to put out," she said, pointing to the blue plastic bins full of products that needed shelving. We'd been slowly reorganizing the store, grouping stuff together in a more logical way instead of the way it had made sense to Old Mac's grandfather back in 1924. It was funny to think that if I had been through here in 1924, which I hadn't, I could have seen Old Mac's grandfather and his shiny new store.

"And look." Meriwether knelt and showed me several

new boxes: homeopathic medicines. I'd been after the old man to stock some of these because people had kept asking me for them.

I clasped my hands together and pretended to swoon, and Meriwether grinned.

"If you gals wouldn't mind getting some work done instead of just gabbing, you might be worth your wages!" Mr. MacIntyre shouted at us from down the aisle.

I picked up a box of homeopathic echinacea gels and gave him a huge smile and a thumbs-up. He narrowed his eyes at me and stomped into the back pharmacy area, where he filled people's prescriptions.

"How do you do that?" Meriwether whispered a few minutes later as we shifted some Ace bandages to make room for the new stuff.

"What?" I whispered back. "Hey, we should probably do this alphabetically, right?"

"Yeah," she agreed. "You know, not freak out when my dad yells at you."

Well, over the years I'd been at the mercy of northern raiders, not to mention Viking berserkers and Cossacks. As long as Old Mac wasn't splitting my neighbor's head open with an axe right in front of me, I could handle what he dished out.

But I couldn't say that.

"Maybe 'cause he's not my dad," I said quietly. "It's

always worse when it's your own dad." I'd lost my dad when I was ten, so I was guessing here. But it seemed like it would be true. "So, got big plans for New Year's Eve?"

Meriwether smiled, and I blinked, taken aback at how it transformed her. She nodded. "There's a school dance," she murmured. "And my dad actually said I could go. For once. I'm going to my friend's house and we'll get dressed up together."

That sounded like fingernails down a chalkboard to me, but she looked happy and I was glad she was escaping her dad for a while.

"No boyfriend?" I asked.

She made a face. "No one will ask me out. They're too scared of my dad. But I'm hoping this guy named Lowell is there." She let out a deep breath. "What about you?" she asked. "Do you have plans?"

I nodded. "Nothing too big." Just a special magick circle with a bunch of immortals. Same old, same old. "Just some friends getting together. I'll try to make it to midnight." Since I got up *before dawn* these days, my head usually hit the pillow before ten. It was…embarrassing. I used to feel so much cooler. But, of course, that coolness had gone hand in hand with feeling half crazy and worthless. So I guess I didn't miss it that much.

Someone came in and Meriwether left me to go wait on them. She was back in a few minutes, carrying some poster-board signs that she and I had made to advertise our new products. I have zero artistic talent, but Meriwether had done a great job, drawing little figures finding things with happy expressions. I left what I was doing and together she and I started hanging the signs with heavy double-sided tape. "What's *your* dad like?" Meriwether asked suddenly as I held up a corner so she could tape it.

I hesitated. No one had asked me that in…ages. A really long time. I quickly compared my dad, who had been a dark, power-hungry king in medieval Iceland, with Old Mac. Not too much in common.

"Well, he's dead," I said, and Meriwether winced.

"Sorry," she whispered.

"It's okay. It was a long time ago." Ha ha, you have no idea. Anyhoo, I let out a deep breath, allowing myself to think about my father, remember him for a few moments. Something I don't usually do. "I…remember him as being kind of forbidding," I said slowly. "My mother was with us more. He seemed like a stern character."

"Did he travel, for work?" She pressed a strip of tape into place, then stepped back to admire our colorful sign, my carefully lettered words arching over the stick figures' heads.

Why yes, it's hard to loot and raid and subjugate other villages from one's armchair. My father had been a king in the way that powerful men were kings over smaller territories, a long time ago. He'd increased lands under his rule by four times during the first ten years of my life. I nodded. "He taught us stuff sometimes," I went on, not even knowing why I was bothering. "He was, um, in the military. He wanted us all to be brave and tough. My older brother adored him." Sigmundur had tried to be just like Faðir in every way. He'd been sixteen when he died, but already hardened and skilled with weapons.

"Did your father yell?" Meriwether picked up the last sign and looked around for a good place to put it. I pointed to the front of the checkout counter, and she nodded. We headed over there and knelt to stick the sign up.

"When he yelled, it seemed like the whole...house shook," I said. "People who worked for him were afraid of him." I hadn't even realized that until just now.

"Like my dad." Meriwether carefully peeled off a piece of tape and stuck it in place.

"Yeah." In a bizarre, completely inexplicable way.

"My dad's always worse during the winter holidays," Meriwether said. We heard Old Mac leave his pharmacy and come our way, and we quickly shut up and separated, busily concentrating on our different tasks. Slowly we drifted back toward each other and continued putting boxes and bottles on shelves.

"You said it was around this time that your mom..." I'm not a delicate or sensitive person, and stomping on other people's feelings is usually not a problem for me. But I liked Meriwether, and Lord knew she'd been through enough without me making it worse.

"Yeah." Meriwether concentrated on aligning each small box just so. "We were on our way back from a Christmas party and it was icy. My dad wasn't with us."

"You were in the same car?" Oh, jeez. That had happened to me, too; in fact, it was how I had first met River back in 1929, in France. But the person who had died had been practically a stranger, and her death had barely made a ripple in my consciousness. Things like that hadn't really affected me—until the cabbie, two months ago. Part of what they were teaching me at River's Edge was how to actually feel things with appropriate weight.

Meriwether nodded without looking at me. Instantly I got it: She felt guilty for surviving. And her dad couldn't look at her without remembering that his wife and only son had died. And she hadn't.

"I'm really sorry," I said—maybe the second time in my life those words had ever come out of my mouth. But I did feel sorry for her—there was no way for her to win in this situation.

I remembered when I'd lived in a small village outside Naples, in Italy, in the 1650s. One of the last waves of the plague came through, and bodies were piling up. Later I read that half the people of Naples had died in that one outbreak. Half the people of a whole city. *Half* of them.

My little village was hard-hit. My neighbors died; their children died; the local priest died. People who had been genuinely good and kind, to me and to one another, all died within a matter of days. On Tuesday your neighbor would be working in her garden, and on Friday you'd walk past her body piled on top of other bodies in the street.

Not me. So many people, so much better than me, had died, and I was left standing to go on my merry way, because, hey, that town had become a big bummer. I kept surviving. Over and over and over.

Next to me, Meriwether sighed, then glanced back at the pharmacy.

"It just—should have been me, you know? It would have been so much better for everyone." She got up and took the empty cartons out to throw them into the recycle bin.

I sat back on my heels, struck by that. Not a new thought—I'd seen it in countless movies, read it in books. Now I knew that Meriwether felt that way, for real, in her real life.

What about me? Had I ever felt that *I* should have died that night, 450 years ago? That maybe my older brother should have lived? He wouldn't have run away, like I had.

He might have seized the family's power, found some followers, and gone after Reyn and his father to avenge our family.

Or one of my sisters? My oldest sister, Tinna, had been so smart and brave. My father's face had lit up when she came into a room. I remembered her and my mother working in the kitchen—we had cooks and servants, but every Oestara—Easter—my mother would make her special egg bread. She and Tinna would knead the dough side by side, laughing and talking.

My next-oldest sister, Eydís, had been the family beauty and my most constant companion. Her hair was long, wavy, and a brilliant strawberry blond, like the sun when it first peeks over the horizon. Her eyes were clear and gray. Even as an eleven-year-old, she'd been known for her beauty, and basically everyone was waiting for her to be four years older so they could see how *really* beautiful she would be as an adult. She and I had done everything together, made up all kinds of games, studied together, slept in the same room.

Then there was my little brother, Háakon. He'd been thin and pale, almost delicate. I'd seen my father looking at him sometimes with a bemused expression, as if wondering how this boy had come from the same union that produced all the rest of us. But Háakon had been sweet, not a tattler, and a faithful follower of me and Eydís as we marched around with sticks on our shoulders or practiced our rock throwing.

When the raiders broke down the door to my father's study, where we'd been barricaded in, I was clinging to my mother's skirts in terror. Reyn's father—the aptly named Erik the Bloodletter—had lunged forward with a roar, and I'd felt the swift jerk of my mother's body as he'd severed her head. She'd fallen backward right on top of me, and I'd lain, covered by the wide skirts of her wool robe, until it was all silent less than five minutes later.

Should I have died that night? Yes. Reyn's father had shouted that none should be left alive. My siblings had all had swords or daggers in their hands, children standing up to an unbeatable foe. I'd been cowering behind my mother. Which had saved me.

Why? I'd accepted the stunning reality that I was still alive, that my family was dead. I'd never questioned why that was or if it should be that way. Until now.

"I don't pay you to sit around!" Old Mac's roar startled me and I was yanked back to the present day, where my boss was standing in the aisle, cheeks red with anger. Behind him Meriwether made an unhappy face. "And what's all this junk?" He gestured angrily to a couple of our new signs. "No one said you could put this crap up!"

Meriwether's face flushed, and then Old Mac *ripped*

down our signs and threw them to the floor. I clenched my teeth shut so I wouldn't start shrieking in fury.

"Dad!" Meriwether said, her face crumpling. "We worked hard on those!"

He whirled on her as if she were a grass snake and he was a mongoose. "Nobody asked you to! I don't need your stupid, ugly posters around!"

Meriwether's eyes flashed. "They aren't stupid—" she began, but suddenly Old Mac grabbed a small plastic jar of vitamin-C capsules and hurled it. It all happened so fast—her eyes went wide, her voice choked, and before I knew what was happening, my hand snapped up, I hissed something, and the jar took a small, crazy zigzag away from Meriwether at the last second. It hit the wall beside her and cracked, then dropped to the ground. The lid popped off and gelcaps rolled everywhere.

We all stood still in the shocking silence. Old Mac looked stunned—more than stunned. He looked kind of gray and he leaned to one side, unsteady on his feet.

"I...I didn't mean—" he said in a shaking voice.

Then I realized: I had made magick quickly, without thinking. Something in me had reached deep into my ancient subconscious and come up with goddess-knew-what spell to deflect the jar.

But I wasn't skilled at white magick. I didn't know enough. So the magick that had come out had been the magick a Terävä would make, which I was: I'd taken energy from Old Mac to do it.

If I said anything, I would no doubt make this situation much, much worse. So Meriwether and I watched as Old Mac shook his head, as if in disbelief that he had done such a thing. Then he turned awkwardly and made his way down the aisle to the back room, trailing a hand along a shelf to help himself balance.

What had I done? Oh God. But what had my options been? Let Meriwether get hit by that jar? It was plastic and not that big, but it still would have really hurt.

Meriwether stood silently, tears running down her face.

"Does he do stuff like this? Throw stuff? Does he hit you?" Because I'd have to go kill him, if he did.

Meriwether shook her head. "He's never done anything like this before."

"He looked pretty sorry," I admitted. "You said he's just—super unhappy right now. Plus, you know, he's a butt." Inside I was shrieking about the harm I might have done with my spell.

"Tell you what," I said in a low voice. "You go to the bathroom, wash your face, try to get a grip. I'll clean up this mess." I gestured to the shiny, honey-colored gelcaps that had scattered in a surprisingly large radius. "If he tries to stop you, knee him in the balls."

That got the barest flicker of less misery on Meriwether's face. She nodded and headed off, then paused and looked back at me. "How did you do that?" Her voice was horribly clear and soft.

A big fist seemed to squeeze my insides. "Do what?"

"You moved your hand, and the jar jumped to one side." Her voice was quiet and solemn, her eyes locked on mine. "I saw it. It would have hit me right in the chest. I was frozen—couldn't move."

I managed an *Oh, please* kind of nonchalant grin, my hundreds of years of lying to people, especially myself, coming in useful. "I wish!" I snorted. I waved my hand dramatically. "Shazam! That Oreo is mine!" I gave a casual little laugh.

Meriwether looked at me for a few more moments, clearly replaying the incident in her head, wondering whether to pursue it, wondering if she had in fact seen anything. I kept my face unconcerned and went to fetch the broom and dustpan. She was gone when I returned, and I started sweeping everything up.

But I was quaking, my panicked wail sounding loud to my ears alone. I had made magick outside of River's property. Dark magick. It was very possible that someone, an immortal, could pick up on its energy and recognize me in its patterns. Someone like Incy.

I tried to breathe normally. No, surely not, I reasoned

with myself. It had taken half a second. It had been just a little thing. A little tiny thing. And I would be really careful in the future and never do anything like that again.

I kept telling myself that, over and over, all the way home. But I couldn't help looking in my rearview mirror, as if the devil were after me.

CHAPTER 4

t had been autumn when I'd first arrived at River's Edge. The trees had been flame-colored, reds and golds and oranges, and the world had been just starting to shut down for the winter. Now as I drove my little beat-up car down the long, unpaved drive that led to River's house, the trees were stark and bare, chilly skeletons with just a few brown leaves still clinging here and there. Two months ago the woods had seemed thick and impenetrable; now I could see twenty yards in. It would be beautiful in the spring.

I stopped, the car rolling to a halt on the crushed gray

rock of the drive, my hands on the steering wheel. I realized in surprise that I planned to be here in the spring. I wanted to be here, wanted to see the changes. That is, if my little screwup back in town didn't have a butterfly effect and completely destroy my life and the lives of everyone around me.

Hey, if I were a Merry Sunshine, do you think I'd be in this place?

As I rounded the final corner, the house came into view, large and square and white. It had seemed severe and forbidding when I'd first come, but now I was aware of a gentle warmth inside my chest as I pulled off the drive and parked next to River's red pickup.

I sat in my car for a minute, "sitting with my feelings," the way Asher had been trying to teach me. Which I hated so, so much. I am extremely skilled at suppressing virtually any emotion. Turns out, even if you suppress an emotion *so* successfully that you truly aren't aware of having any, *it is still there inside you*. This had been one of the more loathsome realizations I'd had since I'd come here. All the emotion I hadn't even been feeling was in fact curled up inside me like black bile, eating its way through my psyche until I was very, very close to being nuts. In the last two months, I'd experienced—and expressed—more emotion than I had in the hundred years before then.

And while I could *sort of* wrap my head around the reality that it was actually better this way, healthier this way, I couldn't get away from the deep-seated conviction that, really, it totally sucked.

What was I feeling? I leaned my head onto the steering wheel and closed my eyes. Panic, of course, like I always felt as soon as my brain realized I was trying to face something instead of running away. *Much* more comfortable with running away.

I was…glad, I guess, to be here. Especially now that Nell was gone and wouldn't be waiting to spring her next ill-wish on me. I was looking forward to going inside and seeing everyone. Except Reyn.

Liar. Your heart speeds up when you see him, your hands ache, your lips—

See, this is why suppressing emotion is so workable for me. Who wouldn't want to avoid that? I sighed, and then someone tapped on the window of my car, startling the hell out of me. I hadn't felt anyone come up.

My head whipped sideways and there he was: Reyn. Six feet of golden Viking disaster.

The very first time I'd come here, I'd been stopped like this, resting my head like this, and Reyn had tapped on my window. He'd taken my breath away, in a surly, unfriendly, gorgeous, suspicious kind of way. Here he was, doing it again.

But I wasn't that same broken waif who'd practically crawled here this past fall. I took the keys out of the ignition and opened the car door briskly, almost whacking him with it.

"You sure do like sneaking up on people," I said snippily.

"I was seeing if you had OD'd or something," he said, mimicking my tone.

"OD'd? Oh my God, are turnips that addicting?" I made my eyes wide. "I'll be sure to avoid them *even more* from now on."

He fell into step beside me as I walked quickly toward the house. The sun had dropped while I'd sat in the car, and it was twilight, that magickal time between day and night. The time of day when it feels like anything could happen. Anything at all.

"Just get back from work?" Reyn asked, and the whole scene was so incongruous that I laughed. He turned his unsmiling, slightly narrowed eyes on me.

"Is that what your wife used to say when you came home?" My voice sounded brittle in the cold air, and even thinking that he'd probably had *wives* was like a sucker punch to my gut. "'How was the sacking today, honey? The looting? Any good pillaging?'"

Just like that, in a flash, Reyn was furious. I felt the change come over him even before I looked at his face, saw the tightness of his mouth, the downward V of his brows. An instantaneous alarm rang inside me and I wondered if I could make it to the house before him.

When he finally spoke, it was clear that he was using all his self-control to not, say, throttle me. "That past is only a small part of who I am." His voice was tense and measured. "Just as all of the stupid, selfish, destructive things *you've* done are only a *part* of who you are."

My face flushed. "But your past is so much worse than mine!"

He paused, struggling again to keep his anger in check. "My past is worse than a lot of people's," he agreed bleakly, and then turned to look at me again. "How's your present going? How does your future look?"

Before I could answer, he strode ahead, and I was left behind.

As soon as I stepped through the front door, I felt a general excitement and energy in the air. At Yule, the house had been decorated with evergreen boughs and mistletoe, but we'd taken those down a couple of days ago. I hung up my puffy coat in the hallway, glad that Reyn was nowhere in sight. River came out of the front parlor just as I passed the door.

"Hi," she said with her easy smile. River was one of the very few immortals I'd met with silver hair. Hers was shiny and straight, falling below her shoulders when it wasn't held back.

"Hi," I said, trying to look calm and unrattled. "Just on my way to check the chore chart."

"Don't bother," River said. "No chores tonight for anyone. But upstairs on your bed there's a list of things to get done before dinner. Not chores, exactly. Things to help prepare for the New Year's Eve circle later on."

"Oh." I still had a love/dread relationship with magick circles. "So...no fireworks? No champagne?"

River grinned, her clear brown eyes lighting up. "There will be champagne at dinner."

"Fireworks?" I love fireworks. I'd seen some amazing displays in Italy and in China, hundreds of years ago. Before all those pesky safety laws.

"No," said River. "No fireworks. Not in these woods, despite all the dampness from the snow. But I bet you won't miss them."

Because the circle would be so exciting? "Ooh, are we learning shape-shifting tonight?"

She laughed and pushed me toward the stairs. "Very funny. Go get ready. Dinner's at eight. Late tonight."

No shape-shifting. I'd been joking, but who knew what powerful immortals could actually do? I headed upstairs and made it into my room Reyn-free. I closed the door and turned the knob on my small radiator to warm the place up a bit. As promised, there was a note on my bed, next to a glass dish of salt and a little muslin bag that smelled like herbs. I picked up the note, recognizing River's beautiful, old-fashioned handwriting. It said:

Drink the mug of tea on your bedside table.
Take a bath with the herb packet.
Put on the robe hanging in your cupboard.
Cast a circle with the salt and meditate inside of it for one hour. Think about the new year.
Open your circle, scatter the salt along the floor, then sweep it all up and dump it out your window.
See you at dinner!

I picked up the mug and sniffed it. It was still quite warm. It smelled like—and I know this will shock you—herbs. Between you and me, I'd be so thrilled to just have a nice cuppa Lipton. If one can get sick of herbs, and I believe one can, then I was well on my way to being sick of herbs.

Down the hatch with the tea. It wasn't very pleasant, and a little shot of brandy would have gone a long way to improving it. But I got it down. Then I went and checked out the robe in the wardrobe. Quick aside: The word *cupboard* is about as descriptive and simple as you can get. It began, literally, as a board to put your cups on, way back in the day. And *wardrobe*? Ward-robe. It would ward, or guard, your robes. Your gowns. Interesting, eh? Stick with me—you'll learn a lot. Not all of it reprehensible.

The robe, which I hadn't seen before, was of heavy white linen, washed to be very soft. It was simple, like a nightgown, and had runes embroidered in white thread around the neckline. I saw kenaz, which meant revelation, knowledge, vision. Algiz, as a ward-evil. Laguz—water? I had just relearned all this. Right—water, dreams, fantasies, visions. Berkano was the symbol for female fertility, growth, and renewal. Fabulous. I turned the gown in my hands and saw dagaz, daybreak or dawn. Awakening, awareness. Finally, at the back of the neck was othala. I let out a breath. Othala stood for one's heritage—literally, the land or estate that one inherited, one's birthright.

The estate that I was the sole inheritor of had been destroyed, razed to the ground, when I was ten. I saw its rubble when I was sixteen. Had never been able to bring myself to go back after that.

I passed Anne on my way to the bathroom. She came out, face flushed from steam, dark, fine hair sticking wetly to her head. She smiled when she saw me and kissed both of my cheeks as if she hadn't seen me in a long time.

"I love New Year's Eve," she said. "I'm very glad you're with us."

I was still unused to all this open expression of feeling and replied with an embarrassed, troglodyte mumble.

"Tonight will be very exciting," Anne said, not put off by my cloddishness. "Be sure to wear your new robe to dinner—everyone else will."

"What will we do at the circle?" I asked.

"A New Year's circle is usually designed to help us clarify things in our past and give us an inkling of what the future holds for us," Anne said. "People often have visions of events that have yet to happen."

"Ew," I said. I myself almost always had visions during magickal circles, and they were pretty much always heinous.

Anne laughed. "It'll be okay," she promised. "We'll all be there together."

I nodded somewhat glumly and went to take a ritual bath.

CHAPTER 5

y post-bath hour of meditation was a failure. I'd been spooked by Anne's prediction of vision-seeing tonight, and was still all jangled and raw-feeling from last night's nightmare about Incy, remembering my family today, the at-work incident that I was done thinking about, and the whole ongoing Reyn thing.

Still, obedient Nastasya made a circle with salt, lit a candle, and sat there till my butt was completely numb. Finally I sighed, blew out the candle, and sprinkled the salt everywhere as instructed. I got the broom from down the hall and swept my room, then dumped it all out the window.

I looked at the robe lying on my bed. I would feel stupid wearing this. It was so...clichéd, the robed witches dancing around a fire at midnight. Maybe I would suddenly come down with something. Stomach flu. Maybe I should just go to bed and stay there all night. Maybe I should—

Knock knock.

It was Brynne—I felt her vibrant energy.

"Yeah?" I called.

The door opened. Brynne stood there, beautiful in a scarlet robe. She was our only black member—we weren't an incredibly diverse bunch (I mean here at River's Edge; immortals in general were of course plenty diverse—just about every culture has them)—and to me looked the most teenagery. Her finely boned face was beautiful, and she was long and lean, like a Brâncuşi sculpture. Only smoother. I felt short, pale, and plain next to her.

Seeing me sitting on my bed, she laughed. "I knew you were in here being a chicken!"

"What does one wear under this?" I asked, holding up the robe. "I'm thinking long underwear."

Brynne grinned. "Why would one wear *anything*?"

My eyes flared in alarm. "Oh, no. No, I've got to have something on under this."

Brynne tucked her hands under her arms. "*Bawk, bawk, bawk*," she chirped.

"It'll be freezing," I pointed out.

"You won't feel it," she promised.

"You don't really mean *naked* under this?"

Brynne made obnoxious clucking sounds and left. I heard one final *bawk!* as she went down the hall.

I gritted my teeth.

At dinner I felt stupid and self-conscious in my robe, despite the fact that everyone there was wearing one. They were in all colors: River's was silvery gray, like her hair; Anne's was a deep cerulean blue. Daisuke's was a dark charcoal. Charles's was emerald green. Brynne's of course was red, and she raised her eyebrows meaningfully at me as she took a long sip of her champagne. I scowled at her.

Glancing around, I saw I was the only one in white. As well as the only one with a fine wool scarf wrapped closely around her neck. I saw River glance at my scarf, but she didn't say anything. She knew I wouldn't go without it.

"Pass the chickpeas, please," said Jess, on my right. His voice had been shredded by his various excesses, and I didn't know if it would ever recover. His robe was black. I wondered about the symbolism.

"All of these dishes are traditional, meaningful New Year's foods," said Solis. "If you eat a bit of everything here, your new year will be lucky, prosperous, healthy, blessed, and full of good fortune!"

I was too busy feeling like a Halloween ghost wrapped in a sheet to focus on what he was saying, but other people laughed and clinked glasses. I saw my champagne and grabbed it. Champagne is meant to be sipped, but I hadn't had any alcohol in almost two months, and I drained that sucker.

Asher grinned and refilled my glass. "Now, sip it," he admonished. "Make it last."

I took a ladylike sip and set my glass down, pretty sure it was eighteenth-century Venetian handblown crystal. It was gorgeous, imperfect, and as delicate as a butterfly's wing.

Someone brushed against me as he stepped over the bench to sit down.

I knew without looking up that it was Reyn. My face froze as I caught a glimpse of his robe, a deep amber color. Quickly I took some sautéed greens from the main bowl and glopped them onto my plate.

"You're late," said River, but she smiled at him.

"Sorry," he said shortly. I swear, that man could charm the skin off a snake!

"Well, now that we're all here, let's talk resolutions!" Asher rubbed his hands together. "I will, of course, resolve the usual."

I was about to ask what his usual was, but Anne said, "To make the perfect chèvre?"

"Yes! This will be the year!" Asher practically glowed, and everyone laughed. I'd walked past the wheels of curing goat's milk cheeses in the root cellar but hadn't thought much about them except, Hoo, boy, glad I don't have to mess with them.

"Next?" River looked at all of us.

Daisuke spoke up. I knew him the least well of all the students. I knew he was one of the more advanced students and often studied one-on-one with River. He was pleasant but shy. "I, too, resolve the usual," he said in a soft voice. "To achieve enlightenment, free myself of all want, and become one with the god and goddess."

Judging from the understanding smiles and nods he got, he was actually serious. He was trying to achieve *enlightenment*. I was such a loser.

And so we went around the table. Some resolutions were small or funny, like to eat less sugar or pat the farm cats more, and some were larger, like to be more patient or more kind. River resolved to be more understanding and accepting, which IMHO was like water trying to be more wet. I didn't see how she could possibly be *more* of those things.

I was racking my brain trying to come up with something that wasn't insulting, like resolving to match my socks more often, but not too ridiculous and ambitious, like to be a genuinely good person someday. My turn got closer and closer, and I started to feel panicky, wondering if I could abstain but knowing that I would be the only one lame enough to need to skip, and here was one more thing that I sucked at, and why was I trying when I barely had any excuse for even living—

"Nastasya?" River's brown eyes were—yes: understanding and accepting.

I gulped down some champagne to buy another few seconds—I was such a waste—and then said the first thing that popped into my mind. "I resolve to...trust more." I had no idea where that had come from. Out of thin air.

All eyes were on me, and I was self-conscious. River looked a tiny bit surprised, her head on one side as she gazed at me. Surprised and thoughtful.

"That's an excellent resolution," Asher said in the silence.

"Yes," said Anne. "Lovely. Good for you."

Now I felt even more self-conscious. That resolution had appeared out of freaking nowhere and yet...I uncomfortably recognized that I meant it. I trusted nobody, not even myself. Not my decisions, my emotions, my plans, my work ethic, my sincerity, my looks—nothing. The one thing about me that seemed rock solid, that I could completely and utterly count on no matter what, was my ability to screw things up. That was as inevitable as the proverbial sun coming up tomorrow.

"And now Reyn," said River.

Come on, someone please refill my champagne glass, I thought. I could feel Reyn's tension, next to me, the warmth of his leg next to mine.

The whole table waited expectantly. I wondered what Reyn had said last year.

"I resolve...to try to be happy," he said, sounding awkward.

Silence. Everyone was staring at him, and I knew why: He wasn't exactly the poster boy for mirth and good cheer. Even now a sidelong glance told me he was almost scowling down at the table, his hands curled into fists on either side of his plate.

"Perfect, Reyn," said River gently. "Thank you."

Reyn uncurled one hand and picked up his fork, beginning to work steadily through the food on his plate. I was sure it tasted like sawdust to him.

So I was the most untrusting person in the world, and he was the unhappiest person in the world.

We were quite a pair.

CHAPTER 6

was ready to just go to bed by nine thirty and skip the whole New Year's circle thing, but again I knew I would be the only one lame enough to cut out, and my pride wouldn't let me. Finally it was eleven thirty—time to get my circle on.

I met Rachel and Charles going out the back door and joined them, glad I wouldn't have to walk through the woods alone. Another circle. Would I barf, as usual? See horrible visions, as usual? Would I feel that glorious starburst of light and power within me that made magick seem worthwhile and even necessary, at least till I started heaving? The darkness, thick and cold, pressed in all around me. I retucked the scarf around my neck, hoping I wouldn't regret my decision to skip my down coat.

"I wonder if this year's circle will be as good as last year's," Rachel said. Her voice was calm and even, and it occurred to me that I couldn't remember her raising it or sounding sarcastic or teasing. It was just always calm and even.

"How was last year's good?" I asked.

Rachel looked at me solemnly. "We made s'mores."

I grinned, and Charles chuckled. The barest smile crossed Rachel's face, and then we were at the clearing, and Solis had already started a fire.

"Welcome," River said as we kicked off our shoes. "Welcome."

The twelve of us stood around the fire, watching as the mesmerizing flames licked the dried wood, crept softly along its edges like a cat, then suddenly devoured it. It was, as I had predicted, freezing out here. I stretched my hands toward the warmth, but I was almost shaking with cold, as well as forcibly reminded of my horrible Incy vision. Great.

"You won't feel it after a while," Anne said, repeating what Brynne had promised.

I nodded, thinking that my bare feet were undoubtedly already turning blue. I would probably lose a couple of toes to frostbite. All I needed was for my nose to start running and then this picture would be complete.

"And here we are," River said, smiling at all of us. "The end of another year. The birth of the next year of our lives. Tomorrow is a new day, a new chapter, a new start." I thought she looked at me in particular, but the leaping fire was bending the air all around it, and it was hard to tell.

"This circle will be mostly celebratory," River went on. "With each of us meditating on the theme of what a new year means to us personally. Then, at the height of our power, we'll each release something that we no longer have need of. In past years, I've released fear or the need to control things or my intense craving for dark chocolate."

Smiles.

"But of course each of you has something within you that you no longer need, something that is holding you back. Some of us already know what we plan to release, but don't worry if you don't have something in mind yet. At the right time, it will come to you. Now, are we all ready?"

No. We should disband and go have some hot tea.

I did not get that particular New Year's wish. Instead we held out our hands, thumbs facing left so that they aligned perfectly when we clasped hands with our neighbors. I was between Rachel and Charles. River was across from me, and His Lordship was next to her, looking amazing in the deep amber robe that he was probably wearing nothing underneath.

Rachel glanced at me. "Did you say something? Or stub your toe?"

"No." Must suppress stupid whimpers.

River began her song, her personal invitation to magick to come out and play. No, *play* wasn't the right word — not with the appalling destructive power that I'd seen too many times. An invitation...to a conversation. That was more how it was.

We walked clockwise around the fire, and after the second revolution I realized I could feel my feet again, feel the cold ground and scattered leaves. With another revolution I was no longer cold and was starting to get the weird kindling sensation in my chest that signaled magick building in me, around me. I began to sing my song.

I'd asked Solis if I needed to be taught a more formal or traditional song to call magick to me, and he'd said no, it couldn't be taught. It just came from within you, no matter what culture you were from or what language you used. In the past I'd simply opened my mouth and sounds came out, sounds that were ancient words. I figured I'd heard them when I was small, from my parents. The words far predated them; knowing now what I did about the great houses, I assumed they went back to the earliest days of magick and immortals, whenever that was.

At any rate, when I opened my mouth, my song appeared and drew magick to me, thrillingly, seductively, frighteningly. Our circle was moving faster now, and mine wasn't the only flushed face. The fire danced in the middle, its flames seeming to become sharper, more jagged as our own dance continued.

Rachel's hand was warm in mine; Charles's felt strong and surprisingly firm. I looked from face to face, seeing the flickering light reflected off of skin and eyes. I saved Reyn for last, drawing out the moment when I would finally let my eyes rest on him. And there he was, between River and Daisuke. He was a good head taller than either of them. The fire cast shadows on his angled cheekbones, those bewitching, almond-shaped golden eyes. He suddenly looked at me before I could glance away, locking his gaze on me in a way that snatched the breath from my throat. His robe, like everyone's, pressed against his skin as we revolved, outlining the hard planes of his chest. His scar was under that robe, as mine was under my scarf. Our matching scars. Not identical but a matched set, the two sides of my mother's amulet.

My song twined in the air, growing stronger and richer. It wove itself into all the others, so that together we created a strong, thick tree trunk of twisted roots that seemed to sink deeply into the ground. It was so...entrancing, so beautiful, this beckoning of magick. I'd forgotten. I guess I'd never really known, not like this. Tiny things, baby spells, yes. But not this full-fledged courtship between me and magick, the promises we were making to each other.... Like a lover, I feared its power and its ability to hurt me. But like a lover, it also promised such incredible joy, such a blossoming of power inside. It was revealing itself to me — and so revealing me to myself.

Whoa, listen to me! Next I'll be writing a self-help book! *Joy through Witchcraft*!

I forced myself to concentrate again on what was happening around me and not the Wondrous Miracle of Self-Realization within. River was smiling widely as she sang. Her hair, loose around her shoulders, flowed like liquid silver. She looked beautiful and happy and strong. I think I've looked like that at some point in my life, but it hasn't been recent.

But I did feel sort of happy right now. I did feel strong. I was full of magick, bursting at the seams with it, and was probably grinning idiotically. I felt physically perfect, not too hot or too cold, but full of lightness and joy. My feet flew over the ground; my hair whipped around my face. I felt included and like I sort of belonged here, with these people.

"Now!" River said, and we all threw our hands in the

air as if we were giving the universe a gift. Maybe we were. Who the hell knows?

Our circle slowed gradually and we came to a gentle stop, settling into our individual places like flower petals resting on water. There were smiles, looks of wonder and even awe as my circle-mates shimmered with the beauty of magick. I felt as if I could float right off the ground, and only the weight of my linen robe was keeping me earthbound.

Magick buzzed and crackled in the air. It was a blissful feeling of well-being, of every single thing in the world being exactly what it should be. I felt that at this moment I could do nothing wrong and that everything would happen the way it was supposed to.

River clasped her hands in front of her, breathed something into them, then flung her hands at the fire. The fire leaped as if in response: River had released what she didn't need, and the fire had taken it, consumed it.

Asher was on River's other side and he went through the same motions. I watched in fascination as the fire actually seemed to grab his wish out of the air. Say what you will, magick, schmagick, but that was downright freaky.

And so it went, around the circle: Anne, Lorenz, Brynne, Jess, Rachel...each cast something out, and the fire claimed it for its own.

Then it was my turn. It wasn't that I didn't know what

to cast off—more like I had way too many things for this one fire to handle. I'd probably make it gag or choke or something. Stupidity, selfishness, sloth, laziness—wait, is laziness covered by sloth or is it redundant? Immaturity, and I said selfishness, right?

Rachel gave me a gentle elbow in the ribs and I looked up to see everyone waiting expectantly. I swallowed, still wrapped in my glorious bubble of light and power. Quickly I clapped my hands together and breathed the first words that popped into my mind. *I cast off darkness.* I flung my hands open at the fire and it almost exploded, jumping to three times its size, making me step back quickly. But the flames mesmerized me, drew me in. I felt their heat but couldn't tear my eyes away.

I cast off darkness. That had seemed to cover everything. I had shed my old life like a lizard's skin; my old friends, my old me. Everything was new. This was a new year, a new start, and I was going to begin by making this conscious decision to release any darkness within me, to open myself to the possibility of good.

A memory came to my mind and floated before me, taking shape in the fire. It was me and Incy, and Boz and Katy were there, too. Then the fire faded away, and I saw the scene clearly.

We were in France, during World War II. We'd tried to cross the border into Switzerland with forged papers, but there had been bureaucratic red tape and we were stuck while we had new papers forged.

The four of us were on our way to a bar run by an immortal who had inexplicably decided to stay in France. We were glad he had, though. His bar was hidden — it was exciting and risky to get to, involving climbing down sewer steps in the dark, practically crawling through bombed-out cellars, and in one short section edging through a narrow, disjointed hallway that ran beneath a boarded-up cathedral.

As we hurried down the street, trying to avoid the annoyance of having a German patrol randomly stop us, we saw a Red Cross truck parked at the curb outside *une poste* — the post office. We were laughing, dressed up, looking forward to the evening and hoping to get our new papers the next day to escape this ruined, pathetic town.

The driver was inside the shop, the door still open. We heard him ask in appalling, American-accented French where the orphanage was. The shop mistress began explaining rapidly, with gestures, and it was clear that the driver wasn't getting any of it. He mimed drawing a map, and the woman nodded and bustled off to get a piece of the inadequate, tissuelike paper that was all one could get then.

"Hey!" said Boz, slowing down.

"What?" I asked.

"The Red Cross truck — it's going to the orphanage." He lowered his voice and pulled us into an alley.

"So?" Incy asked, then his dark eyes lit up. "It's taking supplies. Maybe food."

When we half carried, half dragged the wooden crates into Felipe's place, we were greeted like heroes. They held an unbelievable trove: bars of chocolate, soap, *real eggs*, which made everyone squeal, and actual *oranges*. None of us had seen any of these in months and months. We were magnanimous, sharing with everyone, handing out bars of chocolate as though we all had chocolate every day, blithely giving the eggs to Felipe's wife, who bustled them off as if they were solid gold.

I remember the delicious, tangy scent of an orange as I dug my red-painted nails into the peel, pulling it back. A spritz of juice squirted out and hit my cheek. I laughed, and Boz licked it off. I squeezed some of the juice into the awful, watered-down whiskey that was Felipe's stock in trade, and then I ripped the orange open and bit into the flesh. Nothing ever tasted so good, before or since.

It had been glorious, one of our favorite stories to remember and laugh about. We still congratulated one another on what a fantastic coup that had been.

Now, in the fire, I saw what I hadn't seen then, hadn't ever thought about: how the orphans would have heard the truck coming, would have peered through the windows, some broken and boarded up. How the nuns would have bustled about, giving them permission to run out and see *le militaire*. These were kids whose parents had probably died in one of the hundreds of air raids that German Messerschmitts had rained down on France. They'd probably run out to the truck, jumping on the driver, cheering when they saw the big red cross painted on the truck's side. The driver would have strode to the back, feeling like Santa Claus. He would have seen their torn sweaters, the thin legs showing beneath too-short pants. Then he would have thrown back the olive green canvas and seen... nothing. An empty truck. The orphans would have been dumbfounded. Crushed. It would have been far better if the truck had never come — they hadn't hoped for anything. But the truck had arrived, their hopes had flared up like the fire before me, and then their hopes had been utterly destroyed.

By us. By me. By my darkness.

Darkness, leave me, I pleaded silently. *Darkness, leave me.*

I heard someone cough, and I blinked, coming back to myself, to the here and now.

"What on earth did you cast out?" Rachel murmured, but River said, "Charles?" and the circle continued as if nothing had happened. I stepped back, trembling, and wrapped my arms around myself. Had I been standing there only an instant or for minutes? And how many memories did I have like that one? Things that had seemed wonderful, brilliant, amusing at the time—but that I would now look on with dismay, even revulsion? Many. So many.

Something sharp and bitter rose in the back of my throat and I put my hand to my mouth and swallowed hard.

Next to me Charles blew on his hands, and the fire gave a barely perceptible rise, as though it was a piece of cake after what it'd had to take from me.

My face was hot and I started to sweat; I felt curious looks. I focused on a spot near the fire's base and didn't raise my eyes. After Charles was Solis, and the fire mustered some energy to consume what he cast out. Solis, then Daisuke, then Reyn. I peeped at the fire for his; it gave a medium-size jump. What had he cast out? The longing to conquer people? The need to sack villages? His desire for me?

Then we were back to River, who looked alert and clear-eyed. "Well done, everyone. What a lovely circle. Let's disband it together."

We took one another's hands again. I was embarrassed because my palms were clammy and Rachel and Charles could feel it. The twelve of us simply raised our arms to the sky and said farewell.

I felt the magick fading, paling, felt it start to unwind and slip off into the trees and the sky and the ground. That indescribable sensation of power and strength ebbed also, and I grew panicky, afraid at how diminished I would be without it, how normal.

A gentle arm slipped around my shoulder. River said, "Are you okay?"

I quickly did a self-check for signs of imminent hurling, then nodded. "Don't think I'll barf."

"No, I meant emotionally," she said. "That was an important circle; you raised a great deal of very strong magick. Could you feel it?" She inclined her head to mine as people started to find their shoes and head back to the house, chatting and laughing.

"I felt everyone's magick, all twisted together," I told her, and she looked thoughtful.

"Yours was particularly strong," she said. "How do you feel about what you released?"

"Um, fine." I found my shoes and shoved my sockless feet into them. I was starting to shiver again with the night's chill.

River hesitated as if she wanted to say something else.

I hoped she wouldn't ask any more questions about what I had cast off—I wasn't sure that I had done the right thing, said the right thing. Could one cast off darkness itself? Should I have just stuck with selfishness?

Finally she said, "Okay. We can talk more about it later. Come back to the house—we have all sorts of special treats waiting."

"Okay." I made a big show of slowly tying my laces, and she went on ahead. I didn't want to talk about it, any of it. Not what I had released, not what I had seen, not the horrible, curled-up memory of false happiness.

I got to my feet and realized that *everyone* had gone on ahead, and I was alone. Outstanding. The fact that it was below freezing was just sprinkles on the doughnut.

I gritted my teeth.

An owl hooted, *of course*, sending a chill down my already chilled spine. I heard twigs, winter-dry, snapping from feet not my own. Was that—had someone laughed? Oh goddess. I swear, if a clown jumped out at me, I would flay—

Reyn stepped out from behind a tree, and I almost screamed.

"Dammit! You big...lurker! Is this how you get your kicks? This isn't *funny*!"

"I wasn't *lurking*," he said, looking irritated. "I was *waiting* for you. I know you hate being alone outside at night. I thought you could hear me, knew I was here."

My mouth opened in surprise.

"It looked like you and River were having a private talk, so I waited *here*."

Now I felt terrible, accusing him when he'd been being thoughtful. Even kind. His eyes looked brown in this dim light, and his cheekbones cast shadows along his jaw. Then his face cleared and he looked at me with an expression I didn't recognize.

"Do you really think," he said softly, "that with the history we have between us, I would think it was funny to *jump out* at you?" He crossed his arms over his chest.

I took a controlled breath and put a hand over my pounding heart. "I wasn't thinking," I said stiffly. "I was startled. How do you know I don't like being outside at night?"

"Every time I've seen you outside at night, you're tenser than a bowstring," he said, speaking so quietly that I unconsciously leaned forward to hear. "You hate it. You hate it enough to stand really close to me when we walk." His voice was warm and velvety, as though to keep the cold night away.

"You waited for me?" It was just sinking in.

"Yes. Should we go?" He gestured in the general direction of the house.

I nodded, bemused by how grateful I felt, and by how he looked, standing in these woods with soft bits of snow falling soundlessly around us.

He tilted his head to one side. "Your hair...looks like it was spun from moonlight." He looked away and gave a fake laugh, as if he hadn't meant to say that.

I blinked, thinking, Warrior Poet, and then he turned back, his face solemn, and slowly leaned down to me as my breath suddenly left my chest. No more thoughts cluttered my head as our arms went around each other at the same time, my hands sliding up the soft cloth of his sleeves that couldn't disguise the hard muscle underneath.

"Reyn," I whispered. Then his mouth was gently pressing against mine, his eyes open as he waited to see if I would push him away. Instead my eyes closed and I leaned against his chest, as solid as an oak. This was Reyn, kissing me, and everything felt new and unique, despite my four and a half centuries of kissing. He held me more tightly to him, his hands on my back, and I became thrillingly aware that there was nothing between us except our stupid freaking witch robes, which I had totally known was a bad idea.

With winter raider focus, he deepened our kiss, making my head spin. He smelled like smoke and laundry soap and some sort of unusual, almost Oriental spice that I associated with him alone. I hadn't been aware that he was edging me backward, but now I felt the cold immovability of a big rock sticking up out of the ground, hitting the backs of my knees. So I was officially literally between a rock and a hard place.

It was just...so good. It felt so good, amazingly good, better than anything I could ever remember, though I was freezing and unsure of what had happened at the circle. When I was with him like this, connected to him, I felt safe. Nothing could get to me. Nothing could hurt me now. Except him. And by the time that thought had struggled through the Jell-O of my mind, I had the dim awareness that my arms were around his shoulders, one of my hands was buried in his hair, and I'd curled one leg around his.

I gave in, letting the riptide of Reynness sweep me under, pull me in over my head.

I pressed myself against him as hard as I could, as if I could meld us together. One of my hands pushed beneath the neckline of his robe to feel hot, smooth skin, the straight strength of his collarbone, the sleek muscles of his shoulder. He was big and strong and solid and perfect. I felt him breathing hard and was pleased—I had done that to him. I just wanted to have time *stop*, right now. I wanted to give up, give in, let go of everything except Reyn.

Of *course* I was tempted to do just that. I'd *love* to give up this stupid, difficult, effing struggle toward being Tähti. It would be so much easier to just...*coast* from now on.

To overwhelm my senses with Reyn, letting him fill my mind, my heart, my body.

But—wouldn't that leave me just as much of a loser shell as I'd been when I got here? It completely pissed me off, but the truth was that I had a goal here. Losing myself in all of these lovely, fierce, tantalizing emotions would just be making another placeholder inside where Lilja— the name I was born under—ought to be.

Reyn lifted his head, looking at me. We were both panting, making puffs of smoke in the frigid air. My arms felt cold and stiff.

"Where are you?" His voice was almost a whisper. I thought I could detect the very faintest hint of his original language—some Mongol/Scandinavian bastard hybrid. He stepped back but kept his arms around me.

"I can't do this," I said, knowing I *had* just done it, hating how breathless I sounded.

His eyes narrowed a fraction.

With a sense of loss similar to feeling magick ebb from me after a circle, I made myself say, "I don't know why we're doing this." I tried unsuccessfully to step away from his hands. "I don't know why—" I shook my head, feeling bone-tired and confused and sad and yet somehow triumphant for some reason.

"We're drawn together," he said, his words falling almost silently in the night air. "We have a past together."

"A horrible, disastrous past." Well, someone had to say it.

"Maybe this is the only way to heal it." His chest was rising and falling, but with longtime warrior instincts he was making no sound.

"I don't know." I hated being so indecisive. I prefer to be snappy, even abrasive. I almost always know where I stand on things, am happy to give my opinion about anything. But tonight I couldn't muster a coherent thought.

"You—have feelings for me." He was quiet but insistent.

Oh yes, indeed. Lust, longing. "Dread? Pain?"

I felt his muscles tighten though I wasn't touching him anymore.

"Being at River's is about…being who you are," he said, each word sounding as if it was coming out against his will. "Who you really are. And making that—okay, somehow."

My body, which just moments ago had been singing his praises and urging me to get to know him ever so much better, started to spiral downward. I was coming off my Reyn high just as I had come off my magick high not ten minutes ago. Adrenaline and excitement leached from my veins and I was suddenly shivering with cold again. I crossed my arms over my chest.

"Okay, Dr. Laura," I said, but without real snark.

"It's pointless to lie to yourself." His words landed flatly between us.

I worked up a pretty sincere frown. "Oh yeah? Good tip."

But this was a man who had probably held out for weeks, even months, during icy sieges, waiting for barricaded villagers to starve and break, so my brittle walls didn't pose much challenge for him.

"If you can't face your feelings, all of them, then you're never going to be strong enough to break free of the past."

I was caught off guard by his words as much as by the way he looked against the black trees of the woods, the snow white under our feet, moonlight striping his face and hair and making him look like some kind of exotic tiger-person.

"Oh, like you know." I now felt stupid and vulnerable and not like myself.

Feeling like I had to get away from all this emotion, I pushed past him, and he let me. I headed home *by myself*, walking fast on the snow where other feet had made a path. I didn't know if he was following me, but a minute or two later I was almost running up the kitchen steps, desperate for the light and the laughter within.

CHAPTER 7

ost of the January firsts in recent memory have involved splitting headaches and roiling stomachs and often being surprised about where I was waking up. ("No, Officer, I have no idea why I'm wearing this possum costume. I called you what? Oh. My bad.") Plus a sort of heavy dread about still being here, still being me, still doing whatever. Then one of my friends would call, or roll out from beneath the couch, or offer me a Bloody Mary, and it would start all over again.

This year felt different. I woke up not hungover, not with strangers, but with a wary sense of excitement about a whole new year of possibility. In Iceland we'd always had huge bonfires on New Year's Eve and had made wishes and toasts to the new year. I had done that last night.

I felt...excited. Even hopeful, though I didn't want to jinx anything by admitting that. Lying in the tub in the women's bathroom on my hall, I cataloged my progress. I watched my toes turning pink in the hot water and silently listed ways where I felt I was doing better.

I wasn't fine. I wasn't altogether okay and together and trustworthy and positive. I still had a long, rocky uphill road ahead of me to get there. But I was doing better. And this new year would hold even more progress. Really. Truly. I ducked myself underwater and rinsed off, imagining that I was washing away my past.

Polishing stable tack is high on my list of dislikes, right after piña coladas and walks in the rain. Faced with several harnesses, two saddles, and a couple of girth belts, I could only give thanks that some of the tack was nylon webbing and needed no upkeep.

"Hallo, *cara*," Lorenz murmured as I went past him to the tack room. He and Charles were sweeping the middle aisle of the barn, and the air was thick with kicked-up hay and dust. "Have you seen the lovely puppies?"

"Yep." Everyone was all about the puppies here.

Charles sneezed and drew a clean white handkerchief

from his barn coat pocket. Even sweeping the floor, he looked tidy and kempt. And Lorenz could have been modeling for *Horse Illustrated: The Winter Collection*. He even had a silk scarf knotted around his neck. I myself was dressed to thrill in flannel-lined jeans, muck boots, a sweatshirt, my puffy coat, and a thick wool scarf. Lorenz, his fashion sensibilities offended, tried not to wince but simply couldn't bear it.

"No, not the scarf wrapped many times," he said, propping up his broom and coming toward me. He was only about a hundred or so and still had a pronounced Italian accent.

I put my hands up to stop him, but he firmly pressed them down and undid my scarf, while I stood frozen. My hair had grown out a bit and now covered the back of my neck, but just barely. I felt stuck to the floor and tried to get a grip on the raging panic his action had set off.

"Look. This is the way." With deft hands, he folded my scarf, then looped it quickly around my neck while I tried not to leap away. He tucked the loose ends of the scarf through the loop and tightened it up around me. I controlled my breathing while he futzed with it, draping it and fluffing it up. He stepped back to regard me critically.

"It's better, no?" he asked Charles, and Charles made a noncommittal gesture.

"It's better, but you can't really do much, with that

sweatshirt," he said, not meanly, and Lorenz sighed and nodded.

"True. Nastasya, you have an adorable figure. The sweatshirt does nothing for you," he said definitively. "Jewel tones, yes? More fitted. A little cashmere cardigan."

"I am polishing tack in a barn," I felt compelled to point out.

"Ah," said Lorenz, and nodded. "Yes, true. But you dress like that all the time. Like a man."

My eyes widened. "I don't dress like a *man*," I said. "I dress *practically*. Because I live on a farm. And do icky, farmy things *all the time*."

Lorenz grinned, which was breathtaking. "A cute little man."

I took a deep breath, then headed to the tack room. The two of them chuckled out in the aisle as they resumed sweeping.

"I miss carriages," I heard Charles say.

"They were so elegant," Lorenz agreed.

I took all the metal stuff off of a harness and began to whack at the dirt with a brush. Someone had been riding out in mud, and it was caked on. I knew Reyn sometimes rode—of River's six horses, three of them were for riding—and so did Lorenz and Anne. Probably others. I never did, though she had offered them to me.

Lorenz began humming, then softly singing a passage

from *Aida*. I tried not to listen to the romantic words as I began to soap up a bridle with the aptly named saddle soap. He and Charles actually missed horse-drawn carriages. Here was another reminder of how different we all were, we immortals.

Me + horses = painful memories. I wiped off the saddle soap and started rubbing in tack oil, trying hard not to think about any other time in my life when I had done this. Think about something else. My brain was suddenly awash in memories of the previous night, kissing Reyn in the dark, cold woods. My cheeks flushed with heat and I bent over my task.

Reyn. What was he doing pursuing me? He didn't seem happy about it, like, ZOMG, I met my soul mate and now my life can begin! It was more like he was being compelled against his will. And not that that wasn't fun for me, but still. And I continued to totally resent the fact that I was so drawn to him, found him so overwhelmingly hot.

I'm really good at not thinking about difficult stuff, and I put that skill to use right then. I wondered what was for dinner, how Meriwether's New Year's had gone, what Dray was up to, since I hadn't seen her lately. I wondered why Charles was here, why Lorenz was here....

Why, perhaps I should ask!

"Lorenz!"

A few moments later his handsome head peered around

the doorway, gull-wing eyebrows arched perfectly over deep blue eyes. "Yes?"

"Why are you here?" I gestured largely, denoting "at River's Edge" rather than "in the barn." He blinked in surprise, and I could almost see him weighing the decision to tell me, what he should say, if anything.

He stepped into the stall and stood by the door. I was struck by the change in his demeanor—he was usually brash, cocky, charming; self-confident in the way that an incredibly handsome man can be. He opened his mouth to say something—raised his hand, then let it fall.

I polished a saddle very quietly, my eyes locked on him. This ought to be good.

His fingers plucked the fabric of the Italian wool trousers he had chosen to muck out the barn in. "I…" he said, looking at the ceiling, the floor. "I have…"

I held my breath. Cheerful, lovely Brynne had tried to set someone on fire, so I couldn't imagine what had brought Lorenz here.

"I have two hundred and thirty-five children," he said, and I almost fell over. "Or so." He didn't look at me, was trying to seem nonchalant, but I'm the queen of nonchalant and I saw right through it.

I realized I was gaping at him slack-jawed, so I closed my mouth, nodded, and worked on the saddle some more, my mind screaming questions.

"Wow," I said calmly, as if, oh yes, gosh, I run up against stuff like this all the time! Only 235, you say? Why, I knew a man who...

"That's a lot," I acknowledged. "All immortals?" Holy moly, our numbers were really increasing.

"No." He brushed thick black hair off his brow. "About sixty immortals. I think."

Instantly I saw it: He was facing the death of about 170 of his own children, one after another. Why would he do that to himself?

"I have tried...." He gave the wall an ironic smile. "Vasectomies heal."

Of course. That's what we do. And he was apparently too self-destructive for the obvious condoms or other kinds of birth control. Lordy day.

"And yet you keep going up to bat?" Clearly.

"I'm trying to understand," he said. That's why he was here. To find out why he would perpetrate such pain on himself, on his children, whom he surely wasn't being a father to, not all of them—and the women he abandoned.

"Holy crap—you're only about a hundred!" The thought escaped my mouth before I could stop it.

He nodded solemnly. "A hundred and seven."

Oh my God—say he got started when he was twenty. In eighty years he had fathered 235 kids, that he knew of. Surely some of them were already dead—disease, accidents. But he was facing another ninety years of watching his offspring die. And then there were all the immortal kids, demanding their allowance, *forever*.

"I am trying to understand," he said again, and gave me a polite, distant smile. Then he turned and headed out, and a few moments later I heard the *swish* of his broom again.

Well. I picked up the leather oil and tilted a small bit onto a rag. That had been...reassuring. I mean, not to be all sucks-to-be-you on Lorenz, but the notion that I'm not the worst person in the world was something I clung to like a chunk of the *Titanic*. And I was blowing my whistle in the dark.

Okay, I don't know where I was going with that— have to stop flinging metaphors around—but you get the picture.

Jeez. All those kids. The half-immortal ones would mostly live very long lives—you tend to read about them in the papers because they're more than a hundred or whatever. And either Lorenz would have to pretend to age in front of them so he would seem normal, or he would simply have to split and never see them again. Either way would suck. But the immortal ones...they were his *children*, but he'd probably never have a real relationship with more than a handful of them. Or maybe he could. Who knows? Maybe living forever meant he'd have tons of time to get to know each one. But any way you sliced it, it was weird and destructive.

"Oh, nice-looking aisle, guys," I heard River say. Her booted footsteps *thunk*ed on the brick floor of the barn. I began to polish industriously. Tack has to look nice but not too shiny, because shiny means possible slipperiness, which is the last thing you want to be dealing with as you're trying to get a twelve-hundred-pound animal to do your bidding. It's hard enough tacking them up when they're not slippery. And sometimes you can't take the time to tack them up at all....

In the 1860s, I was in England, in some dinky little town up north. I was there, like, waiting to catch a train to London or something. I think I had to wait another two days. What had been my name? It wasn't that long ago... what was it? England, England, after the gold rush in America...Rosemund? Rosemary. Rosemary Munson. Yeah, Rosemary. Oh my God—I remember the name of the inn where I was staying. The Old Blue Ball Inn (I am not making that up).

Anyway, in the middle of the freaking night (this stuff always happens in the middle of the night), I woke up because people were yelling and screaming. So I jumped up and threw open my window, looking out into the darkness for the fire or the invading army or the escaped circus tiger. And saw nothing.

But, you know, when people all around you are running and yelling, it makes a person sit up and take notice. I mean, you can keep your head while others lose theirs, but for God's sake figure out what's causing the shrill screams of panic. My two cents.

Then I saw it. It took a while to figure out what the hell I was looking at, but I put all my context clues together and cottoned on to the fact that people screaming "The dam broke! The dam broke! It's coming this way!"—plus an enormous gray slug rushing down the valley, weirdly fast—meant we were all about to die.

I grabbed my jacket and threw it on over my nightdress. (We're talking a Victorian-era nightdress—lace, yards of fabric, long, the works.) I raced downstairs and found the innkeeper and his wife throwing everything they could into the back of their old box wagon. The horses were neighing and rearing and kept almost toppling the wagon.

Much pandemonium. I remember it was cold, and my feet were bare. I ran out to the stables and found about eight horses freaking out and trying to kick down their stalls. In a split second I tried to figure out which one was the least likely to kill me, and then I undid its stable door bolt. It was a mare, a dappled gray with beautiful lines. I had no idea whom she belonged to. She reared and kicked and I whipped around her slicing hooves and looked for some kind of saddle. But most people took their saddles into the inn with them, because of thieves.

The screaming was louder, and then I heard a series of explosions that rocked the ground like thunder, almost shaking me off my feet. I read later that the rushing flood broke a gas main that had then been ignited by a spark — the showering flames had set most of the buildings on fire. I grabbed the horse's nose halter and clambered onto her back while she tried to throw me off. But I had been riding horses since I was three years old, so I grabbed her mane with both hands, clamped my knees to her sides, dug my bare feet in, and shouted, "Go!"

And she leaped right out of the barn into the fire. I had no reins, no way to steer this horse. I yanked her head sideways, my fist in her mane, and she turned like a ballerina, swinging left on her two hind feet.

And we raced out of that town, running through the fire, only a hundred yards or so ahead of a great, gray wall of water that was crushing everything in its path. We tore out of there as if creditors were chasing us and ran and ran uphill for what seemed like hours.

At one point I looked back, and all I saw was the flooded valley and the rooftops of buildings, a few still burning and sticking oddly out of the churning, rushing river.

My nightgown and the sleeves of my jacket were charred and singed; I had some blisters on my arms and legs. But I had made it, had escaped being badly burned (immortals feel pain just as regular people do), escaped having to fight the flood, get knocked around, drown but not die, etc. Most people hadn't survived. Sheffield. That was the name of the town.

I came out of it fine—the jacket I had grabbed had all my worldly goods sewn into the seams and the lining, so I was quickly able to buy new clothes, sell that pretty, lovely, brave mare, and get a new ticket to London. It had made quite a story. I had been victorious over disaster!

Now I couldn't swallow, sitting here in the stall at River's Edge. I was still, my hands aching, my chest about to burst. The clean saddle in my lap seemed like it was mocking me, my pathetically tiny penance.

The other horses. All the other horses in the inn's stables that night. What had happened to them? I could have set them all free, in seconds. They could have run to safety. I probably could not have, in all actuality, saved any people. Maybe another small one, on the back of my horse. But the people had all been trying to take care of themselves, and at the time it never even occurred to me to bother about them.

Or the horses. I'd gotten my ass out of there, leaving

trapped and panicked animals behind. I sank miserably into the barn floor. I'm just—such a waste. Such a failure as a person. I couldn't think of words bad enough to describe me. That, my friends, is *only one* of hundreds of similar tales, tales where I came out on top, happy and lucky and in good shape. Leaving death and destruction and victims all caught up in the dust cloud on my tail.

CHAPTER 8

h-oh. Are you having a moment?"

I looked up to see River grinning at me from the doorway. I rubbed my hand over my eyes and couldn't muster a smile.

"A whole lot of moments?" Her voice was kind. She came and sat next to me on the dusty floor, littered with bits of hay and stains from tack oil.

I bobbed my head with my usual suave sophistication. I didn't know why these old memories were affecting me this way—I was literally remembering them differently, from a more acute angle than I ever had. And it was so, so awful.

I looked away from her, still loathing even the suggestion of crying in public.

She rested one hand on my filthy knee. "Drag all the skeletons out where we can see 'em," she said softly. "That's the only way to get rid of them. They hate the sunlight."

Oh, like I would ever admit stuff like this to anyone. No way.

"Maybe I'm not worth saving." I hadn't planned to say it—it came out in a whisper. I'd felt guardedly optimistic this morning; now I wouldn't be surprised if River kicked me to the curb and told me not to come back.

River was silent for a moment. "You don't believe that."

I shrugged. I didn't know what to think. I was writhing inside, like an ant under a magnifying glass.

"I think...I'd like to show you something," she said.

I squelched an unhappy sigh. Here was another teachable moment, hurtling toward me like a freight train.

"I'd have to link our minds together," she said, and I felt a flicker of interest.

"Why?"

"I have to show you—I can't just tell you about it." She waited for my answer.

I couldn't pass this up. I nodded.

We swept a space clean on the floor, and River drew a

perfect circle freehand using some of the rock salt we put on the walkways to make them less icy. An old green candle stood on a shelf; River blew the dust off it and kindled its flame. I made a mental note to ask someone to teach me to do that.

"Now we sit, our knees touching," she said. Just like we had the night she had stripped all the black dye out of my hair, making me look like the real teenage me.

"Okay."

"And we'll call our power, and I'll cast the spell, and I'll put my hands on your face," she explained.

"And you'll suck my consciousness out through my eye-balls?"

The corners of her mouth turned up. "No. Promise."

"Okay." I let out a deep breath, then closed my eyes and tried to concentrate. I heard River singing, chanting, and after a while I joined in, following along. I inhaled deeply, as if I were breathing in lights of many colors, enough to crowd out the blackness that was coiled inside me, aching to get out.

I inhaled again, filling with serenity and beauty, peace and joy. A leftover tear leaked from my eye as I felt the miracle that was magick casting its radiance over me, over us. Filled with magick, I felt only awe, only a brilliant, crystalline perfection drawing me to it. And then River's cool fingers touched my face. I wondered what she was going to show me at the same moment that I had the nauseating *duh* that this mind-meld might very well work two ways. Would she be able to see the random and mundane grotesqueness inside me, as I could see inside her?

"No," said River, and then she was standing in front of me, holding her hand out toward me. I looked around—it was daytime; we were outside somewhere. The scene had a dreamy feel to it, but I felt like we were really there. I reached out, seeing my hand take hers as if from a long distance away.

"I won't go into your consciousness unless you ask me to," she said as we walked. "And you know how to block me or anyone else, even if I tried."

I was digesting these thoughts when I saw we had come to a tall stone building, the kind you find in old European cities. This one looked pretty new—it wasn't weathered or chipped. The stones were smooth and stacked together with perfect precision. I heard voices as we came out into a square, a piazza, because we were in Italy—I recognized it.

A crowd of white-robed, foreign-looking people were swarming around a raised platform set up at one end of the square. Flags showing coats of arms hung from several of the buildings. River and I stood at the back of the crowd. I tried to make out what the shouting was about, but I could only barely understand the occasional word, sort of.

"Why can't I understand them?" I asked River. "I speak Italian."

"They're speaking Middle Italian," she explained. "This is Genoa, the year 912. Come on."

We moved easily among the crowd—not like we were going right through people, and not like we floated over them, but just that we went forward and somehow eased our way through. Sharp, strong smells filled my nose. The bright colors, the loud shouting, the scents—it was in complete contrast to, say, present-day western Massachusetts.

I remembered that River was from Genoa. She'd been born in…718? And she was from one of the main houses of immortals, the Genoa branch. So she'd inherited a lot of power.

"Oh…"

I could see now. The platform was maybe eight feet off the ground and had a flag on the front: a coat of arms in red and green, featuring a three-headed snake, hissing. Nice. There were at least twenty people on the platform, and it took a minute to understand what I was seeing: the bargaining, the calling for bids. It was a slave auction. I'd seen them before, in different times, different parts of the world—it was amazing how common slavery had been in so many places until relatively recently. These looked like ragamuffin white people being sold to…

"Who's buying them?" I asked River.

"Mainly men from the Muslim countries to the east," she said.

"Where'd the slaves come from?"

"All over. A lot of Slavs. Some Baltic, some Turkish. Mostly Slavs."

I was wondering why she'd wanted me to see this, when my eye was caught by a flash of red. Up on the platform, behind everyone, stood a woman. Her back was to me, and she seemed to be directing the order of slaves being sold. At her word, beefy guys dispassionately hauled people forward. There were men, women, and children. The auctioneer was yelling constantly, working the crowd, describing a slave's attributes and trying to get the bids up. Two tall men with dark hair and eyes stood over on one side. One of them spoke to the woman, and she turned around, laughing.

It was young River, not quite two hundred years old. She was beautiful, with long black hair hanging down her back in complicated braids. A small white linen cap was tied under her chin. Her dress was simple but luxurious, and compared to the rest of the crowd, she was clearly of a higher class.

She called something back to the man, and they both laughed. Then she turned and spoke to the auctioneer's assistant, who bowed and nodded. Her clear brown eyes scanned the crowd shrewdly—she was gauging her audience. She quickly counted the slaves yet to be sold this day and almost absently touched the brown leather pouch tied to her waist.

I turned to the River at my side. She was watching the scene calmly, but there was deep sadness in her eyes.

"We were very successful slave traders," she said. "My brothers and I. We operated as different branches of a large, mythical family and were able to stay in Genoa for almost three centuries before the witch rumors started."

"Who are those men?" I pointed to the tall, dark men at one side.

"My brothers," she said. "Two of them."

One of the men called, "Diavola!"

The River on the platform turned and raised her eyebrows, then called back an answer to his question.

"Was Diavola your first name?"

"My third," River said. "The name I was born under was Aulina."

It only sank in gradually: River, one of the few actually truly pretty good people in the world—certainly the most good person I'd ever met—had bought and sold human beings. For centuries.

On the platform, a sobbing woman slave was being torn from her squalling infant. Diavola watched dispassionately nearby. River turned away.

"I'm ready to go," she murmured, and again I was aware of her fingertips touching my temples. With the next breath, I drew in reality and the scene faded away.

I didn't open my eyes. I don't think they were ever closed. It was more like River came into focus in front of me.

She lowered her hands and began to dismantle the spell. As much as each spell was created layer upon layer, so it was taken apart, layer by layer. I got my usual panicky horror at the feeling of bliss fading, leaving my world washed out and grayer, leaving me incomplete and flawed. That's why people would kill other people to take their power. I saw it now. Of course people would want more of that feeling, want to have it more often, have it last longer, be stronger. If I were truly Terävä, I would kill River right now and seize her power for myself.

I blinked and drew in a shocked breath, awed by my horrible thoughts. But you won't kill River, I thought quickly. You would never do that. Never. You're not all bad. You're not someone who would do such a thing. You know that.

I was barely aware of when River blew out the candle.

"Everyone is worth saving," she said softly, not looking at me. Her slim hands rested lightly on her knees.

I felt my butt frozen to the floor, the ache in my back and along my legs. For future reference, I would prefer to do magick wearing sweatpants, on a water bed. Enough with cold floors.

"You told me once that you used to be dark. Was that what you were talking about? That your family used to be slave traders?" I asked.

River gave a short, sardonic laugh, making me blink. I'd never heard her do that. "Yes, that was part of it. But sadly that wasn't even the darkest part of my history. Slave-trading was bad, it was really bad, and it put my karma in the toilet. But my story goes deeper and gets much worse, I'm afraid."

I had trouble believing that, but in my mind I saw Diavola, young and beautiful and without feeling as she split families apart and consigned people to wretched futures with slave owners.

"My point is, everyone is worth saving," she said, more firmly. "If I didn't believe that, I couldn't go on. I'd have ended it all a long time ago."

I nodded as we got up, brushing hay off my seat and wiggling to get some warmth going. "Yes, I mean slaving was not good. But slaves were everywhere back then. That society considered it normal. No one thought you were awful for being in that line of business, at that time."

Her eyes were thoughtful. "You think that makes it all right, not evil?"

"I think it makes it less evil," I said honestly. "You can

only be formed by your society." I came up with a quote I had heard once: "'Nothing is good or bad, but thinking makes it so.'"

"Hmm," said River. "That could make for some very interesting dinner conversation. So if you think that the nature of the society helps determine the relative evilness of a thing, would you say that Reyn's marauding and plundering was less bad, because it was so common back then? So many tribes did it?"

I stared at her. How neatly she had turned the tables on me. I looked for spite in her eyes but saw only warmth and compassion.

I couldn't craft a coherent, well-reasoned reply. Instead I stiffly hung the cleaned tack and saddles on their pegs and tried to squash my immediate urge to lash out at her.

"That was different," I said, knowing how ridiculous it sounded, and knowing that she had me. I couldn't make excuses for her without making excuses for Reyn, and I would *never* make excuses for Reyn.

"Hmm," she said again, and looked at her watch. "It's late. And I think you're on the dinner team."

She managed a slight smile at my unenthusiastic look, but she seemed tired or withdrawn, as if visiting that past had drained her.

I felt a little less bad.

CHAPTER 9

uring my centuries of debauchery and wastedness, I had lost most of my practical skills. Now I found a quiet, surprising satisfaction in my ability to do things somewhat competently. Even if I had to do them side by side with Jess and the unsmiling Butcher of Winter.

As long as I didn't have to stand too close to Reyn, I was okay. We hadn't spoken since our Winter Wonderland experience. Perhaps if I didn't get a whiff of the fresh-laundry scent of his shirt, I might possibly be able to not throw myself at him and make out right on top of the kitchen table.

"Here." Jess set a basket of already (thank God) scrubbed turnips, carrots, and potatoes on the kitchen table. He'd put a big roast in the oven hours earlier, and the room was filled with delicious-smelling steam.

"You want 'em cubed or in big chunks or what?" I asked.

"Big chunks. I'll add them to the pot," he replied, and turned to open a bottle of wine. Without asking, he filled a wineglass halfway and put it at my elbow. No one here drank much at all, and I knew that some of us, like Jess for example, had had huge substance-abuse problems at some point.

But I wasn't going to look a gift glass in the mouth. I picked it up quickly and inhaled its sweet, rich tang. Then I took a sip and let it linger in my mouth. So, so lovely. I tried not to think about times when I'd chugged half a bottle in one gulp.

Jess put most of the bottle into the great big pan in the oven. A wave of roasting meat filled the room, and my stomach growled.

I chopped at one end of the table and Mr. Golden Sunshine set up shop at the other end. He dusted the table with flour, took out a plastic bin of rising dough, and set about forming a pile of dinner rolls as if I wasn't there.

Seeing some of River's past had been weird and kind of disturbing. I guess I hadn't really believed her when she'd said she'd been dark, before—she was so patently amazing now. I frowned, cutting the tops off the turnips. If she was just as flawed and awful as me, why would I believe anything she said? Could someone really get past all that and be a better, completely different person?

And then, Lorenz's startling admission about the million Lorenz Juniors running around. That was messed up. And Jess here was obviously a train wreck of a person. Reyn was the personification of someone tortured by his past and never really getting over it. Why were any of us even trying? I kept hoping I was done with all the past-reliving, and then something happened that brought it all up again, like a cat eating grass. My past was standing in the middle of the road, waving its arms, screaming *Look at me!* But why? Why did any of it matter anymore?

Out of the corner of my eye, I watched Reyn's taut, strong forearms as he kneaded dough and shaped rolls expertly. I tried not to think about him kneading or shaping me.

"Hi hi," said Anne, pushing through the kitchen door. Her fine black hair swung around her cheeks, and she shoved the sleeves of her green sweater up to her elbows. "I'm setting the table—there will be thirteen at dinner because..."

The door pushed open again, and Anne made a ta-da gesture. "My sister is here! Everyone, this is Amy. Amy, this is Jess, Reyn, and Nastasya."

"Hi," said Amy with a smile. She was Anne Lite, with slightly younger features, longer, unstyled mink brown hair falling around her shoulders, and a less polished look altogether. Anne was a teacher; Amy seemed like a student still, if that makes sense.

I realized she was really, really pretty, in a fresh, unmade-up way. Why could some women skip makeup and look "fresh and unmade-up," but when I skipped it, which I did every day, I looked like I'd been embalmed?

"Wow, it smells great in here!" said Amy, taking the stack of plates that Anne handed her.

"Yeah, we rock," I said, and took a sip of my wine. It left a warm trail all the way down my throat, and I suppressed the urge to gulp it.

Amy smiled, and then I watched as she caught sight of Reyn, and everything went into slow motion.

Her eyes visibly focused on him. Her smile faltered for just a second, then became wider. It occurred to me that even though I didn't want him, it had been annoying when Nell had, and now Amy seemed to be falling into the vortex of Viking fabulosity. It burned me. No one but me should see how intensely appealing he was, how beautiful, how deadly. Clearly, Amy could.

"Any hopes for dessert?" she asked Reyn, doing everything but batting her eyelashes.

And Reyn, who was taciturn and tortured with *me*,

gave *her* an easy smile back. I blinked, practically hearing angels sing. Amy was hypnotized and thrilled, staring into his eyes like a stunned rabbit.

"Yes," he said, throwing a dish towel over one broad shoulder. "Something chocolate."

"Excellent." Amy gave us all another smile and pushed through the doorway after Anne. The kitchen seemed smaller without her.

Many dismaying thoughts whirled through my head like trash on an empty street, but what I came up with was: "Chocolate?"

"I'll think of something," he said, and I started to feel totally irrationally furious that he would make something *chocolate* for *her*.

I turned my back to him and finished chopping the vegetables, pretending that each one was Reyn's self-confidence and I was whacking it into bits. I gave them all to Jess, ripped off my apron, then stalked out.

I was 459 years old and full of schoolgirl jealousy over someone I didn't even *want*.

Crap.

You'll be interested to hear that the previous scene was the *highlight* of my week. Yes. It all slid downhill from there, like a Popsicle off a hot car hood.

I headed to work the next morning, knowing that

Meriwether was back at school—it was just me and the charm of Old Mac until that afternoon. Mr. MacIntyre was even angrier and more hostile than usual. I wondered if the holiday had pushed him over the edge.

I did my usual worker-elf routine: putting away stock, tidying, sweeping, sorting out the day's receipts, and keeping a log of checks to go to the bank. MacIntyre's Drugs: the store that technology forgot.

Mostly I kept well out of Old Mac's way, and he spoke hardly two words to me all day. At four, Meriwether came in, her pale hair wind-tossed. She smiled, looking genuinely happy to see me, then headed into the back to clock in and drop off her schoolbag. Her own father made her clock in and keep a time card.

I'd saved some restocking so that she and I could work together without Mr. MacIntyre yelling at us. Soon we were settled down in aisle four, unpacking medicated foot powder and arch supports.

"So how was the New Year's dance?" I whispered. Old Mac was behind his pharmacy counter, and I didn't want to waken the beast.

"Both good and icky," said Meriwether, keeping her voice down. "I had a good time, at first. Lowell was there—he's really nice, and the DJ was good. And I really liked my dress. I couldn't believe my dad even let me go. So those were all good."

"What was bad?" I slid packages onto their little metal supports.

Meriwether made a face. "A bunch of kids crashed the dance. And they were drunk, wasted. They made a big scene, and Mr. Daly tried to kick them out, and then they broke up stuff."

"Oh, bummer," I said. "They actually broke things?"

"Yeah. Like one of the DJ's big speakers, and they fell against the food table and the whole thing collapsed, so all the food was ruined. We were all so pissed."

"That's awful," I said, as images of myself doing similar things to similar nice, undeserving people rolled through my head. "Did you know them?"

"A couple of them. They used to go to my school, but they dropped out. A girl named Dray and some guy named Taylor. Some others I didn't know."

My hand paused in midair. Dray? The Dray I was trying to fix? I hadn't seen her in several weeks, but we'd had a really good talk the last time we'd run into each other. She reminded me uncomfortably of me, and if I saved her before she totally self-destructed, I was adding more points to my side of the board, so to speak.

"That's too bad," I said. "They used to go to your school?"

"Yeah. Taylor was a senior last year, but he got kicked out for smoking pot, like, two months before graduation.

Dray was in my grade. She was such a bitch. But I always thought maybe she had it bad at home, you know? My dad wouldn't let her mom shop here anymore, because her checks always bounced." Meriwether looked unhappy. "But still. That doesn't mean she can come wreck the only dance my dad ever let me go to."

"Yeah, I know. What a bummer. Do you think you'll actually go out with Lowell?" What kind of modern kid is named Lowell?

"I don't know if my dad will let me. But I can see him at school. We could sit together at lunch sometimes." Her face brightened, and we finished unloading that crate. The sun had gone down outside, and the dark sky looked gray and sullen because of the clouds hanging low over the town.

"What are you doing?" Mr. MacIntyre's gruff voice almost made me jump. Since his jar-throwing incident, he had been more subdued, as if that had shocked him into trying to repress his anger a little bit. Meriwether didn't seem to be holding it against him. I wished I could do more to help her situation. I gestured to the empty plastic crates.

"Taking these out back," I said, doing just that.

When I returned, Meriwether was dusting the shelves. As Meriwether stuffed the feather duster back under the counter, we heard something drop. Frowning, she leaned down and picked it up. It was a small frame, and her face fell when she looked at the picture in it. I was dying to see what it was but pretended not to notice, in case she wanted to stuff it out of sight again. Instead she came over and held it out to me.

"This was my mom," she said in a tiny voice.

In the photo, Meriwether was sitting on a green corduroy sofa, smiling at the camera. She seemed about twelve or thirteen, so it must have been right before her mom died. Her mother looked a lot like Meriwether, but older. I mean, a *lot* like her. As in, Meriwether would be her twin when she was that age. No wonder Old Mac could hardly stand to be around her. Speaking of Old Mac, my jaw almost dropped. I'd never seen him so normal, so healthy. He was smiling hugely, gazing at his wife, his arm across the back of the sofa. I couldn't believe how happy he seemed—a completely different person.

"This must be your little brother," I murmured. He, too, looked happy, sitting securely between his father and Meriwether. Where Meriwether was pale and fair, like her mom, her brother had dark hair and eyes, like Old Mac.

"Yeah. That's Ben," she barely whispered, her face tragic.

"What the hell is this?!" The roar surprised us both, and I almost dropped the frame. Mr. MacIntyre stood there, all temporary restraint gone, almost shaking with rage. He shot out a hand and yanked the picture from me, scraping my palm. "How dare you! How *dare* you take this—" He made the mistake of glancing at the picture, and in a cartoon, he would be the figure that someone had punctured, letting his air out with a hiss. Then he recovered, clutching the picture to his chest and slamming his other hand down on the counter.

"Don't you *ever* mention his name again!" His voice, huge and incensed, filled the small store. Meriwether, already stretched thin by his tirade, burst into tears. I wanted to snap my hand out, hiss something strong and dark, make him crumple to his knees. Of course I wouldn't, shouldn't, but I was taut, vibrating like a string, ready to leap into action. But I was so mad, *so mad* that he got to yell at her like this, with no one stopping him. So mad that he blamed Meriwether for being alive. My palms tingled with the urge to just—Taser him with magick.

"You quit yelling at her!" I shouted. "It's not *her* fault she didn't die!" It wasn't what I meant to say, and of the three of us, I'm not sure who was the most shocked. Meriwether abruptly stopped crying and stared at me, and Old Mac went pale. Then his eyes almost bugged out of his head.

Of course I trundled on. Why would I develop discretion now? "She's all you have left! You guys have each other! Should she have died, too, so that you'd have no one?"

Meriwether hiccuped in the unnatural silence.

"You shut up!" Mr. MacIntyre screamed, and I took a step back at the look on his face. He was winning the Who's Madder? contest, hands down. Did that stop me? Nope.

"You're ruining what life you have left!" I yelled back. "Your business is in the toilet because no one wants to deal with you! Your daughter is afraid of you! You seem like a crazy old man! Is that what you want?" This may have been pushing it. A vein throbbed in his temple, and I wondered if he was going to have a stroke. He seemed speechless, so enraged that he literally couldn't spew hate fast enough.

Finally his mouth opened, and I braced myself.

"You're fired!" he bellowed. "Fired! Get the hell out of here! I never want to see your face again! And you stay away from my daughter!"

I blinked. Naively, I had not actually expected to get fired. I thought we would all yell for a while, then fume silently for several days, followed by a month of passive-aggression. But fired? Crap. I was supposed to have a job. For my personal growth.

"Fired?" I tried to sound brave.

"Fired!" he shouted again. "Get your stuff and get out!"

"Fine!" I turned and stomped to the back, where I grabbed my coat and my time card. Then I stomped toward the front. "Here!" I said, smacking my time card down on the counter. "You owe me for six days, since before New Year's!"

"Get out!" he screamed.

I faced Meriwether, who looked like nothing so much as a trembling aspen. "Hang in there," I told her. "Sorry your dad's such a bastard."

Her eyes widened, and Old Mac drew in a furious breath. I stomped outside into the dark, only to remember that I now had to go home and admit I was fired. That I was unable to keep a job that a reasonably bright chimp could do. Ugh.

As soon as I was out of sight of MacIntyre's Drugs, I slowed down. Stupidly, I had walked in the wrong direction—my car was parked behind me. But there was no way I would walk past that bright picture window again.

I gritted my teeth, angry and agitated. What a terrible scene. He'd actually *fired* me. And had I also hurt Meriwether with my words? Her face had been bloodless. Crap. I saw that I was in front of Early's Feed and Farmware, our local general store. I went in.

What was I going to tell River? Everything is a *choice*. *Everything*. Including shouting awful things at one's boss, causing one to get one's ass fired.

I headed to the candy section, and after some agonized

deliberation got some sour apple Now and Laters. Which everyone knows should be called Now *or* Laters.

I was in the middle of checking out, giving the cashier my money, when I happened to glance toward the back of the store. I saw a familiar flash of green-streaked brown hair. Dray!

The boy was counting out my change, so I couldn't go over to her, but I tried to catch her eye. Which is why I saw her boosting some batteries, slipping them off their holder and shoving them under her jacket.

My heart fell.

"Miss?" The boy held out my receipt.

"Thanks." I took it and headed for the exit, going over all the ways this day had sucked. Outside I leaned against the building and unwrapped a Now and Later. It had started to snow; fine white flakes were drifting down, already sticking to the cars parked along the street.

I didn't have to wait long. Dray came out a few minutes later, walking casually through the doors and then hooking a sharp right and starting to speed up.

"Yo."

She turned at my voice and saw me. I held out an N and L. She hesitated, not quite stopping.

"It's sour apple," I said in a coaxing, singsong voice.

She made a face and took it from my hand.

"How are things?" I asked.

She shrugged, not looking at me. "Fine."

"Me too. Thanks for asking."

She shrugged again and put the candy in her mouth.

I decided that quizzing her about her holidays was probably a bad idea. "So . . . what have you been up to?"

"The usual. Volunteering at church. Reading to the blind." She chewed with her mouth open slightly, watching the snow fall.

"Have you thought more about getting out of here?" The last time we'd talked, before the holidays, I'd urged her to leave West Lowing in her rearview mirror.

Her heavily rimmed eyes shifted to me. "No. What's wrong with being here?" Her tone was belligerent. It was like looking into a mirror from six months earlier. Or even from a week ago. Gosh, it must be so rewarding for other people to interact with me.

"I thought you want to get out of here, get away from people who can't appreciate your inner beauty," I said. The sour apple tingled in the back of my throat.

She was bored. "I'm fine." It was like she had taken the online correspondence course called "You Can Be Nasty, Too!"

And just as people dealing with me soon lose their patience, I lost mine.

"Is that why you're nicking batteries from Early's?"

She frowned. "Nicking?"

"Stealing."

She rolled her eyes. Snowflakes were landing on her head and melting against her hair. It was supercold, and I'd just gotten fired and possibly really hurt Meriwether's feelings.

"Dray, c'mon, we talked," I said. "I told you that you should get out of this one-Wal-Mart town. Why are you here, stealing stuff?"

"Who are *you*?" she snapped. "My social worker? What gives you the right to tell me anything?"

Probably a regular person would have realized the truth in her words at this point and backed off. That's so not me.

"I'm someone you should listen to!" I snapped back. "I know more than you, have done more than you, have been more worse-off than you! I'm more *you* than you'll ever be! And you know and I know that this town is going to drag you down! You're hanging around with losers, doing stupid-ass stuff like crashing school dances and lifting *batteries*, for God's sake — and now you're standing here like everything's fine? Come *on*!"

Dray stared at me, furious. "Screw you!" Her voice was loud, and some women leaving Early's looked over at us. "You're so together? You have no family, no friends — you're in *rehab* at some stupid farm, and you're working at a freaking drugstore in the middle of East Jesus! And you're lecturing *me*? You never even graduated high school! You're a big *joke*!"

My mouth opened to defend myself, then shut abruptly. I had no family, I'd left all my friends, I was in a much more serious rehab situation than she knew, I'd actually gotten *fired* from my pathetic job, and I have not ever actually graduated from any high school, as it turns out.

When you put it that way, maybe I should curl up in a snowbank and not freeze to death.

She sneered at the look on my face. "Truth hurts, huh?"

"That is such a cliché," I muttered.

"*You're* a cliché," she said coldly. "You're going around trying to help people, but you're such a screwup yourself! And you can't see it!"

"I can see I'm a screwup!" That didn't come out the way I'd intended.

I totally recognized her mean, defensive face. "Yeah, I bet. Go off and take care of your own problems. Leave me alone." She turned and headed off into the night.

"Dray!" I yelled, with zero plan for anything to say after that.

Without turning around, she shot me the finger.

Yeah, that had gone well.

CHAPTER 10

ince this day was the hill that crap kept rolling down, I still had to admit I'd been fired. I darted past the lit window at MacIntyre's Drugs, casting a fast glance inside. I was relieved to see only an empty store and skittered over to my car.

River's Edge had many lit windows, promising warmth. In the yard, snow coated everything like powdered sugar. I climbed out of my car and trudged toward the house, wondering if I could slink upstairs and into a hot bath without anyone noticing me. I climbed the stairs and quietly opened the dark green front door—

"Hey! Nastasya! They're making Chinese food for dinner!" In the front hall, Amy actually bounced on her heels a couple times in excitement. "And Charles lived in China, so he knows the real way!"

How did she know that Charles had lived in China? I didn't. She'd just gotten here!

Anne came forward with a smile. "Hi—how was your day? It's bitter out there."

My plan of sneaking upstairs and faking illness evaporated.

"I got fired!" I blurted, and felt my chin quivering, my face crumpling. Because I hadn't been humiliated enough today, we were going to go the extra mile of crying in front of everyone, including Anne's adorable sister whom Reyn had made chocolate dessert for.

"Oh, honey," said Anne, and immediately came to hug me, patting my back as if I were a child with a scraped knee. "I'm so sorry. I know Mr. MacIntyre must be awful to work for."

"What happened?" River's voice.

"James MacIntyre fired her today," Anne said over my shoulder. I kept my eyes closed, not wanting to face River.

"Oh, goodness," said River. "Well, you lasted an amazingly long time. It was only a matter of when you would sneeze wrong and he would give you the boot."

They were taking my side. Instantly, without hearing

the facts. They *knew* me, and they were still sticking up for me. I straightened and opened my eyes, dragging the back of one hand under my nose. "I didn't sneeze wrong."

"What happened?" River asked.

"He was screaming at Meriwether, his daughter who works there, and she was crying, and I thought he might actually even hit her, and I didn't want to use magick to stop him—that would be wrong," I put in virtuously, "so I lost it and shouted awful things at him and said he was ruining his life and that his own daughter was afraid of him." I took a breath. "Then he yelled that I was fired and to get out and he never wanted to see me again."

Actually, I didn't come off too badly there—defending the innocent, etc. And it was all true. I hadn't captured the depth of the awfulness, or Meriwether's shocked, pale face and the fact that in trying to hurt her dad I may have hurt her, too. But that was the gist.

"Hmm," River said. I couldn't read the expression in her eyes. It wasn't anger or condemnation or disappointment.

"How awful," said Anne, patting my back again. "But I have an idea about what might make you feel better."

"Ice cream?" Hope flared in my chest.

"No," she said, grinning. "A nice meditation session. We just have time before dinner. Join the four of us." She gestured to herself, Amy, Rachel, and Daisuke, who had gathered in the hall while I was pouring out my story.

Oh God, no, I thought.

"An excellent idea!" said River, wearing the slight smirk that told me she knew exactly what I was thinking. "Go along now. I know you'll feel much more centered afterward."

Anne started up the stairs, followed by the others, and I lingered, hoping River would say she was just kidding and what I really needed was a Scotch and a hot bath. She smiled and smoothed my snow-damp hair. "You really will feel better afterward," she said softly.

I sighed and headed up the stairs. They were insidious with their niceness.

I hadn't tried to meditate since my self-introspection flop on New Year's Eve. This was the last thing I felt like doing. Would I ever be well enough to be able to say, *No, thanks, no meditation for me right now?* Surely I would get to a point where I wasn't so obviously damaged that people wanted to fling me into meditation circles every time I turned around. Right?

I breathed in and out. My washout day ebbed away from me. My stomach unknotted; my shoulders unhunched. This moment was serene and perf—

Nastasya's power is so amazingly strong. I worry—

My spine straightened a little — who had thought that? It had already been pointed out how unusual it was that I could sometimes hear people's thoughts during meditation. Apparently your run-of-the-mill immortal was not burdened with knowing what people thought about them. But who here was worried about me? Surely Anne, as the only teacher here. But maybe Rachel or Daisuke, both of whom were really advanced? I calmed my breathing and opened myself up to receive more.

I should give away Shiro's pot.

This I recognized as Daisuke. His thought came to me in a flash: He had a small, beautiful bowl that his brother had made. His brother was dead, and this was the only thing that Daisuke had of his. He was agonizing about his need to divest himself of all belongings and his desire to keep a little part of his brother with him always.

Should go home and see Mom soon . . .

That was Rachel. I wondered where her mom was. I knew Rachel was originally from Mexico.

I'm going to be all over Reyn like ugly on an ape.

I almost choked on my spit and forced myself to swallow slowly. That would be Amy. She was *facing* her emotions. She was not refusing to *deal* with things. Because the thing she was *dealing* with was her intense desire to ~~be a normal person with a hot guy~~ jump on some stranger she didn't even *know*.

Nastasya, you are such a chickenshit.

What? Who was that?! Oh, wait—it was me.

What?

You are such a chickenshit. You act so tough, but really you're a gooey marshmallow of schoolgirl fears. You keep saying you want to get better, but only if you don't have to do anything hard.

What does that mean? I am working hard!

No. Your "working hard" consists of not fighting everyone about everything. And that's a start. But you have to do more than just not say no.

What the eff?

You have to be active, not passive. You can't just storm away from Meriwether, from Dray, from Reyn. You can make things right. You, Nas, actually have to grow the hell up. At last.

Well.

I guess we're just walking in the truth here.

I was practically hyperventilating with anger. How dare my own subconscious turn on me? How dare—

You're deflecting what you need to do by focusing on being angry.

I almost snorted, furious.

"Okay, let's start to come out," said Anne softly.

Who did my subconscious think she was? I opened my eyes, mad that Anne had suggested I do this, that River had made me. Daisuke, across from me, looked troubled, no closer to an answer about his brother's bowl. Rachel looked thoughtful. Anne had her eyes on me. And Amy? The jonesing-for-Reyn Amester? I glanced at her, then stifled a shriek, jerking backward.

Amy had Incy's face, handsome and unearthly. She had Incy's dark, intense stare, his dark curls, his eyes locked on mine. I saw my visions of him, my dreams. . . . It was all I could do to not leap to my feet. Instead I blinked and sucked in a quick breath, and then Amy was just Amy again.

Everyone was looking at me.

I brushed my hand against my mouth. It was trembling. "Sorry," I muttered. "Optical illusion." He was haunting me, stalking my mind, and I felt scared. Dreams, illusions, were hard enough to deal with. If he was going to be around during a normal waking day, then I was going to be seriously wigged-out.

I almost wept with joy when the dinner chime rang just then. I scrambled to my feet, tossed my buckwheat pillow on the pile in the corner, and headed out after Rachel.

Not so fast, Grasshopper.

"Nas? A minute?"

I turned with extreme reluctance to face Anne. The others filed out — lucky bastards — leaving us alone in the small workroom.

Anne looked like she was thinking of how to say something. Finally she asked, "Is everything okay? You seemed really upset for a second."

"Oh, I'm okay," I said unconvincingly.

Anne waited for a couple moments to see if I would break down and tell the truth, but when I didn't, she went on. "I remembered you'd heard people's thoughts, in an earlier meditation class. I guess—I wasn't sure if you could always do it or whether that was a fluke. But—it's actually not okay to eavesdrop."

"Is there a way to stop it?" I asked.

Anne blinked in surprise. "Yes. You don't listen in on purpose?"

"No. I just...sort of feel my mind opening." I remembered the cutting things my inner Nasty had thrown at me. "Sometimes too much."

"Okay, that will be our next lesson," said Anne. "I've never had to teach someone how to not do that—almost no one can. But it makes sense for you—I should have thought of it earlier. I'll teach you how, okay?"

"Sure." I started to walk out, but she wasn't done.

"Nastasya—you really did seem frightened at the end. When you looked at Amy. What was it?"

I glanced at Anne quickly, remembering that Amy was her sister. "Nothing! I mean, Amy's fine. It was just— my mind playing tricks on me. For just a second she looked like someone else—the friend I left in London. Incy."

Anne frowned. "Had you been thinking about Incy?"

"Not just then. But it's nothing about Amy. She doesn't remind me of him or anything."

"Hmm," Anne said, walking with me out the door.

I shrugged my shoulders, self-conscious and not wanting to talk about it. Had my mind been telling me that I was hopelessly dark? As dark as Innocencio? As dark as my parents had been? Was it in my blood, inescapably? And...would there be any point to me being here, if that was true?

CHAPTER 11

e active, my subconscious had said. Make it right. Grow up.

If I had my way, my subconscious would never get another gig as long as I lived. Wait. Crap. Never mind.

I had no idea what it had meant. I pondered it all the way through Charles's fabulous Chinese dinner, then through a shower, then for about two seconds after I fell into bed, exhausted. When I jolted awake at 5:29, one minute before my alarm went off, I knew that forming any kind of make-it-right plan was a not-happening thing.

I was on egg-gathering duty that morning, appropriately enough, given the chickenshit reference. The devil chicken gave me the evil eye, and I didn't even try to get her eggs. Someday I would come in here with asbestos fireplace gloves up to my elbows, and there would be a reckoning. But not today.

I put the last warm egg in my basket, imagining my brain overheating from thinking too hard, smoke coming out of my ears. Make it right. Try one little thing at a time. Maybe. Okay, how about... I would try to... um, not judge people too harshly? At least not right away, I amended in a nod to reality. I groaned at coming up with the lamest thing ever and left the warm, feathery coop to head back to the house. About forty feet ahead of me was Reyn, carrying two metal pails of milk from our two milk cows, Beulah and Petunia. He looked tall and strong, carrying the pails as if they were empty. I forced myself to see him as: Man Carrying Milk Pails. He was not *only* the person I remembered from long ago, and he was not only the superficial, physical object of my fevered fantasies. He was a whole, real person — and, actually, I barely knew him.

We ended up at the kitchen steps together, and he looked over at me.

"Good morning," I said. Big-girl Nastasya.

"Morning." I felt his surprise. Then we went into the kitchen.

• • •

So, if you try to make things right with someone, and they dis you, it's so humiliating. Which is why I had never, ever tried. I'd written off any number of friends, had left any number of towns, rather than try to mend a hurt or a misunderstanding or a wrong. I had no idea how to make things right with anyone, much less…Old Mac, for example.

I had no idea what to do, but my rookie instinct told me that I probably had to be in proximity to Old Mac to even try.

So I drove myself to work. The drugstore was unlocked, and my time card was where I had thrown it on the checkout counter. For a second I wondered if Mr. MacIntyre hadn't even locked up the night before, but then I saw him behind his pharmacy counter, and he was wearing different clothes. He looked up when the bell over the door jangled and seemed both surprised and angry to see me. I just went to the back, punched in my time card, and started sweeping.

He came out to stare at me, hands on hips, but I kept sweeping. Sweeping seemed like a very *active* thing. I swept my pile all the way to the front door and out onto the sidewalk. Then I turned the CLOSED sign to OPEN and got out the feather duster. After a while he went back behind the counter, though I felt him watching me, off and on, most of the morning. Meriwether was in school, and he didn't have anyone else. I did my usual tasks: straightening shelves, marking off what stock needed replacing on the inventory list.

Toward noon the bell jangled and I looked up to see a couple I didn't recognize, a man and a woman, dressed as if they did not live in West Lowing. Boston, maybe. New York. Paris. Most of our customers were locals, and I recognized literally about 98 percent of them. These were strangers.

"Hey," I said from my position on the floor. "Can I help you find something?"

The woman looked at me, and for some reason, right then, I shivered. Her hair was corn straw yellow and cut in a feathery cap all around her head. Her eyes were a very light blue. The man looked from-India Indian, smooth-skinned and polished, well dressed, with blunt, handsome features and a mouth that looked...cruel.

I stood up. They were probably tourists, had gotten lost, just as I had once. But something about them felt— not right. Hinky. My skin crawled and I suddenly felt chilly. It was dumb—I didn't know them; they didn't know me; it was nothing. But still.

"Allergy medicine," said the woman. She had a slight British accent.

"First aisle, in the middle," I said, not smiling.

"Thank you."

I kept my distance as they stood in the cold-and-allergy aisle and read labels. They talked to each other in low murmurs, and I felt like—like they weren't even reading the labels. Like they were killing time by being here. Almost as if they were waiting for someone. Could they... be friends of Incy's? Surely I would have seen them before?

My fists clenched at my sides. I stayed standing, as if I might suddenly have to run. It was weird, and probably stupid, but I felt like a gazelle being eyed by two cheetahs. My breaths were shallow; my heart was beating fast. I sidled toward the back and saw Old Mac engrossed in deciphering a doctor's handwriting.

I edged around the end of the aisle, as if I was casually walking toward the front of the store, and when I quickly glanced up, they were watching me. My heart started pounding.

"There are so many different kinds," said the woman, holding up a box of Benadryl.

"Yes," I said, not going any closer. "Some make you sleepy; some don't. Some work more quickly, but some you have to take every day for them to work well. It depends on what you want it for." I realized I was jabbering on because I was nervous.

The woman nodded. She and the man met eyes again

and murmured. I have really good hearing, like, beagle-good hearing, and I couldn't make out a single word they said. Was it a different language? I didn't even recognize the basic patterns and cadences of speech, and I know bits of *a lot* of languages.

"We want the kind that makes you sleepy," said the woman, and I wondered hysterically if they wanted to *dope a victim*. With…Benadryl. Unlikely, right?

"Benadryl would do it," I said, my voice cracking. I coughed and headed toward the front counter. My hands were shaking and clammy. I'd never had such a visceral reaction to a person—not to anyone. It was freaking me out. I couldn't even tell if they were immortal or not.

The woman put the box on the counter. Usually you have to look in someone's eyes, or maybe touch them, to "feel" if they were immortal or not. But everything in me refused to look her in the eyes. I was seriously wigging.

I rang up the medicine, the woman paid in cash, I made change, and they left.

I saw them get in their car and drive away, but stood there and watched the front door obsessively, as if they might suddenly reappear. After a few minutes I hurried to the back, pulled that door tightly shut, and locked it. Finally I felt myself relax a little, as if my body no longer sensed a threat.

That had been really freaking weird. I hadn't gotten

any magickal vibes from them, no spark of recognition. But they had just been the scariest people imaginable. I shook my head at how nonsensical it was and then found myself something to do.

The day went on. I was already feeling kind of beaten down and weary when Dray came in. Another chance to be active, make things right! Oh boy!

"Hey," I said. Could I do my one thing with Dray? To not judge her?

She nodded and started cruising the aisles. If she was here to steal something, I was going to be seriously pissed. Which was, you know, *judgmental*. I hovered around her, my arms crossed over my chest. She spared me withering glances every so often.

"So what's going on?" I finally said in a burst of activeness.

She looked at me, then continued to read the instructions on a box of Band-Aids.

"Are you okay?"

Her eyes narrowed a bit at that. "What do you care?" she muttered unhelpfully.

"I care if you're okay."

She shrugged.

I waited. In general, I have about a minute and a half of patience, maybe three minutes if I pace myself. I was running out. I gritted my teeth.

"My boyfriend broke up with me," she said finally, not looking at me. "The day before Christmas. I'd already gotten him a present and everything."

"Oh no. That sucks. Why did he do that?"

"I wouldn't help him take the 7-Eleven over in Melchett."

Melchett was the next town over. Take? Like, rob?

"Um, and he got mad?" I ventured.

"Yeah. So he broke up with me. Now he's going around town talking trash about me, telling stories. That aren't even true. Everyone's looking at me funny."

I waited for her to tell me that he then did a drive-by shooting and popped a cap in her grandmother, but the story seemed to be over.

"And you're really upset?"

That earned me a full-on glare. "Yeah, I'm really upset! The whole town hates my family, and now all my friends hate *me*!"

"So get out of here!" I said once again. "What do you care what your loser boyfriend says? To hell with him! He's trash! Ditch this place and all the assholes that make it tough for you here! Go someplace else; start over. They're *nobodies*!"

My stomach fell when Dray's eyes filled with tears. She threw the box of Band-Aids down. "You say it like it's so easy!" she shouted at me. "Like you know *any*thing! But it's not! It's hard! I don't have any *money*, I don't have a *car*—" Her jaw clenched as if she couldn't bear to say more. So she spit on the linoleum tile by my foot and slammed out, making the door bell jingle violently. Then she stuck her head back in and yelled, "Screw you!"

I was getting to be an old hand at this "making things right."

I rubbed my fist over my forehead, feeling a splitting headache burst into full flower. Then I looked up and saw Mr. MacIntyre standing at the end of the aisle. I braced myself to get yelled at again.

Instead he shook his head, seeming as tired and dragged down as I felt. "Just go home," he said. "And don't come back."

That hurt so much more than him shouting. I was crying by the time I got to my car.

See? That's what happens when you take a chance. I could have stayed home—I'd been *fired*—but nooo, I had to go be all active. I *should* have stayed home. Now both Dray and Old Mac had fired me out of their lives—*twice*. This time I was going to stay fired. Subconscious? Bite me.

Of course at home I was put to work, since I had no job to go to. I was grumpy and out of sorts and didn't feel like being around anyone. I hated to admit it, but my feelings were hurt. I don't make an effort for many people or many situations. I had made an effort for Mr. MacIntyre and Dray. And they couldn't care less. So to hell with them.

The next day I was in a spellcrafting lesson, just me and Jess, being taught by Solis. I took some notes:

> *Major Classes of Spells:*
> *1) Divination*
> *2) To effect change on a person or thing*
> *3) To effect change on an event*
> *4) Celebration and fellowship*

What? I have nice handwriting. I might not have graduated from high school, but that doesn't mean I write like a peasant I'm not educated.

We were in the main workroom on the first floor, practicing a healing spell. It would encourage the body to strengthen its response to infection, like from a wound or, say, if Amy stepped on a rake. Solis had led us through the limitations, which were for the specific person, the length of time, and the general nature of the response.

Jess crafted his spell slowly but carefully. It was interesting to watch someone else make magick without having to participate. When it was over and he had dismantled the spell, I asked, "Do you feel any different?"

Jess thought for a second, rubbing his hand over his grizzled gray stubble. For someone as young as he was, he looked about a thousand. Could hard living have aged him so much? I didn't know.

Then it was my turn. I'd just seen Jess do it, so I was a total whiz. First I drew the sigils of limitation in the air: I specified myself and no one else as the recipient, the response to be mild, and the effect to be open-ended, beginning now and lasting until I ritually broke the spell at a future date. The limitation of response specified that it was to bolster only my germ-fighting response — not to change anything else, like give me great eyesight or other senses. When all the limitations were in place — I glanced at Solis quickly to see if his expression clued me in to any problems — I started to call on my magick. Holding my moonstone in one hand (Jess had used his topaz), I began my song, softly at first, then more confidently.

I could almost feel the spell as an actual structure, as if I were building something with physical form. Mentally I went through the steps: It felt whole and complete and even elegant, like a painting with every dab of paint in the right place. I was pleased: evidence that I was actually learning stuff.

I was deep in concentration. My eyes were closed and I felt focused and content. I felt the magick all around me, as if it were the heavy scent of lilies. No sound disturbed me; I wasn't aware of anything except myself and the feeling of magick shimmering through me. Had my mother worked magick like this? I remembered her chanting over our garden, singing softly as one of our horses foaled. I was connected to her in this way. I was congratulating myself on a job well done—the only thing that had gone right—when suddenly it went not right.

Solis cried out, my eyes popped open, and something hit the back of my head, hard. My head snapped forward and I shrieked something bleep-worthy.

"What did you do?" Solis yelled, diving behind a chair.

The air was full of...flying books. Not cute books with little wings, zipping around like the Golden Snitch, but, like, demonic, possessed books hurling themselves at everything, out for blood.

"Nothing!" I shrieked, ducking from one, then another. A third one whapped me in the shoulder, like a brick. "Goddamnit!"

Over and over I heard heavy *thuds* as books—some thick and oversize—hit things. One slammed Jess in the side, and he swore loudly and scrambled over to hide behind the desk. I had no time to dismantle my spell—just covered my head with one arm as I scuttled over behind the desk next to Jess.

More books sailed past me, knocking objects off every surface. Crystal globes shattered on the floor, a glass inkpot

spewed deep purple ink across the antique rug; empty tea-
cups, bits of parchment, chunks of minerals, lumps of copper and gold...all went flying in the crazy storm I had
somehow created. A tiny pot of powdered copper flew
open and scattered shiny glitter across the pool of ink.
Other books flew violently at the window, breaking it with
a huge crash. Still others landed in the fireplace, where
they caught fire.

"Undo it!" Solis shouted.

"I don't know how!" I wailed, cowering under the desk.
Books slid off its top and tumbled onto Jess, who swore again.
"I don't know what happened! *You're* the expert! *You* fix it!"

Solis was already spitting words out, his deft fingers
drawing sigils and runes and other magickal symbols in
the air. It seemed to take for-freaking-ever, but suddenly
every book dropped heavily to the ground right where it
was, all at once. The books made a tremendous noise, but
in the deafening silence afterward we heard footsteps running down the hall toward the workroom.

Solis jumped up and ran to the fire, snatching books
away from the flames and rolling them in the hearth rug.

"What the hell did you do?" Jess roared, ten inches
from my face.

"Nothing!" I screamed back. "You saw me do the spell!"

The door burst open. Asher and Brynne stood there,
eyes wide. They looked around the room: the shelves

almost empty, books strewn everywhere, the window broken. Everything on a surface had been knocked over or pushed off; small pots and bottles of oils and essences were smashed on the floor. Solis was on his knees looking at the burned books to assess their damage.

"What in the world happened?" Asher asked. "Are you all okay?"

A frigid gust blew through the broken window, swirling with the overpowering smell of flower essences and herbal oils.

More people came: Charles, River, Anne.

I stood slowly. I had done this. I had caused this.

"What happened?!" River asked.

The three of us were silent. The old Nastasya would immediately blame Solis, for teaching me incorrectly, or Jess, for distracting me, or life in general, for not going my way. Which was clearly the path to choose here—this was a whole world of bad.

"It was me," I said, touching my puffy eye. "I truly don't know what happened. We were doing a healing spell. I thought I was doing it exactly right."

"You were," said Solis, standing up. He looked at River. "Jess went first, then Nastasya right after. I was there, watching and listening. She did it perfectly, and everything was fine until the spell was supposed to go into effect. Then all the books started . . . flying off the shelves."

"Like in *The Exorcist*," Brynne said unhelpfully.

"Except we don't believe in the devil," Charles said, examining all the wreckage.

"You used limitations?" River asked.

"Of course," I said.

Solis nodded. "She did—she set up all the proper limitations. I really have no idea how this happened." He gave me a thoughtful look, and my heart sank: Unless I'm hopelessly dark. The thought came to me instantly, fully formed, and seized my heart like a cold fist.

River came into the room, stepping over debris carefully. "So, normal spell, everything fine, then books fly off shelves, go everywhere, break everything."

I shivered and wrapped my arms around myself. "Yeah." Oddly, the person I felt like seeing was Reyn. I flashed on the feel of his arms holding me, how illogically safe I felt with him. I didn't know why I felt that way, but I did.

"I'll clean it up," I said, stating the obvious.

"I'll help," said Solis.

"Right now let's find a piece of wood to board up that window," said River.

"I can do that," Jess said.

I looked at the ruined room, felt my various bumps and bruises, and thought that so far, the new year was kicking my ass.

CHAPTER 12

t took me eight hours to clean up the room, even with Solis's help. While we worked, he walked me through the steps of the spell again, and we both examined every bit of it to see where it had gone wrong. We still couldn't figure it out.

Unless the thought I'd had was true, that my magick is inherently dark, like my parents'. Unless I *can't* choose to *not* be dark.

Just a week ago, I'd felt so much more hopeful. I'd seen progress. Now I couldn't do anything right. A dark, heavy cloud of Teräväness was hanging over my head, following me wherever I went. Every time I caught a glimpse of myself in the mirror, my puffy, purpling eye reminded me that I couldn't be trusted to do a simple spell by myself.

When Reyn saw me, his eyebrows rose. "What does the other guy look like?"

I wanted to come back with something witty and brave and casual, but I couldn't think of a thing. In general my head felt fuzzy, as if I wasn't getting enough sleep. But I was hitting the sack by nine thirty, just to make these awful days end earlier. I had no other symptoms except listlessness, a foggy brain, and a desire to spend all day, every day, in bed.

I went to classes, though I refused to work any actual magick, and, tellingly, no one pushed me to try. I did my chores.

One night Reyn, Brynne, and I were on the cooking team. I found being with Reyn both comforting and tension-producing. It was exhausting.

In my attempts to see him as who he was now, I was noticing how other people acted around him. With surprise I realized that everyone seemed to like him and feel comfortable with him. I hadn't really seen that before. At first glance, he seemed bossy and abrupt, forbidding and humorless. I was coming to realize that he was just— really self-contained. Withdrawn, even. Quiet, wrestling with all his inner demons. I still didn't know why, specifically, he was here. What had brought him to River's? How long had he been here? What was he hoping to get out of being here?

The answers to these and other questions may or may not be revealed later on, in *Eternity: The Ongoing Docudrama*.

"Oh! Turn that song up," Brynne said, pointing to the small, old-fashioned radio on a kitchen shelf. I turned up the volume, and Brynne started dancing as she chopped garlic. She seemed to know the words to any song that came on, reminding me again of how unaware I was, how little I paid attention to things.

"Baby, you know you got it going on," Brynne sang, chopping in rhythm.

I smiled and looked up to see Reyn also smiling. We met eyes and Had a Moment; then I went back to work.

A few minutes later, Amy came in and perched cutely on a stool near where Reyn was cutting sausages to grill. "Can I help with anything?" she asked.

Reyn shook his head. "You're a guest."

I stirred the onions and garlic I was sautéing. I wished that it was just Reyn and me in the kitchen.

"Nastasya?"

It took a second to realize Amy was talking to me. I turned around.

"Is this your first time at River's?" she asked. "I was

here ten years ago, and there was a completely different gang. But most people seem to come and go and then come back."

"No, it's my first time," I said. "Do you visit Anne here often?" Time to brush off the rusty ol' social skills. I had gathered that Amy was actually a nice person. It wasn't her fault that she'd fallen under the spell of the Golden Glory. Probably most women did, I thought wistfully.

Amy smiled. "I come here every so often, but I last saw Anne three years ago. Every once in a while our whole family gets together somewhere, spends a couple weeks catching up. Last time it was Prince Edward Island. So beautiful there."

"Your whole family gets together?" I detected amazement in Reyn's face, even though it was subtle.

"Yep." Amy picked a piece of lettuce from the salad bowl and ate it from her fingers.

"Mine does, too," said Brynne. "Every four or five years. My parents, all my siblings."

"Isn't it great?" Amy asked her. "I mean, crazy and hectic, but great."

I glanced at Reyn again and found him looking at me. We understood what the other was thinking: We were both orphans. Our families had wiped one another out. He shook his head, as bemused by that thought as I was.

"What about you, Reyn?" Amy asked. "Does your family get together?"

"No," he said. "It sounds nice." He put the last sausage on the platter, then went out into the awful weather to use the big grill outside.

"You?" Amy asked.

"No," I said. "My family died a long time ago." I dumped a ton of diced potatoes into the onions and stirred. These people were into their potatoes—you could never make enough.

"Oh." Amy looked taken aback.

"It was over four hundred years ago," I told her, and she looked surprised. "I can't even imagine what they would be like nowadays. I can't imagine how they would have changed, modernized through the years, you know?"

Reyn came back in, stamping snow off his feet.

"Yeah, I see," Amy said.

"They're kind of frozen in time for me," I said, and felt Reyn stiffen as he realized what I was talking about. I never blurt out info about my family, preferring instead to cover my pain with scathing retorts. But I felt beaten down these days, little bravado in store. So I was dragging their skeletons out into the sunlight, as River had suggested. "I can only picture them as they were in the fifteen hundreds. It's weird."

"Yeah, I can imagine," Amy said, looking uncomfortable.

"Has it been interesting, seeing your family change through the years?" I asked politely.

"Not really 'interesting,'" Amy said, absently picking another piece of lettuce out of the bowl. "It just seems normal, you know? Clothes change, hair changes, cool new things get invented—but it doesn't happen all at once. It's all gradual, so nothing seems sudden or shocking. Just normal life."

I'd never heard anyone describe the immortal experience as normal, so this was a whole new concept for me. I went back to pushing potatoes and onions around the pan, making sure nothing burned, but inside my mind was a quilt of new thoughts. To me my life had always seemed like an unending disaster—one long series of awful experiences intermittently broken up by something good or fun, then descending into tragedy again. The tragedies were what I remembered, what dogged me. I'd never been strong enough or determined enough to kill myself, and I'd also never been together enough to see my life as a positive thing, a long line of opportunities, chances taken, people loved, if only for a while. Normal. What a freakish concept.

I ate dinner like a zombie, barely able to pay attention to what anyone was saying. So much to think about. So many new ways to see so many things.

When I went upstairs, I couldn't remember the lock-door spell on my room.

Back when Nell had been roaming the place, Anne had taught me a basic lock-door spell so no one could leave ill-wishes inside. Nowadays I almost always used it, whether I was in my room or not, because I felt too vulnerable to leave my door unlocked. Not that anything could get to me here. But...you never know.

Now I was standing here, exhausted, overwhelmed by new concepts, and I couldn't get into my own room. When I tried to remember the spell, my head clouded over, as if full of a swarm of bees. I started and stopped several times, my hand freezing in midair as I tried to trace a sigil I could no longer visualize.

Crap. What was going on? I heard footsteps coming up the stairs. I didn't want to be found out here like an idiot, especially after my room-destroying event of the week before. Think, think, *think.* It suddenly came back to me in a flash, and I murmured the short spell and drew the appropriate sigils and runes as fast as I could.

I turned the doorknob and nipped inside, quickly closing the door behind me. I had cold sweat on my forehead. What was the *matter* with me? Shakily I recited the lock-door spell again, then crossed the room to draw the insulated curtains against the cold black night. I turned the knob on the small radiator, hearing the steam start to hiss through its curved pipes. I kicked off my shoes and my jeans and crawled beneath the covers. The sheets were freezing.

My head was pounding. I closed my eyes.

"Darling, how well you look." Incy's voice, warm and friendly, made my eyes pop open again. He was sitting in a sleek modern chair, white brocade and dark wood, in what looked like the living room of a hotel suite. I thought I recognized it—was it the Liberty Hotel in Boston? A heavy silver tray sat on the glass-topped coffee table in front of him. "Tea? No—you're getting enough tea these days. Coffee, then." He poured me a demitasse of espresso and dropped one cube of white sugar into it. "Remember in Russia? We drank hot tea through sugar cubes in our teeth?"

My hand, as though disembodied, reached out to take the china cup. I nodded. The Russian tea had been strong and bitter, explaining the custom of sipping it through a sugar cube. It had taken several tries before I'd quit making slurping sounds or had tea dribble down my chin.

"What are you doing here?" My voice sounded as though I were hearing it through tissue paper. I still felt hazy, foggy-headed.

Incy leaned back in the chair and crossed his legs, elegant in black Armani trousers and a custom purple silk shirt. "Come to see you, of course." He smiled and sipped his own coffee. "You see, I'm rather dependent on you."

"Why?" My throat tightened and I forced the coffee down. It left a heated trail and kicked up some acid in my stomach. Why was he here? How had he found me? I'd tried to disappear, thought I was safe at River's.

Innocencio shrugged and examined the oil painting over the side console. "I thought I'd just gotten used to you," he said slowly. "But actually, it's much more than that. You and I are soul mates, two sides of one coin. There can be no me without you." His face changed, darkening, and his eyes were glowing coals when he looked at me. "And there can be no *you* without *me*." His smile was beautifully cruel, and I shivered as if icy fingers were drumming down my spine. He was saying everything I was afraid of, everything I wanted to not be true.

"We're not soul mates, Incy," I said. I drank some coffee to show how unconcerned, unconvinced I was, and almost gagged on it. "We're not lovers. We were best friends for a long time. But I think...I need to take a break."

The room grew dark, as if suddenly covered by an eclipse. Incy's face was thrown into sharp relief, the room's small fireplace flickering ever-changing shadows across his symmetrical features. He got to his feet, looking at me, then threw his cup against the wall, where it smashed.

Coffee ran down the yellow wallpaper like a bloodstain. My heart throbbed irregularly and I felt like I couldn't breathe.

"No, Nastasya." His voice was tightly controlled. "No, Nastasya. No, *Sea*." Sea had been my name before Nastasya. "No, Hope. No, Bev. No, Gudrun." He was scrolling through my identities, going back in time, decades. "You see, Linn, Christiane, Prentice, Maarit—we *belong* together. You remember, Sarah? You remember when we met? And I was..."

"Louis."

"Yes. I was Louis to your Sarah. Then I was Claus to your Britta." He pronounced it the German way: klows. "Then I was Piotr to your Maarit. And James to your Prentice. Then Laurent. Beck. Pavel. Sam. Michael. Sky. Remember when we were the Sea and the Sky, together in Polynesia? Now I'm Innocencio to your Nastasya. And you are. Not. Taking. A. Break. From. *Me!*" He ended with a roar, kicking over the table, swiping a crystal lamp off the sideboard. He stood right in front of me, chest heaving, eyes bloodshot, and he looked totally out of his mind, like a junkie, like—

Like he was a junkie. Like he was addicted...to me.

It was a stunningly clear realization, one that I wish I'd had, say, eighty years before.

I got to my feet, trying to project strength. He had

never hurt me in a hundred years. It was hard to believe he would physically harm me now. "We're not *soul mates*, Incy," I said, feeling my own anger finally igniting and squashing my fear somewhat. "I've *never* thought that—I don't know why you would. And of course I can take a break—from you, from everything. I'm going to rest up, hang out for a while, and then maybe we can get together in Rio or something. In time for Carnaval." Throw him a bone—Carnaval was in February.

"I don't think so, Nasty," Incy said with a hard smile. "I don't enjoy being alone. And given the price of leaving me, I'm sure you'll change your mind."

He made a graceful gesture to the right, as if demonstrating what was behind door number one.

I glanced over, and my whole body jolted in shock. It took seconds to comprehend what I was actually seeing. There were...heads sitting in a thick pool of dull blood that was scudded over and clotting. It was hard to see the features as human—but I saw past the drooping gray skin, half-open eyes, and slack mouths, and recognized Boz's face, and Katy's. A pasty hand showed from behind the couch—their bodies were there. Incy had killed them.

And then Incy was holding a huge, curved blade, like a scimitar. Blood had dried on its edge. He was smiling as he walked toward me. The fire in the fireplace had gone out, and a thick, oily black smoke was coiling through the room. I could smell it. I could smell the suffocating, coppery scent of the congealing blood.

"Come here, Nas," Incy said softly. "Come here, darling."

I stood stock-still, frozen. I hated crazy Incy—wanted fun Incy back again. The smoke was choking me; I was wheezing, sucking in air, suffocating—

And then Incy was standing over me, eyes glittering as he raised the scimitar. I couldn't make myself move, couldn't leap out of the way, couldn't attack him—

And with a smile, he brought the blade down hard.

Then I was jackknifing up, bolting awake so fast that I tumbled out of bed to land on the floor, my shoulder and hipbone thudding painfully into the chilly wood. I lay there, still and quiet, as if moving would make Incy materialize right in my room.

I inhaled slowly, silently, then checked all four corners of my room. Same room at River's. Empty except for me. Window closed. Door closed and spell-locked? I couldn't remember. Inhaling again, I smelled only the lavender we put in the laundry water and a trace of the white vinegar we used on mirrors and windows. No blood. No choking black smoke.

The floor was cold. I pulled myself into a sitting position, flicked on my reading light, then collapsed again and leaned against my bed. My face and back were damp with clammy sweat. I brushed my hair off my face with a trembling hand.

What was *wrong* with me?

This had started at New Year's...at the New Year's circle. Laughably, I had committed myself to being good, making Tähti magick. I mean, I had—*oh my God.* I had cast off *darkness.* What if—what if I had only *released* darkness, *unleashed* it? What if I had sent my darkness—which was considerable, given my family history—*out into the world*? Now it was coming back like a rabid dog, nipping at my heels, scaring me with threats of so much worse.

Then I had another bad thought. I crawled under my bed and used my fingernails to pry out a piece of loose floor molding. There was a small space behind it, chipped out of the wall plaster. Reaching in, I grabbed a colorful silk scarf, all wadded up. I pulled it out and leaned against my bed again. Still feeling trembly, I unwrapped the object inside.

The ancient, burnished gold gleamed at me, warm in my hand. It never felt cold. It was half of the amulet that my mother had worn around her neck always. To find it, possess it, was why raiders had stormed my father's castle, killed everyone except me within. But they'd found only half of it. I still had the other half. I'd picked it out of the fire, wrapped it in a scarf and tied it around my neck so I could run with my hands free. It had burned through the scarf, burned its pattern into the skin on my neck, the design, the symbols, everything. That burn had never healed—just as the one Reyn had on his chest had never healed.

I'd kept this my whole life—it was the only thing that I had from my family, my childhood.

But it was a tarak-sin: the ancestral object that helped channel tremendous magick for my parents, the rulers of one of the eight great houses of immortals. Each of the houses has or has had its own tarak-sin. It didn't have to be an amulet—it could be almost anything. Some of them have been lost. I hadn't had a clue about any of that until I'd come to River's Edge. I'd also learned that everyone believed that the tarak-sin of the House of Úlfur had been lost forever.

I had no idea if this broken half still had power, could still magnify my own power. For 450 years, I'd kept it solely because it had belonged to my mother.

Now I held it in my hand, wondering if it was the cause of my darkness, my failures. It had channeled dark magick for centuries, for who knows how long. Was it intrinsically dark itself? Was my carrying it around one of the reasons—the main reason—my life had, for the most part, sucked?

It was the *one* thing I had of my mother's. The *one*

thing I had from a life that had literally been wiped off the face of the earth. Of the several fortunes I'd gained and lost over hundreds of years, this secret thing had always been my greatest possession. And maybe the key to my eternal downfall. Maybe an inescapable source of evil.

It was possible that the one thing I most valued was the one thing I couldn't have.

 stayed awake till it was light, then replaced my amulet in its hidey-hole in the wall. I traced a quick sigil for invisibility over the molding, not that anyone would look at the floor molding behind my bed. Several weeks ago, I'd had the insight that I wanted to claim my heritage as my mother's daughter, my father's heir. Somehow I had missed the inescapable inevitability that I would reveal myself to be just as dark as they had been.

I felt uncomfortable in my own skin, as if I were glowing with the plague and everyone would be able to see it.

People were laughing in the dining room as they set up for breakfast. I didn't want to be around people. Goddess knew I didn't want to be in the barn or the chicken coop. Going to a class this morning would be awful, and what would happen the next time I made magick was anyone's guess.

I just needed—

I had no idea what I needed. But I had to move, had to do something. Fortunately my hair-trigger impulsiveness was still part of the Nasty mosaic, and it told me to put down the broom, grab my keys and my coat, and slog through the snow to my little car. Which I did, immediately, feeling a sense of relief at the thought of escaping these undark people, this undark house. I desperately needed to be somewhere else, doing something else, not talking to anyone.

Ice on windshield, hard-to-start engine in frigid weather—here's a time when some magick would come in handy, you know? Did I know any *useful* spells? Why no, I sure didn't. But go on, ask me the Latin name of, like, foxglove. *Digitalis purpurea.* You're welcome.

Crap! My car skidded all the way down the long unpaved driveway until I reached the secondary road, which, thank God, had been plowed. From there it was another couple miles to the also-plowed main road that led to town.

Yeah, because the *town* held so much for me, right? There was the combo Chinese food/falafel joint, the abandoned buildings, the place I had been fired from *twice*.... There was one yucky bar, one grocery store, one rundown Laundromat. Main Street was four blocks long. I've been to museums bigger than four blocks long.

But where else would I go? I'd taken a few steps forward and fifty steps back. My stomach rumbled and clenched, and I remembered I hadn't eaten anything yet. I drove past MacIntyre's Drugs and of course couldn't resist looking in. The store was lit, the OPEN sign was up, but I saw no one except a woman standing at the empty front counter, looking around as if hoping someone would come help her.

I bet Old Mac was sorry he'd fired me *now*.

Main Street petered out, and a quarter mile down the road I was back to empty lots, the occasional small house, an easement for the big electrical lines.

I turned around with a sigh. Maybe I would go get something from Pitson's, the one grocery store, and then return to River's Edge. It was barely eight in the morning—what else was I going to do? As I drove past MacIntyre's Drugs again, I saw the woman leaving the store, her hands empty. No one had waited on her. Hadn't she called to Old Mac? He should have been back in the pharmacy.

I rolled forward and, without even really meaning to, came to a gradual stop at the curb.

I sat there for a minute, not thinking, not doing anything, tapping my fingers on the steering wheel. Then I got out of the car, locked it, and walked to the drugstore. The bell over the door jingled with a deceptively cheerful sound, as if trying to make me believe I wasn't entering my personal hell. I looked down each aisle but didn't see Old Mac. Tentatively I walked to the back. The pharmacy door, always kept locked, was open, a ring of keys still in its lock. The light was on, but Old Mac wasn't there. I'd never seen that.

I locked the pharmacy door and pocketed the keys. Old Mac wasn't in the supply closet on the store's back porch, but footprints in the fresh snow led to the small storage building by the side fence. The door was open, and I crept up, afraid of what I would find. I'm so totally not the hero type, but I could call 911 with the best of 'em.

Then I saw him. He was standing inside the shed, leaning his head against a cardboard box on a shelf. He was muttering to himself. Was he praying? Had he gone crazy? I mean, crazier? This was not good. I decided to give him a couple minutes, see if he snapped out of it. I retraced my steps back to the store. I'd lost many people in my life, of course. I'd lost a son myself. The son that Reyn had found, that time, so long ago. It really had been a long time ago — I'd lived many lifetimes since then. And yet when I closed my eyes, I could still smell my son's baby-fresh scent, still hear his laugh that always made me laugh, too....

ᚼ ᚼ ᚼ ᚼ ᚼ ᚼ ᚼ ᚼ ᚼ ᚼ ᚼ ᚼ ᚼ ᚼ

It had been in Norway. I was married. My husband was awful and I hated him, but back then young women didn't live on their own. My son had been a miracle. He'd been fat and cuddly, his perfect health a shining contrast to the high infant mortality rate back then. His hair was thick and fair, and his eyes were the blue of a crisp spring sky. I'd called him Bjørn, which means "bear," because he was like a little bear cub. He made everything worthwhile: my husband, our poverty, how hard everything was. I used to put him in a woven basket and carry him around with me as I hung laundry out, milked the goats, picked blackberries.

Bear's gurgling laugh, the way he played with his toes — everything was fine then, in my world. We were so poor — my husband drank up the few coins I earned by selling eggs and goat's milk, and cow's-milk butter in the summer. When he was sober, he farmed unenthusiastically, borrowing our neighbor's ox to break up the hard, stony ground. Each year our anemic crops of barley and oats got smaller and smaller. He could have earned more by trapping animals and selling the skins, but that would have involved actual effort.

Still, I was happy with my lovely Bear, and it was mostly me and him, day in, day out, in our rough house with the thatched roof.

Then the raiders came. One of Reyn's men had buried an axe in my husband's head. I found him just outside the empty pens, where my goats and one milk cow had been. The Butcher of Winter had taken every animal in our village, every store of grain and ale, almost every wheel of cheese. The pathetic store of money I'd managed to hide from my husband was worthless, for there was nothing to buy within ten leagues.

It had been horrible, the way my husband had died, but also a relief. I was glad to be a widow, for it to be just me and Bear. Then Truda, a local girl orphaned that day, came to my door with nowhere else to go. Having escaped from being forced into whoredom or slavery, she was thrilled to come live with us and be my helper. God knows she worked harder than my husband ever did. My life was good.

Bear had gone on to become a bright, sturdy toddler, always laughing, getting into everything. I managed to raise a small crop of oats, and we ate them as porridge and bread and ale. Then a flu epidemic swept through the town. The starvation that the winter raiders had caused had weakened everyone, and many people died. Truda had died, at thirteen years old. And Bear had died, even though half-immortals are often able to fight off illness. I would have gladly given my worthless immortality to him, gladly died in his place. Instead I bathed his hot little body, tried to get him to drink water. Anyway. He had died. I'd never had another child after that. Would never go through that again.

"Oh, there you are." The voice startled me, and I realized I'd been standing just inside the door, lost in my thoughts. I took a shaky breath and wiped my hand across my face. A woman was waiting by the pharmacy counter. She was a regular—Meriwether had called her Mrs. Philpott.

"Oh—" My mouth opened to explain that I didn't work here anymore, but Mrs. Philpott said, "I'm glad to see you—I'm in a bit of a hurry. I'm on the way to the airport, and I realized this morning that I needed to pick up my prescription. I'll run out before we get back."

"Um—Mr. MacIntyre is…unavailable right now," I said. "Maybe in five minutes?"

Mrs. Philpott looked concerned. "I'm so sorry. I don't

have five minutes," she said firmly but not rudely. "I've got Eddie's cab waiting."

She pointed out the window and I could see the local burgundy-colored taxi, its lights on.

"Okay, let me check." I went out back again, hoping to see Old Mac storming toward the store. But he was still in the shed, his head against the cardboard box, and now it looked like he was crying.

"He's still unavailable," I said. "Maybe you could get your prescription refilled where you go?"

"I can see my bag right there." Mrs. Philpott pointed to the rack behind the counter. She still wasn't being rude, which was amazing, but she had a determined no-nonsense quality that probably defeated most people. I could feel myself crumbling.

"I'm not allowed back there."

"It's for tamoxifen," said Mrs. Philpott. "I need it right now, and you're going to get it for me even if you have to climb over the counter."

Tamoxifen was a cancer drug. I'd read about it ages ago in a *Reader's Digest* in the waiting room of my favorite mani-pedi place in New York. Mrs. Philpott's steady gaze punched holes in my resistance.

I took the keys out of my pocket, unlocked the door, and prayed that Old Mac would continue to have his breakdown for another seven minutes or so. I zipped into the pharmacy area, snatched up the bag, and handed it over, along with the required sign-in sheet saying she had picked up her prescription.

"And it says your insurance has covered this," I told her, glancing at the label.

"Damn straight," Mrs. Philpott said, signing her name.

I grinned, and she straightened and grinned back.

"Thank you very mu—"

"What the hell are you doing?" Old Mac yanked the door open and thundered into the pharmacy area, which was way too small for the two of us together.

Great. He had to get a grip on his sanity *right now*. He would have me arrested for sure.

"Now, James, quit yelling," said Mrs. Philpott briskly. She stuck the small paper bag in her purse. "I practically held a gun to her head to make her give it to me. She told me she wasn't allowed back there."

"She isn't!" Old Mac roared, in fine form once again. "I'm calling the police! This is illegal!"

Mrs. Philpott slammed her hand down on the counter, making both of us jump. The steely reserve she'd only hinted at with me came out in full force. "Jamie MacIntyre," she said in a low, controlled voice, "I've known you since high school, and you don't scare me. I *made* her get my prescription for me. You are not going to do *anything* to her. Now quit being a *butthead*. You hear me?"

Old Mac stood there, nothing to say. I tried to radiate innocence and helpfulness as I sidled out behind him and slipped into the store area.

"Is that a yes?" Mrs. Philpott said. Outside, the taxi driver honked his horn, and I winced. I never wanted to ride in a taxi again.

"Yes," Old Mac finally ground out, totally hating this.

"Good. Bye. See you when I get back." She turned and strode toward the door, flashing me a final smile. I smiled back.

After she'd left, I decided to take off before he did call the cops. I took one last look at him. He seemed pathetic, deflated, standing behind the counter in an empty store. For one second I wanted to say something. But he'd probably just roar at me again, and *then* call the cops.

So I just turned and left him standing there. Outside the cold wind whipped my breath away. Time to go back to River's Edge. I had no idea what purpose my little jaunt had served, except it had gotten me away from there for a while.

I started my car and used the wipers to get snow off the windshield. I felt terrible, as if there was a grim winter day inside me as well as outside. Why had I thought about Bear? I had trained myself not to. It was more than four centuries ago, Nas. Move on.

I headed down Main Street, and to make my morning

just a little bit brighter, saw Dray. She looked freezing, wearing a short jacket with cheap, fuzzy fur around the face. I waved and she blinked at me. No other cars around meant I could do a U-turn right here, and I did, swinging the small car around with no problem.

Dray was gone. I looked up and down the street. There was nowhere she could have disappeared to—except down a narrow alley between two buildings. To get away from me.

I had FAIL stamped on my forehead, stamped on my life.

I was amazed to see it was still only a bit after nine o'clock. I'd been missed by now, of course. I turned off the main road onto the secondary road and soon saw the leafless maple tree that stood at the entrance of the driveway to River's Edge. And…as soon as my car was on River's land, I felt weird.

Today, with the snow and ice, I went even more slowly than usual, remembering how I had slid around earlier. But it wasn't the road conditions that were bothering me. I felt…dread. A feeling of dread. Not for anything real. My heart fluttered; I felt anxious—to where I actually turned and looked all around, as if a gang was chasing me, about to attack the car.

It was stupid. It was just my stupid emotions, getting the better of me. I was still fired; Dray still hated me. I'd tried to help today and almost had the cops called on me. I'd thought about Bear. Everything was going wrong. Everything hurt; everything was painful.

I was working myself up into a lather of pointless despair when I realized that the car wasn't responding. I had tapped on the brakes to crawl around a turn, but nothing happened. I pressed the brake pedal more firmly, ready to start skidding. Nothing. I'd sped up a bit during my internal rant, and now really needed to slow down. I was coming up to the last turn before the driveway broadened into the crushed-rock parking area.

It was like holding the reins of an out-of-control horse. Gripping the steering wheel, I smashed my foot down on the brake pedal, and nothing happened. Jeezum — this was bad. I needed to stop! I grabbed the parking brake and yanked up on it. It did nothing!

Was my darkness overtaking even this *machine*? Now I was hurtling right toward River's old red farm truck — I was going to cream it.

What to do, what to do? Then the steering wheel turned by itself. I felt it spinning in my hands even as I tried to haul it the other way. And there it was, the enormous oak. Getting bigger, bigger, so fast...

"Is anything broken?" The voice seemed to come from far away. Maybe underwater.

"I don't know yet. Let's turn the engine off."

Solis's voice. And Lorenz's.

I didn't want to open my eyes, just wanted to go back to sleep, but my nose was clogged and my mouth was full of blood. I blinked blearily as strong hands unfolded me from the car.

"What happened?" That voice was Reyn's. Did he sound upset?

"We don't know," said Solis. "I saw her tear into the yard too fast, and then she aimed right for that tree."

I did not, I thought as someone swung my legs out of the car and onto the snowy ground. I bent over and spit out blood. Even with my hazy vision, the bright red was shocking against the white.

"Nastasya, what happened?" Solis knelt in the snow and tipped my chin up.

"The engine won't turn off," said Lorenz. I heard the keys jingling. "The keys are out, but the engine is on."

My nose was bleeding, and I wiped it away before it dripped into my mouth again. I know—ew.

Since I was leaning over anyway, I scooped up a handful of snow and put it in my mouth. It felt lovely, and I tried to figure out how to put my whole head into a pile of snow. I heard the car's hood open.

"Solis," said Reyn. His voice was odd. "I took off the battery cables. The engine's still on."

Solis's hand stilled where it was feeling my arm, checking for broken bones. "That's not car failure," he said. "That's magick. Dark magick."

"I'll go get River," said Lorenz, and I heard him running to the house.

I blinked again. I couldn't breathe through my nose.

"Can you stand up?" Solis asked. "I want to get you away from this car."

I nodded, which hurt, and slowly stood. Solis quickly ran his hands down both legs impersonally, as if he were checking a lame horse. Since my knees didn't buckle, I assumed I was okay. Again he tilted my chin up and looked at my face.

"Your nose is broken," he said. I saw River running toward us, her face showing concern.

"The car is spelled," Solis told her shortly. "Can you stop it?"

River nodded quickly and moved past us. I heard Reyn say something to her but couldn't make it out.

"So what happened?" Solis asked.

"I don't know," I said, but because of all the gore it came out "Ah dun oh." I spit more blood out onto the snow (gross). "Ah wash drahvin an de cah wooden thtop."

"Okay. Let's get you fixed up." He helped me up to the front porch.

Inside, Solis took me upstairs to my room. I had just

gotten my coat off when Anne hurried in, holding a basin, some rags, and a first-aid kit. And, of course, a mug of steaming tea, because you couldn't sneeze around here without someone rushing over with a mug of tea. Arm get cut off? Have some tea. Legacy of darkness slowly destroying every facet of your life? Tea.

"Her nose is broken," Solis told her.

"Oh, crap," Anne said. "Anything else? Ribs? Teeth?"

"Everything else seems okay."

"Let's get this scarf off—it's covered with blood."

"No! Ah mean—ah take ih off ater." My hands clutched it.

"Drink this. Wash the blood out of your mouth." Anne pushed the mug at me. My hands were trembling, but I managed to hold it. The warmth did feel good, and it did wash away most of the taste of blood. Dammit. Right again.

"Okay," Anne said, taking the mug from me. "Lie down."

I did. Very gently she swabbed at my face with a warm rag. I smelled calendula and elder leaves in the warm water.

"You're going to have two black eyes," Anne said. "And just as your library black eye had healed. The air bag must have gone off. That's what broke your nose."

"Ah don wamembah."

"Well, you're starting to puff up. Let's fix your nose before it gets any worse."

Before I had time to tense up or realize what she was doing, she pressed her fingers firmly on each side of my nose.

"*Yow yow yow* nooo!" I yelped, then heard a loud clicking sound as new pain exploded in my nose. My back arched and my hands flew in the air. "Oh, Jethus! Cwap! Dammit!"

Her fingers were still pressing my nose tightly. "Be still!" she admonished. "You'll knock it out of joint again." She began to murmur rapidly under her breath. One hand held my nose in place and one hand gracefully drew sigils and runes in the air with amazing rapidity. Healing spells. Again, useful spells that I did not know. Then I remembered that I'd been learning a healing spell when I had made the library vomit books.

"Okay," she murmured a minute or two later. "Now let's tape it into place." She quickly tore off a piece of white bandage tape and carefully placed it across my nose. She looked at her handiwork and smiled. "You look like a little boxer," she said. "After a prizefight."

"Bantamweight. I was just thinking that," said Solis.

I had zero response to this. Ze-ro.

"Now, sit up and finish this tea."

I did. Already the pain in my nose was lessening.

When the mug was empty, I didn't sound like Elmer Fudd anymore.

"Now, what happened?" Solis asked just as River and Reyn came into the room.

Could Reyn see me just once in decent clothes, with my hair brushed? Apparently not. "What happened?" he echoed, looking pretty forbidding.

I didn't want to talk about the wreck. I was pretty sure it was my own darkness that had caused the car to become suicidal. "I went to town," I began reluctantly, with the instant, oops, recollection that I'd run off without telling anyone. "Everything was fine, car was fine. Then, on the driveway, the car picked up speed without me noticing. I tried to slow down, but the brakes were out." I paused, trying to remember exactly. "I realized I was going to wreck — I was going to cream River's red truck. But the steering wheel turned, and I couldn't stop it. It aimed me right at the tree."

"Did you try the parking brake?" Solis asked.

I nodded. "I yanked up on it, but it didn't do anything."

River came over and smoothed her hand over my hair. The longer pieces in front had blood drying on them. "How come you went to town?" she asked gently.

"I had to get something. Really quick."

"The car was spelled," Reyn said.

River looked concerned. "I was able to stop the engine. I felt dark magick, strong magick, but it was very well done. I couldn't pick up on any signature. Where did you park, in town? How long were you away from the car?"

"Not long," I said. "I parked at the curb, outside of Early's. I couldn't have been gone more than ten minutes?" Then my eyebrows rose as I realized what she was saying. She thought that maybe someone had put a spell on my car in *town*. And then I remembered: In my last dream about Incy, he had been in the Liberty Hotel, in Boston. In my previous visions, when I could tell where he was, he'd been in California. Was Incy actually in Boston? Maybe even closer? Could it have been him? Him, and not me? After a moment, I shook my head, which was a mistake. I was so tired of thinking about all this.

Asher came in. My small room was really crowded. "I just heard," he said, looking at me, then at River.

"Go look at Nastasya's car, will you?" River asked him. "I couldn't get anything, but maybe you can."

He nodded and left, his footsteps echoing down the hallway.

Anne stood up. "Rest for a while," she said. "Come down for lunch."

"Okay." Everyone filed out and my room became peaceful again.

Reyn lingered by the door. He didn't say anything —

just looked at me. I felt embarrassed. It would probably be comforting to have his arms around me. Did that show in my eyes? Could he tell what I was thinking?

After a couple seconds, or maybe an hour, he turned and left, silent as an assassin.

I slept.

CHAPTER 14

 s he coming?" I whispered to Eydís.

Eydís peeked around the heavy tapestry. "No," she barely breathed.

We grinned at each other in delight. I was seven; she was nine. We were hiding from our pesky younger brother, Háakon, who always wanted to follow us. We didn't hate him, but he was only not-even-four yet, and he was making us crazy. We'd found an excellent hiding spot: The walls of my father's castle were made of stone. In Iceland. So almost all of them were covered with huge hanging tapestries through every season except summer. Eydís and I were both really skinny, and if we stood on tiptoe and inhaled, we made barely a ripple in the fabric. It had been working splendidly for days— Háakon was losing his mind with frustration.

"Riders! My lord, riders!" The loud shout came from the bailey outside. Instantly, Eydís and I heard the clink of weapons and shields, the neighing of horses. We ran to a nearby window and cranked it open, unable to see through the wavy glass. Far in the distance, rising over the crest of mountain that defined my father's land, was a small group of riders. They didn't look like a huge threat, but still—they could be merely a scouting party.

"Pull the gates!" people were shouting below. My father's steward was making sure we were locking sheep and goats and all our horses inside our walls before six men pulled on the chains, as thick as my arm, that closed the bailey gates.

Eydís and I watched for hours. Háakon found us, of course, and I pulled a stool over so he could stand on it and watch also. No more riders came—we counted seven when they were close enough. Slowly, slowly, their details came into focus: One was carrying a color standard, showing what clan they were from.

By the time they stopped outside the city walls, word had come to us, by runner: The riders were carrying the standard of Úlfur Haraldsson, my father. It had been unmistakable, the runner wheezed—five black bears on a red background, crowned with a wreath of oak leaves.

There was tremendous excitement: The riders were my uncle and his men! I hadn't even known I had an uncle!

We all raced downstairs and waited with my father in front of his hrókur—*castle* is too big a word. Like a big stone manor house that looked like a small castle. To my surprise I saw that my father was wearing his crown—a thin gold circlet set with rubies and pearls, with one brown diamond in the center. He almost never wore it. I guessed he wanted to look fancy for his brother. My mother had on her second-best gown—a deep blue heavy linen with slashed sleeves laced up with gold threads. Beneath her linen cap, her hair was in two braids, long enough to sit on. She was wearing the amulet she always wore, and looked beautiful and solemn.

The gates opened with groans and creaks, and then my uncle and his men rode in. They had big black horses, and, yes, one of the men was carrying the same standard that my father's man carried when Faðir rode to another town to visit, or when there was trouble and he had to bring his army someplace.

I began to run to meet them, but my father clamped his hand on my shoulder with an iron grip. I looked up at him, and then my mother pulled me behind her. "Wait, Lilja," she murmured. "Your father goes first."

The man in front swung off his horse. He looked like my father, big and fair, but younger and less hardened by battle. He came and made a sweeping bow before my father, which people did all the time.

My father stepped forward and held out his arms. "Geir! It's been far too long!" They hugged, patting each other hard on the back. I was practically jumping up and down with excitement.

When my mother introduced us—my two sisters, my two brothers, and me—I blurted, "I didn't know I had an uncle!"

Uncle Geir made an unusual face and glanced at my father. "You used to have several," he said. "But now there's only me."

"Come in, Geir," said my father. "You must be tired from the journey."

We had a special dinner that night. I fell asleep while my father and Uncle Geir were still talking. Not long after dawn I woke up in my bed, threw on my clothes, and raced downstairs. Uncle Geir had told such interesting stories. I had forgotten to ask if he had children. Maybe they could come to visit.

I was about to knock on my father's study door when I heard raised voices coming from inside. I knew they had to be raised, because this door was four inches thick—you had to shout to be heard outside Faðir's study.

"Lilja, what are you doing?" My mother stood there with the housekeeper, her arms full of linens.

"I wanted to see Faðir," I said. "But listen: Why are he and Uncle Geir arguing?"

In our language, we had different words for an uncle from the father's side and an uncle from the mother's side. It translated to, literally, "Father-brother" and "Mother-brother."

"Shah," my mother said, taking my hand and pulling me away. "They're not arguing. They're both big bears of men and talk loudly. Now go have breakfast. There's cold rabbit from last night."

So I ran off. The next morning, my father and my uncle and my uncle's men and some of my father's men set off to go hunting for the wild boars that ran through the woods.

It was sunset before my father and his men came home. My father looked weary and heartsick: A tragedy had occurred. Uncle Geir, though unfamiliar with our land, had laughingly challenged my father to a race. My father shouted a warning at him, but Geir refused to listen. "He was ever headstrong," my father said.

Uncle Geir and his men had rushed on ahead through the woods, despite my father's shouted cautions. As we all knew, in one place the woods stopped suddenly, dropping away to a steep cliff. The sea had reclaimed the land there, and the huge, sharp boulders below were lapped by white-capped waves. My uncle and his men had been unable to stop on their fast horses, and they had all gone over the cliff. By the time my father and his men had climbed down with ropes, they had already been washed away.

I was crying by the time my father finished the story, and so were Eydís and Háakon. My oldest sister, Tinna, and my older brother, Sigmundur, bore the news stoically, as befitted the children of Úlfur the Wolf. But I sobbed into my mother's skirt. My one and only uncle, and now he was gone forever. What a tragedy.

I blinked slowly, leaving behind the severe, beautiful stone cliffs of Iceland and awakening to my cozy room at River's. I hadn't thought about my uncle in centuries. Now, with a grown-up's hindsight, I saw the truth. My uncle and his men had not died in a tragic hunting accident. My father and his men had killed them, so he would be the only brother left and have all his family's power.

I put my fist up to my mouth, overcome with sad horror. Until Geir came, I hadn't even known he existed. And apparently there had been others—also killed by my father, or by Geir? My mind darted from one ancient conversation or snippet of knowledge to the next: Growing up, I'd had no cousins, had thought both my parents were only children and that their parents had died when they were young. Now I had no idea if that was true. Maybe they had each systematically ensured their positions as sole heirs.

My mother had known the truth about my uncle's death—I was sure of it. She had looked grim and determined all that day. I'd always thought of my father as the harsh, ambitious one. Now I realized that my mother had been an equal partner to him.

Oh goddess. Until I was in my twenties, I'd had no idea I was even immortal. Just *that* had been a huge shock. Until I'd come to River's Edge, I hadn't put all the clues together to realize that my father had been the head of one of the eight major houses of immortals. And it was only now, today, that my brain was admitting what he and my mother had probably done to ensure their position.

I was the child of murderers.

I had another thought: Knowing what they did about ruthless, deadly sibling rivalry, why on earth had my parents had *five children*?

I sat up in my bed and hugged my knees to my chest, now wide awake. My breathing became shallow as a possibility occurred to me, and though I would never know for sure, as soon as I thought it, it sank like truth to the bottom of my stomach. My parents had five children, knowing that, most likely, only one of us could be the head of our clan.

My brothers and sisters and I had loved one another. We had shared and played together and cooperated.

It was one thing to kill a stranger or an enemy. It was another thing altogether to have enough ambition to kill someone you loved. A person strong enough to kill siblings he or she actually loved—that would be a very strong person indeed. That person would be ruthless enough, determined enough to actually be the head of the House of Úlfur.

I was shaking with cold all over again and untangled myself from my blankets to turn up my radiator. I got a glimpse of my messed-up face and grimaced. I put on a clean flannel shirt since it buttoned and wouldn't have to go over my head. With an immortal's typical recuperative powers, I'd be fine in a day or two, all trace of injury gone. But right now I felt like...um, like I'd been in a car wreck.

I'd just looped and knotted a scarf around my neck, trying to remember what Lorenz had done, when a gentle tap on the door alerted me to River's presence.

"Come in," I called.

"Hi," she said. "Feeling a little better?"

"Not really."

"Do you want some lunch? There was chicken soup."

I nodded. "That sounds good." Then the juxtaposition

of this normal conversation and the horrible thoughts I'd just been having sort of clashed in my mind, and I burst into tears.

Here's a tip: Try not to cry when you have a broken nose. It's a big, painful mess.

I was so tired of crying. Tired of having huge, soul-crushing realizations about a life that, while stupid, selfish, and pointless, had never before forced me to face any truths about myself.

"Nastasya," River said at last. *"What's going on?"*

"I don't know." I sat up and got the box of tissues by my bed. People here tried to use cloth handkerchiefs instead of these, but I hadn't drunk that Kool-Aid yet. I mean, it's a tissue. Please.

I started lobbing used tissues into my wastepaper basket.

"What do you think happened?"

I couldn't look at her as I said out loud the words that had been eating into me for days. "Maybe…it's just my darkness? I feel like it's coming out, like it's affecting everything around me. My job. My magick. Everything."

River was silent for several minutes while I played with the fringes on the end of my scarf.

"Hmm," she said at last. "And our other option is to wonder who would try to hurt you."

I looked up, wishing I could blame this on someone

else. "Incy, I guess. That's the only one I can think of." Would I feel him, if he were nearby? Would River pick up on his darkness? She could sense mine.

"Okay. Now, why do you think *you* caused this?"

"I don't know," I said, then I blurted the inevitable. "I'm just dark! I'm the dark child of dark parents, from a long line of dark ancestors. I can't escape it! It's useless to try." I started crying again.

River's hand stilled on my shoulder. "You believe that?"

"There's no believe or not-believe," I choked out. "It just *is*. That's how it *is*. That's the *reality*." Oh my God, I hated reality so, so much. I would take fantasy any day. When River didn't say anything, I went on, telling her about what I'd realized about my father, my uncle, my parents.

"That's who I'm descended from," I said. "That's the blood in my veins." I looked at River's face and saw compassion but also a thoughtful stillness, as if I were a puzzle she was trying to figure out.

"And I wanted to be his heir?" I said. "I wanted to be the daughter worthy of Úlfur the Wolf? What was I *thinking*? I must have been crazy! And Reyn!" I was getting more and more worked up, thoughts and pain spilling out of me like blood from a wound.

"What about Reyn?" River asked.

I took a shuddering breath. "That...thing we have between us. I don't know what it is. But we have this... thing. He's the winter raider, the *Butcher of Winter*, responsible for the deaths of who knows how many! *I'm* the sole heir to the House of Úlfur the Murderer! That's *us*. If we actually got together, the world would explode! I knew it would be a disaster, but I mean it really *would* be a *disaster*!"

"You feel that you're so dark that there isn't any choice anymore?" River asked.

"There never was a choice," I said bleakly. "That was... an illusion. Or wishful thinking. But there's no escape." This hurt much more than I would have expected.

"Nastasya, listen to me." River sounded very serious and put her hands on my shoulders, forcing me to look at her. "There's always, always, *always* a choice. You have to believe me. Most of us start in darkness. Many of us stay there. I don't know if it's just an immortal thing, but I've found that to be true, across the world. But it is also true that there is *always* a choice. No matter how dark you are, no matter what you think your heritage is or how inevitable your fall is, you can always make a choice in the *next second* to be different."

I'd heard it before. She just didn't understand. Yes, her family had been slave traders, which was bad. My parents had eliminated their *siblings*. And probably done even worse things. Things I prayed I would never find out.

"You don't believe me," she said when I was silent. "You think I don't understand and that you and your family were so much darker than mine."

Dammit. "My face is not that expressive."

"Nas, I *know* you." Her voice was gentle but insistent. "I really do know you. I know you *all the way down*. I see everything you are, light and dark and everything in between. I see things you haven't even discovered yet. And I love you, as is."

My throat closed up. She was lying. I wondered if I could leap out the window before River could stop me.

"Forget it, it's locked," she said.

"You're eavesdropping!" I accused her angrily.

"Please. You hate talking about emotion. Right now you're so uncomfortable you're practically writhing, you have a 'shut up' expression on your face, and your eyes flicked toward the window. A kindergartner could have put it together."

"I need to get out of here." I stood up so quickly, I almost knocked her over. Lightning fast, she grabbed my hand and yanked. I sat down hard on my bed, jarring my nose and everything else. I was shocked—hadn't even seen her move.

"You will sit and listen to me," she said. My eyes widened at the thread of steel in her voice that I'd never heard. "I need to show you something."

I opened my mouth—I don't even know what I was going to say—but in the next moment River put her hand on my face, her fingers outspread. She muttered something and drew some sigils on me with her free hand.

And in a few moments, I began to see...a scene. It wasn't like before, where I felt I was actually there and could smell things and feel the air on my face. This was shallower—more like watching a movie. The edges were blurry, and if I looked at something too long, it faded.

Once again I saw River in her youth, black-haired and beautiful with a hard smile and eyes the color of a rock in an icy stream. I saw the two men I'd seen at the slave auction, her brothers, and there were two more men there. I say men, but they all looked very young, in their late teens or early twenties. The family resemblance told me these were her other two brothers. The guys had goofy haircuts and wore clothing styles that had been ancient by the time I was born.

I was aware of River next to me, now singing softly under her breath.

The younger River and her brothers were in a small, dark room with walls of blackened wood. They were on a boat. A single candle flickered on the table between them.

"So it's decided, then?" one brother asked. I could understand his speech, though he must have been speaking Middle Italian.

"Yes," said Diavola. "When they're on the road to Savona, in the woods, two hours' ride from here — there." Her long, slim finger pointed to a place on a parchment map. "We can ambush them."

"Who will actually do it?" one of the younger brothers asked.

The oldest-looking brother (a small distinction) said, "We must all do it. Diavola will set the flare and startle the horses. Mazzo, you will dispatch the driver and the two outriders. Outriders first, then driver. Michele, you take the two hind-riders. Then we'll all converge on the carriage and—" He clasped his hands together and swung his arms in a fast arc, right to left, as though holding a sword.

I understood. They were planning to kill someone. A handful of people.

The youngest brother, Michele, nodded slowly. "It's a good plan. Then the five of us will rule together, like the five fingers on one hand."

It hit me: Diavola and her brothers were plotting to kill their *parents* and seize their power. *Their own parents.*

I was speechless at this realization, and then I saw Diavola and the oldest brother, Benedetto, exchange a glance. In an instant, it was all clear to me: Diavola and Benedetto had another plan, a secret one. The two of them would then kill the three younger brothers. So that the family power would be divided by only two, instead of five.

This was so painful to me, seeing it. The five immortals of the Genoa house reminded me of the five of us from the Icelandic house. I'd wondered how my brothers and sisters and I would have grown up, if we would have turned on one another like vipers. Here it was already being played out.

So inherited darkness did consume a person, in the end. In the end, there was no escape, and the darkness would have consequences that you would never be able to live down. To live with. To forgive.

My breath was coming fast and shallow—I wanted to leave this scene. I didn't want to see any more of River's horrible fall.

River sensed my feelings and slowly drew us out of the half spell, the vision.

When our heads had cleared and we were firmly in reality again, I stared at River, trying to see a trace of cruelty in her sad and haunted expression.

I cleared my throat, the sound loud and startling in the quiet of my room. "You...killed your parents?" Please deny it.

My heart fell as River nodded, an ancient anguish on

her face. "Yes." One side of her mouth rose in a bitter smile. "A thousand years of therapy isn't enough."

"And you and Benedetto killed your other brothers?" Wait—I remembered her saying that she has four brothers. Still *has*. Not had.

"No, thank the goddess," said River. She drew in a deep breath and let it out, as if releasing pain and memory. "Amazingly, we didn't. It didn't happen that—same night. Like it was supposed to. And before we had another opportunity, I was...saved." Her eyes met mine, and a little of the pain had lessened, eased by the remembrance of who she was now, today. Not a thousand years ago.

"Saved? So...you accepted the Lord as your savior?"

"There's more than one way of being saved." Her voice sounded more like herself. She straightened her shoulders and seemed familiar again, only the barest, faintest shadow of Diavola in her eyes. "A teacher came. And if you think *you* were resistant—well. I was much more so. But she broke through. At last. She saved me. Set me on the path toward light. Taught me all about...choices. And slowly, I convinced my brothers." She looked up. "And now I'm teaching you and others. Sometimes I think that maybe this helps with the karma of...killing our parents. And then, maybe someday you'll be teaching someone else and sharing your own story."

I snorted reflexively, then winced with pain.

"And you're friends with your brothers today?" I asked.

"More than friends. They're my brothers. We share the same blood, the same history."

"And they've forgiven you, for wanting to kill them?" Or maybe they didn't know.

River smiled wryly. "They still throw it in my face at holidays."

I didn't see how she could be so...normal today. After all she had been.

"Most of us start in darkness," she said, echoing her earlier words. "Some of us raise darkness to an art. I'm trying to help people who don't want to be dark. One person at a time. Right now, it's your turn."

I didn't know what to say.

River stood gracefully, as if she hadn't just stunned me with her revelation. "Why don't you rest some more? Then come down to dinner?"

I nodded slowly, and she left my room. I drew my knees to my chest again and carefully rested my bruised cheek on one knee. Too much to take in.

CHAPTER 15

ave you ever been making something in a blender and you have just a little extra and you don't want to waste it, so you go ahead and put it in, and then when you start the blender it totally spews out from beneath the lid?

That's how my brain felt. For most of my life, I'd had maybe one or two new ideas or concepts introduced to me *a year*. Like *electricity*. That was a big year. In the last two months, there had been several huge, earth-shattering, sanity-testing revelations *every day*. Now it was all leaking out through my ears. Metaphorically.

The dinner bell rang. I sighed, tucked my scarf around my neck, and headed out my door.

Reyn was just coming out of his room two doors down. I started to force myself to smile, to not act like a paranoid loser, but my smile froze in place as Amy, laughing, came out of Reyn's room also.

"And you just left him there?" she said to him.

Reyn nodded, looking younger and lighter than he usually did. "For a day and a half."

Amy laughed again, leaning against him.

Then they saw me.

Here's an example of how I was rocketing toward maturity: I went ahead and forced the smile. It probably looked like a pained grimace, but it was the best I could do.

Amy immediately came up to me, genuine concern on her face. "I heard what happened," she said. "I'm so sorry! But Anne fixed you up, didn't she?"

"Yes." I had peeled off the nose tape, slowly and painfully. But I still looked distinctly raccoonish.

Amy leaned her head toward mine conspiratorially. "Did she make you drink tea?" Her eyes were full of warmth and humor, and I couldn't help liking her. It wasn't her fault that Reyn and I had a horrible, confusing history and that I was a complete moron emotionally.

"Yes."

"I know," Amy said. "It's, like, enough with the tea. Tea does not actually fix *everything*."

I really did smile this time.

"Are you feeling better?" Reyn asked politely. He'd already seen the big gorefest of my face, so it wasn't a surprise.

Such a relative term, *better*. I shook my head. "I just don't even know."

Reyn opened his mouth as if to say something else, but then we were at the top of the stairs and were joined by Charles and Jess. Jess made no comment on my appearance, but Charles nodded. "That's a good look for you."

I punched him lightly on the arm, and he grinned. It struck me: These people were nice. Nicer than most people I had known. I was the one instrument that was out of key in this little orchestra.

In the dining room, Anne bustled through the kitchen door, her oven-mitted hands carrying a large enameled stew pot. She set it heavily on the table and turned to me, examining my face. "It already looks better." She stepped back and smiled. "Damn, I'm good."

"It was the tea," Amy said solemnly, and Reyn grinned. For a moment there was a glowy warmth in the room — his face was so transformed when he smiled, when his eyes lit up.

Soon we were all seated, passing bowls of stew and

baskets of bread and serving spoons. I felt self-conscious—everyone must have known about my accident—and when I caught sight of myself in the large gilded mirror on the wall, I recoiled, surprised at how ugly I looked, how unlike myself. I had felt out of place before all this. Now I felt like a neon sign blinking glaringly in a soft desert night.

I was taking a piece of bread when movement caught my eye. I dropped it quickly: There were maggots on it, in it. Live maggots, writhing through the bread.

Brynne shrieked and dropped her bread, too. "Look at the bread!" she cried.

"What in the world—" River began.

"I made that bread today!" Rachel said.

Charles had just eaten some stew, and now his eyes widened. He leaped back off his bench and ran to the kitchen. We could hear him spitting it out into the sink.

"Taste the stew," Asher said quietly to Solis. "Just a tiny bit."

Solis barely dipped his spoon in and then licked it cautiously. His face screwed up and he put the spoon down. "Um..."

Standing quickly, Anne stuck a finger into her bowl and tasted it. She spit it right back into her bowl—no niceties of running to the kitchen to spare us. She looked shocked. "That stew was perfect five minutes ago in the kitchen," she said.

"I tasted it," Rachel agreed. "It was delicious."

"Now it tastes like we used carrion. Toxic." Anne sat down limply.

"And the bread," River said. Her face was solemn. "When did you make it, Rachel?"

Reyn had gotten to his feet and was gathering up all the maggoty bread. When he had all of it, he pushed through the kitchen door, and then we heard the slam of the back door.

"I made it this afternoon," said Rachel. "Just a while ago. That's why it's still warm."

"And you didn't use the maggot recipe," said Solis, making a weak joke without smiling.

"No," said Rachel. She and Anne looked stunned.

I was as freaked out as the rest of them, but then it finally hit me: my darkness. I had done this. The food had been perfect until *I had come downstairs.*

"Oh my God—it's me," I muttered.

Next to me, Jess said, "What?"

I glanced around the table, already pushing off my bench. "It's me. I did this. I made the accident happen. I made the library explode. *I'm* making all the bad stuff happen."

"What are you—" Asher started, but I interrupted.

"On New Year's Eve, I tried to cast off my own darkness," I admitted, getting more and more upset. "But I just *released* it. Don't you see? It's me! I'm the cause of all this! It's *me!*"

"Nastasya," said Solis, "I don't think—"

"I can't stay here!" I cried, and fled the dining room. I ran up the stairs as if the devil we didn't believe in was chasing me. I was ashamed of my past, my stupidity, how much I had resisted knowing for so long. Horrified about my parents, whom I had loved so much, and my heritage. If I'd thought reflecting on my life was painful before, now it seemed like searing, burning pain, the raw agony of acid thrown on my brain.

When I'd left here before, I had *needed* to stay but hadn't *wanted* to stay. Now I both needed *and* wanted to stay. But obviously I was bringing destruction down on everything and everyone here. After a lifetime of running, my past was catching up to me.

I burst through the door to my room, feeling like my head was going to split open in huge shards. Inside I looked around wildly, no idea what to do. Now that I knew about my own darkness, there was no way to unknow it—and this knowledge was going to make me crazy.

I turned at a sound and saw that River had followed me into my room. She took my arm.

"Nastasya, listen to me!" she said strongly. "You should—"

"I should—*what?*" I was aware of a hysterical unraveling happening in my psyche. I thought of everything River didn't know about me. Including—"Oh God!" I put my hand to my mouth, then dropped to my knees and squirmed under my bed.

"What are you *doing?*" River said.

I pried open the molding and shoved my hand in, then wriggled it back out, holding the knotted scarf. I'd never, ever shown anyone else my mother's amulet. I quickly untied the scarf, then practically threw the heavy gold object at River. "Here! You take it! It's dark—evil! I can't have it anymore." I was wild-eyed and breathing hard. Part of me felt like a bystander, watching this scene play out but unable to stop or affect it.

River caught it, then slowly uncurled her hands and looked at my amulet, broken and without a stone. Her eyes widened. Weirdly fast, she went over and shut my door, tracing her fingers along the doorjamb so no one could open it from the outside.

"What is this?" Her voice was hushed.

"You know what it is," I said shakily.

She stared at me, astonished, and then examined it again. Her long fingers slowly traced the ancient runes and other markings on it. "The tarak-sin of the House of Úlfur.

I can't—it's...very beautiful," she said, sounding odd, then tried to hand it back to me.

"I don't need it," I said bitterly. "I carry it with me always." I whipped my scarf away, turned, and held my hair off my neck. Another first: willingly showing my scar to someone else.

River actually gasped. "Oh, Nas," she breathed. "How—"

"It was burned on there. By accident," I bit out. "So you keep that one. Away from me."

"It's broken," River said, turning it over in her hand. It seemed to glow with a golden warmth, as if coming alive in the presence of a strong immortal.

"There were two halves. And a moonstone." I swiped my hand across my eyes. "You have to destroy it—it's evil. It's brought evil here." I chocked. "It brought me here."

"No, you're wrong," River said, seeming transfixed by the amulet.

The idea that my tarak-sin might be dark enough to seduce Diavola out of hiding revolted me as soon as I thought it—and I didn't know what to do. *Everything* I did was bad, with bad consequences. I was poison, as toxic as that stew downstairs, and I had to get out of here before I destroyed everything that River had worked for.

I'd never left my amulet—had always had it with me or nearby—and the thought of it staying in River's hands made me feel like shrieking. But I wasn't strong enough to deal with it—maybe River was. I hoped. If she wasn't—

"I've gotta go," I said, and brushed past River. I opened the door and raced down the hallways even as River started to come after me again. I sped up, pounding down the stairs, and then shot through the front door into the night as if pursued by wraiths.

CHAPTER 16

ran.

I ran through the thicket where Reyn had kissed me just, like, *last week.* The cold air seared my lungs and made my eyes water. I'd hoped that running would warm me up, but I was already shaking with cold or emotion or fear.

Thin branches whipped against my face and arms. The snow crunched underfoot and deadened my footsteps. I had a sudden flashback to that awful dream I'd had about Incy, where I had warmed my hands on a fire made of my friends. I hit my shoulder hard against a tree and raced headlong out of the woods. I saw I was way at the back of the farm, in a pasture no one used. I ran along the fence for a long time, until each breath was like a shard of ice being shoved down my throat. Cold sweat froze on my brow; my lungs were working like bellows because I never run and was totally out of shape.

I staggered to a plodding walk, then finally stopped, unable to go on. I was horrified and panicked. I was outside alone at night. With humiliation I realized that a small part of me hoped that someone would track my footsteps and come find me—but then that would be worse because I would have to go back. Again. Have to face whatever awful stuff awaited me in Reality Land.

I started to cry.

Just a few weeks ago, I'd seen a tiny crack of sunny promise splitting through the dark tarmac of my soul. I'd been able to count the things I was doing right. I'd seen progress—I really had. What had happened? Everything felt ruined: my whole time at River's Edge, my relationships with *everybody*, my magick, my learning.... I'd faced so much—my heritage, my past, my emptiness. I had faced it all, and for what? I was worse off now than when I'd come, because now I actually understood how bad off I was.

What was wrong with me?

I slumped onto the icy grass, which crumpled stiffly under me. Freezing to death was, sadly, not a possibility. I would get hypothermia and pass out, but I wouldn't die. I blinked tiredly, feeling my tears ice-cold against my lashes. Just like in London, I'd reached a point where I couldn't handle the pain.

I cried until my ribs ached and I felt like I might throw up. The grass scratched my face, which already stung from the branches in the woods, and my salty tears burned in the scratches.

I closed my eyes. Maybe I would wake up, find myself back in Tahiti, find this had all been a wretched dream. I had been Sea Caraway, in Tahiti. Incy had been Sky Benolto. I'd made stuff out of seashells, sold it at local shops. This had been back in the 1970s. After I'd been Hope Rinaldi, in the sixties. Before I became Nastasya Crowe, in the eighties.

My head ached. The cold made it throb more insistently.

I just wanted to be happy. When had I been happy?

I remembered laughing.

When had I laughed?

My head swam and I tried to remember laughing, tried to hear what my laugh had sounded like.

I heard the tinkle of crystal champagne glasses gently touching one another on a silver tray. One of the servers was moving through the crowd, penguin-y and proper in his tux. I reached out and snagged my sixth glass, feeling the golden bubbles tickle my nose.

"Dearest." Incy smiled and raised his glass at me.

"Love." I smiled back at him. James. His name was James. We'd been friends for about thirty years. Best friends for twenty-eight.

"Prentice! Darling!" Sarah Jane Burkhardt pushed through the crowd and we air-kissed. Sarah Jane was a savvy, sophisticated twenty—one of the daughters of our hosts. We'd met some months ago at a house party out on Long Island. She held her ivory cigarette holder out to the side so it wouldn't spill ash on my gold evening dress.

"How did you ever get away from Sir Richard?" I giggled, remembering how I'd gaily waved good-bye as Sarah Jane had been forced to listen to that blowhard's war stories. It was 1924. The Great War was long over, never to be repeated. America had had five years of no longer conserving food, no longer being urged to buy war bonds or send extra grain to England or France. It was a time of beautiful parties, beautiful people, once again. Sure, the ridiculous Prohibition had required people to be careful about sloshing liquor around, but there were so many workarounds that it was almost as if it didn't exist for some people. People like us.

"I pawned him off on Dayton MacKenzie," Sarah Jane said.

"She deserved it," James/Incy said. "Did you see what she wore to 21 last week?"

Sarah Jane and I both laughed meanly. Then Sarah Jane's eyes widened. "Goodness gracious. Who is that *lovely* man?" She drew on her cigarette holder and blew the smoke out through her nose, which we'd been practicing all day.

I looked. An unusually handsome man was standing in the foyer. A huge palm in a marble planter partly obscured his head, but he was tall and blond and wearing a beautiful, beautiful linen suit.

"I don't know," I said. "I've never seen him before. James?"

"No," said James. "But he looks like someone we ought to get to know. Do you agree, ladies?"

"Yes indeedy-do," said Sarah Jane, and James boldly led us over to meet the stranger.

The man turned, as if sensing us approaching, and I heard Sarah Jane's slightly indrawn breath. He was too pretty for me, with smooth skin, blue eyes, and long lashes that would have looked better on a girl, but clearly he was Sarah Jane's dream come true.

Sarah Jane held out her hand, palm down, at chest height. The stranger obligingly kissed it. She almost purred.

"Delighted," the stranger murmured. "I'm Andrew. Andrew Vancouver."

"Sarah Jane Burkhardt. This is Prentice Goodson and James Angelo."

I saw, when we met eyes: Andrew was immortal. He recognized us also—some instantaneous flicker of expression that no one else saw.

"Sarah?"

We turned to see a girl with Sarah Jane's features and coloring but more refined, prettier. Sarah Jane was attractive, elegantly dressed and skillfully made up. This girl was maybe sixteen, young and untouched, but she held the promise of becoming a truly beautiful woman eventually.

"Yes, Lala, what is it?" Sarah Jane's voice was kind.

"Is that champagne?"

Sarah Jane laughed and held out her glass. The girl named Lala smiled shyly and took a tentative sip while we all watched, amused. She swallowed and her large blue eyes became larger. "It's like...drinking flowers."

"What a pretty way to put it," said Andrew. "Miss Burkhardt, your guest is charming."

Sarah Jane laughed. "She's not a guest. This is my younger sister, Louisa. Louisa, say hello to Mr. Vancouver, Miss Goodson, and Mr. Angelo."

Louisa shook Andrew's hand, then mine, then took James's and looked into his eyes.

And that was how Incy had met Lala Burkhardt, and put in motion that awful scandal with that poor girl. After her suicide attempt, I think she'd ended up in a sanatorium in Switzerland. The whole thing had been abominable. She must be dead by now.

And Andrew Vancouver? That was how we had met Boz. Boz was working on another heiress at that party, very successfully, at least for a while. But just short of his completely ruining her, her father caught on and kicked Boz to the curb.

After that the three of us hung out together: birds of a feather.

The twenties had been such a fun, glamorous time. Parties and summer homes and all the brand-new cars (horseless carriages!) just starting to hit the market. Women were at last done with corsets for good, thank God, and in some places we could vote. Incy and Boz and I had had such a great time. The thirties were less fun, after Black Friday; the forties were grim; the fifties kind of weird and high-pressure and artificial. Things in America wouldn't get fun again until the sixties.

Lying here now, all my senses were deadened—I was practically frozen stiff. Moving was going to hurt. And I was still: alone, dark, homeless, coatless, and friendless. I took in another icy, shuddering breath, wondering dimly how this would all play out. I didn't have the energy to move or make any decisions.

Gradually I felt a prickle of awareness, a very slight disruption in my field of energy. An animal? A person? River or someone from River's Edge? Reyn? I closed my eyes, awash with despair. Maybe if I was very, very quiet, they wouldn't find me. Such a pointless hope.

It was impossibly dark out here, with no moon, and clouds scudding over the stars. But I definitely felt some-one moving closer to me, and I opened my eyes. I could barely make out the edge of the tall grasses, where they were bent and heavy with snow. Then a dark figure emerged from them, walking toward me.

Not Reyn. Not River.

I lay motionless, watching. It was Incy.

CHAPTER 17

ncy.

I'd met him right before the turn of the century, in 1899. You'd think that with such a long friendship as ours, and how bound up we were with each other, we would have had some dramatic beginning, like he'd saved my life or I'd stolen his horse.

But we'd met when he was peddling forged artwork in New York City. I'd gone with a friend to examine a "recently discovered" print by del Sarto. This was before sophisticated forensic techniques were used to determine the age and authenticity of artwork. Though legitimate experts were often consulted, it was so easy to perpetrate fraud. Ah, the good old days.

"Mrs. Humphrey Watson," the doorman announced. "Mrs. Alphonse North."

I liked Eugenia Watson, and we'd been close friends for at least five years by then. There was no Mr. North — I'd made up a dead husband for myself because a married woman, even a widow, had more freedom than a single woman.

We took Eugenia's carriage to our friend's house, and her footman helped us haul our stupid full skirts and layers of petticoats down the little carriage steps and onto the sidewalk. Bustles were finally smaller, thank God, but my waist was cinched to a fashionable eighteen inches. Make a circle eighteen inches around, with your hands. Yeah. It was a wonder my digestive system worked.

"Coral!" Eugenia said, and did the double-cheek kiss with our friend Mrs. Barrett-Smith.

"Eugenia!" said Coral. "And dear Sarah. Thank you both for coming."

"Thank you for inviting us. We're *most* interested in this print you've found," said Eugenia, and I knew she was telling the truth: Her husband worked for one of the city's leading auction houses. If Coral had discovered a new source for previously unknown sixteenth-century European prints, Eugenia wanted to know about it.

"First may I introduce the man who has brought it into my life," said Coral. She gestured gracefully, and an elegant man stepped out of the shadows of an alcove. "Mrs. Watson, Mrs. North—this is Louis Carstairs."

And that was Incy. He was very handsome, beautifully dressed, somewhat foreign-looking, and, as I realized when he kissed my hand, immortal. The answering spark of recognition in his eyes went unnoticed by my friends.

Anyway. The print was fake, but no one told Coral that. She bought it and was intensely proud of it. She and Incy embarked on a torrid affair that lasted several years, and he and I became friends. We both liked living well, were amused by the same things, and generally got along like a house on fire. We had the occasional spat but would soon make up. Everything was more fun with Incy, more interesting, more outrageous. It was he who pushed me to be bolder in my personal appearance, and he who made me feel comfortable with increasingly outré behavior, both mine and his. I'd always loved traveling, but it was Incy who decided we should branch out of our comfort zones and go to Egypt, Peru, Alaska.

All those years I'd felt that being with Innocencio allowed me to be the real me, the full and complete me. It had really felt like that. How could I have been so wrong? We'd been stuck together like peanut butter to the roof of your mouth for a century. Could I really have been so misguided all that time?

And now here we were. And I'd been hiding from him for two months.

Seeing Innocencio's silhouette coming toward me over the white field didn't instantly put memories of all our fun times into my head. Instead my mind seized on all my devastating visions, my appalling dreams, my increasing fears about him. Were my nightmares coming true now?

My heart had slowed like a hibernating squirrel's, but it now gave a couple of thuds, kicking itself into gear. I was an emotional and physical mess — in no shape to fight Innocencio or outrun him, too far away for my screams to be heard. I drew in a breath of searingly cold air and tried, creakily, to sit up.

Innocencio. Every time I'd imagined him lately, he'd been covered in blood, pushed over the edge into stark, horrifying madness. Now he was here, my worst fears materializing in the darkness, as if my memories themselves had created him, brought him to me.

Ideally I would have been able to leap up and assume a threatening fighting stance, but as it was, I projected more of a victim vibe. I struggled to a sitting position and leaned heavily against the fence post, my hands fluttering nervously on my pants leg.

"Incy?" It came out as barely a croak.

The tall, slim figure came closer, and my breath clotted in my throat when I caught the first ribbon of scent from his cologne. He'd been using the same one since the thirties— it was called 4711. Every cell in my brain recognized it.

"Nas—I can't believe it. It's really you. I've been looking for you." Now he was upon me, and I pointlessly tried to throw my arms up to somehow protect myself. But my muscles were sluggish and cold and I could barely move. I tried to project strength, but every fear I'd had coalesced into a barbed-wire whirlwind that was shredding my ability to think.

At that moment, the heavy bank of clouds suddenly drifted past the moon, and the fingernail-thin crescent shone an anemic light on us. I looked up at him, my heart in my throat...and blinked. Incy seemed...amazingly normal. In my visions he'd been like a wild man, an asylum patient, his eyes too bright with anger and intensity. But he looked *fine*—well dressed, hair brushed back from his elegant forehead. He was clean-shaven, with calm, concerned eyes.

"I've been searching everywhere for you," he repeated. "Then I was driving past, and I...just felt you." He gestured to the great outdoors. "I thought I was going crazy, but the feeling was so strong—and now here you are." He peered at me and frowned. "What are you doing out here? And what happened to your face?"

Freaking out and *car accident* didn't seem like smart responses. But he didn't wait for an answer.

"Oh God—look at your hair!" He chuckled softly. "I haven't seen that color since—ever. But you're freezing!" he said, and slid out of a thick cashmere overcoat that probably cost four thousand dollars. He draped it over me, and I was reminded of a time not too long ago when I'd been outside crying, and River had draped her coat over me. Like then, I was immediately shocked by its warmth.

"I was just going back in," I said, and cleared my throat. "They're expecting me at any second. So what do you want?" My voice was shaky and rough from crying.

He gave a laugh, slightly embarrassed. "I'm sorry, babe. Not to do the whole stalker thing." He knelt down in the snow, beautiful handmade boots crunching on the frozen grass, and offered me his hand. I was leery of touching him and instead struggled to my feet, every muscle protesting and calling me bad names.

Incy stood also. I was more alert now, thawing under the incredible toasty warmth of his coat. I examined his face carefully, but if he had gone completely insane since I last saw him, I could find no evidence. Then maybe all my dreams and visions were, as I'd feared, only a projection of my own inner darkness—products of my deep, previously hidden well of self-loathing? The thought was crushing, and I almost groaned.

"The thing is, Nas," Incy went on, "that, well, I was just really worried about you."

"Worried? Why?"

"Nas—you disappeared without a word." His tone was kind and infinitely reasonable. Of the two of us here in this godforsaken field, I was the one who seemed crazy.

When I didn't say anything, he went on.

"Look, we've always taken little trips on our own. But I'd leave you a message. Or you'd call me from Bali or whatever. This time you simply disappeared, and no one knew why or where or if anything was wrong."

An icy wind crept under the edge of the coat. I saw Incy shiver, and he rubbed his hands together.

"We've hung out, you and me, bread and butter, for a century, darling. If you've moved on, if we've broken up, okay. But *tell* me, you know? Don't let me worry about if someone came and chopped your head off." He sounded so rational. Confusion crept into my brain. It seemed unbelievable that he wasn't as I had pictured him. I'd run away from him in fear and disgust because of the cabbie. But the Incy that night bore no relation to the man standing in front of me. Had I truly just imagined everything?

I licked my cracked, dry lips. "I just needed a little break."

He held out his hands: a sane man dealing with a wing nut. "Okay. That's fine. I accept that. But do you see why

I was worried about you?" He exhaled, leaving a roiling smoke trail in the night. "I've been asking everywhere for you. I even tried scrying!" He laughed, showing even, white teeth. I remembered when he'd had them fixed, in the eighties. "Of course, that got me nowhere. But, honey—I've been so worried." He shook his head. "I couldn't rest until I made sure you were all right—saw you with my own eyes. Even if you've just wanted to go off and do a walkabout—I had to make sure that nothing horrible had happened to you." He blew on his hands, rubbed them together. "If I'd just blown it off and found out later that you'd needed my help—I wouldn't be able to live with myself."

"How could you live with yourself after what you did to that cabbie?" I blurted.

He cocked his head, thinking back, then his face cleared. "Oh, the *cabbie*," he said, as if things were falling into place. "Why, Nas—were you upset about that?"

"You crippled him! Forever!" I stood up straighter, my blood starting to run warm in my veins.

"I did," he said slowly. "I did. I was so...furious. He hauled Katy out of the cab, and she was sick, and he was so hateful. I remember feeling that he was spewing venom at us. And I just—snapped."

He didn't make a huge protest of innocence or justify his action. He didn't try to laugh it off. Instead he looked off into the distance, as if remembering the whole night. He sighed, making another cloud. "Babe, is that why you left?"

"It was a bunch of things," I muttered.

He was silent, as if mentally reviewing. "Okay," he said again. "I'm sorry to hear I was part of it. I wish you'd talked to me about it, then. Anyway. So you're here — at this farm. Have you been here the whole time? Is it… going well for you?" He gestured in the general direction of River's Edge.

"Well" was not how I would describe my stay here. I shrugged.

"Look, if I know that you're healthy and happy here, and among friends, I can leave with a clear conscience," he said, and smiled. "Because I'll know my friend is fine."

Friend. We *had* been friends, for such a long time. My relationship with him seemed to be the definition of friendship. I called him in emergencies, and he always came through. When he needed help, I was glad to pitch in. We went shopping, influencing what the other wore. For so long, my endless days had been bearable because Incy had been there. When I was down, he would do anything, crazy things, to cheer me up. I mean, the male-stripper-gram hadn't been a good idea, but still. We sent each other candy and flowers and little gifts we'd seen that had reminded us of the other. He'd given me a Studebaker once. I'd given him a Corvette. He'd wrecked it.

We simply...always preferred each other's company to any other. I looked up into his eyes, so dark they looked like part of the night sky. I'd looked into those eyes a million times, right before falling asleep, over a dinner table, on countless ocean liners, in an emergency room.

Who could I call my friend at River's Edge? With uncomfortable surprise, I realized there wasn't anyone. No one hated me, but no one was really a good friend, not anything like Incy and I had been, or even Boz and Katy. I thought of how Anne and Amy walked arm in arm, how Brynne and Rachel studied together, their heads close. I would have thought Brynne's flamboyance would be a bad foil for Rachel's natural studiousness, but in magick, it seemed, they were more alike.

I'd been an outsider when I arrived, and I'd remained that way for more than two months. And maybe that had been my fault, I admitted, thinking of the overtures I'd rebuffed, invitations to walks, to movies—once, to spend the afternoon making cookies. I'd never accepted, usually heading up to my room instead.

I remembered River telling me that I'd never be able to love anyone else until I loved and accepted myself. That still seemed just as unattainable a goal as it did when I'd shown up like a hungry mongrel.

Oh God—I'd screwed up so bad, wasted the last two months. I'd been kidding myself. All of my sincere attempts, my stupid, pathetic job, my bumbling struggles to learn, to fit in—it was one painful memory after another. What had I been thinking? Why had I even tried? I recalled the patient smiles, the measured explanations of basic, A-B-C stuff that every immortal in the world knew except me. They must have been laughing themselves sick.

Incy let out another breath and stood up. "I don't remember Massachusetts being this cold," he said. He glanced up as a fine snowflake drifted down, swaying back and forth like a tiny feather. Another flake joined it. Perfect. Because I needed to get snowed on, on top of everything else. I still had nowhere to go, nothing to do with myself. And I would have to give Incy his coat back.

Then what? Yep, I had really thought this through. Was making great choices. Had learned so much.

Incy smiled suddenly and looked at me. "Do you remember that time in Rome—when was it? Like the fifties. Late fifties? We were at that restaurant, and Boz was telling a story, and the waiter put down that huge platter of spaghetti, and we were so hungry?"

I could see it at once and smiled involuntarily, knowing what was coming next.

"Of course Boz was three sheets to the wind," Incy said.

"Montepulciano," I said, remembering the wine we'd been drinking.

"And he was waving his arms around, telling that stupid story about the sheep," Incy said, starting to chuckle. "And then he slammed his fist down on the table to make a point—"

"And the plank of the table flew up, launching the spaghetti platter," I said, grinning. "Oh my God, spaghetti everywhere. Jeez, what a mess."

"But we wouldn't know," Incy said. His smile seemed to light up the area around us.

"Because we sped out of there, leaving Boz to take the blame," I said, snickering.

Incy tilted his head back and laughed, and though I had seen him laugh a bazillion times, it was still fun. The crazed, blood-drenched Incy of my visions seemed almost incomprehensible right now. Yes, he had crippled the cabbie—but now I wondered if it had been Incy's own inherent darkness bursting out of him without warning. As mine had. Or had my own darkness even made him do it? It was a nauseating possibility.

I shivered as I contemplated giving Incy his coat back. I was so deliciously warm. Without thinking I slipped my arms into the big sleeves and wrapped it around myself.

Incy gave me a sweet, loving smile. "I'm so glad— relieved—to see you're all right, babe," he said. "I was worried, but you're doing fine. So…give me a call, next time you want to hang out, tell stories about Boz."

"How is Boz?" In pieces somewhere? I still couldn't shake that frightening image.

"He's fine." Incy shook his head: silly Boz. "He, Katy, Stratton, and Cicely are all waiting for me back in Boston. They've been worried about you, too. Anyway—we were thinking of hanging out there for a while, and then at the end of the month catching the new sixty-day cruise that Halliday just announced."

I *love* cruises. No driving, no looking for hotels, no finding restaurants. Plus, you can get drunk and the worst thing that could happen to you is you fall overboard. Which is really hard to do.

"It goes to the Far East—China, Japan, Thailand, Vietnam. Then down to India—all around in there. It has some great day trips." He shrugged. "Sounded fun."

It sounded like freaking paradise.

"Huh. How much does it cost?" Not that cost was ever an issue for us.

Incy snorted. "Practically nothing. Twenty-two thousand for a suite. For sixty days."

"You're all going?" I remembered other cruises with the gang. They had been so, so fun.

Incy nodded. "Stratton's still on the fence—depends on this girl he's chasing."

"Oh. It sounds fun. It leaves at the end of January?"

He nodded and put his hands into his corduroy pockets. He must have been freezing and was shifting from foot to foot. "Yeah. Like January twenty-fifth or something. Katy says she needs all new resort wear." He rolled his eyes. "But we can do some shopping in Boston, and then take the red-eye to LA in time to catch the boat." He gave me another sweet, somewhat wistful smile. "They'll be so glad to hear that you're okay. Just hiding out in the backwoods, chilling. Literally."

I gave a tiny laugh. "How did you get here?" I asked.

He gestured vaguely over one shoulder. "I have a sweet ride, a Caddy. The latest Incymobile. The road isn't too far from here, actually. I concentrated on you, seemed to feel your energy. I thought I must be crazy, but something told me to stop there, get out, and walk. And then there you were."

"Oh." I licked my lips again. My car was totaled, of course.

Incy looked at me. "Honey — you're happy here, right? You're fine? I can leave and be happy for you?"

My eyes filled with tears again, and Incy looked alarmed. I was not known for being a big crier, and he hadn't been around for the last two months of waterworks.

I didn't know what to say. My mind was splitting in two. There was no way I could go back to River's Edge, face all those people, look like such a failure, and have them realize how inescapably dark I was. But would being on my own be any better? I'd have to come up with a whole new life for myself. What would I do? Where would I go? While I'd always had my own apartment or house—Incy was a huge slob—still, I'd known who I would be with every day. Knew basically what I would do. Being at River's Edge had, in some ways, been more of the same: a pattern.

If I left River's Edge, and I wasn't going to be with Innocencio, what would I do? The thought filled me with panic as I pictured myself living in a new place, maybe knowing a couple of other immortals I wasn't close to. It was the last thing I felt like doing.

But what choice did I have? After all, I was still kind of afraid of Incy—wasn't I? I didn't even know. He seemed so... himself. Totally himself. Easy and fun and really, sincerely concerned about me, and oh yes, *sane*. Because obvious insanity would be a deal breaker for sure.

I rubbed my hand across my eyes, which burned and felt gritty. Snow was falling more heavily now.

"Nas. Now I'm worried again. Was anyone mean to you? Do I need to kick some ass?"

That thought alone was hilarious; he would never risk ruining his outfit. I gave a leaky smile.

I was frozen, not with cold but with indecision and

utter confusion. If I'd been lost, not knowing who I was two months ago, I was doubly so now.

"Listen," said Incy, really looking concerned. "Do you want to just get out of here? You could come get in the car. I'll crank the heater; we'll be in Boston in two hours. You can take a nice, hot bath with a brandy, to warm you from the inside out. We'll get room service. You'll feel like a new woman. And tomorrow you can decide what you feel like doing next."

It all sounded so intensely appealing that I almost whimpered. But how could I possibly just hop in his car like I'd hit a reset button? I'd spent the last two months going to extreme lengths to hide from Incy. But I *know* I couldn't stay *here*.

"I don't want to push you. I know you're doing this... experiment, or whatever, for yourself, and I want to support that," Incy said kindly. It reminded me of the time I'd decided to study ballet, in Paris, in the late forties. He'd gently pointed out that most successful ballerinas began their studies at early ages, five or six, maybe seven. And I was... you know, already more than four hundred. But he'd still been supportive, had gone with me to get my leotard and shoes. Even came to a recital, before I finally wised up and dropped the whole thing.

"But I'm just saying, if you wanted, you could come hang out. You don't have to stay with us, or me, if you need more space," he said quickly. "You do what you want to do. You could fly out of Boston tomorrow, go anywhere else. But of course you'd be *welcome* to stay with us. I'd love for you to come on the cruise. Who else could truly appreciate the cross section of humanity that one sees on cruises? Pretty much only you." He and I were always merciless, dissecting wardrobes and hairstyles of fellow passengers while we sat at the bar, slugging back gin rickeys. Ha — like I should talk about anyone else's clothes or hair, right?

That was the coup de grâce: The cruise sounded like heaven. Sixty days of people-watching and seeing fabulous things and not having to think at all. Not having to work, or learn, or prove myself worthy in any way. Not having to look at Reyn, to see Amy's face shining up at him. Not having to see River, giving me chance after chance.

I'd run away from Incy before. I'd become convinced he was evil and dangerous.

And I'd run away from River before.

I was quite the runner. Never the soldier-on-through type. For some reason I pictured Reyn being disapproving of my cowardice, unable to respect my need to flee. He would think I was being a sissy, a big baby.

Good thing I didn't care what Reyn thought. That whole situation was impossible, anyway. I knew that.

Nothing seemed certain, rock solid. No decision, out of my three choices, seemed like a good idea.

I truly did not know what to do, but whatever I decided would have a huge effect on me, on my life.

Give me a sign, I pleaded silently. Goddess? Universe? Anyone? Anyone? Give me a sign. Tell me what to do.

Please, someone tell me what to do....

"Nas?" Incy's voice was gentle. "Come on and get in the car. I'll take care of you. Okay?"

hree hours later we were facing the million bright lights of Boston. We'd stopped a while back and bought wine and some Twinkies — and let me say that they are two great tastes that taste pretty vile together.

Every once in a while Incy would look over at me and smile.

"What?" I asked.

"I'm so happy to see you," he said. "I know it was stupid. You're a big girl, after all, but I just couldn't shake my worry. And also, you know, it was hard on *me*." He gave a wry laugh. "I mean, enough about *you*. Let's talk about *me*. I'd gotten so used to doing everything with you that I was out of balance for a while."

I took another swig of wine — the finest that a 7-Eleven on Highway 2 had to offer — and felt my first tingle of alarm since I'd gotten in the car. *How* out of balance had he been? Was getting into this Caddy the stupidest thing I'd ever done? Well, yes. I mean besides the *general* stupidity of it. Had I blithely gotten into a car with a killer?

"What do you mean, out of balance?" Here was some personal growth: pursuing something I might not want to hear but should probably know. It was something new and different for me, all of this lesson-applying. I watched him out of the corner of my eye, in case he suddenly became visibly insane or started morphing into a werewolf or something. Again, werewolf = deal breaker.

Instead he chuckled sheepishly. "I hadn't realized how dependent I'd gotten on you," he said frankly. "I was so used to consulting you, planning stuff with you, thinking of us doing things *together*. With you gone, I wandered around bleating pathetically until Boz slapped me and said, 'Pull yourself together, man!' "

He said the last bit in an English accent, as if quoting a movie, and laughed.

"Huh," I said, still watching him.

Incy shrugged. "I always missed you—didn't stop missing you—but I did figure out how to dress and bathe myself."

No, I had *not* done that for him. For God's sake. He was *exaggerating*.

"Oh."

"Then I started, you know, just planning for one." Another sheepish shrug. And he seemed so freaking normal. Incredibly normal and healthy, even more than when I'd left. Maybe my leaving had been good for him? Broken a bad pattern between us? Maybe I *had* been radiating darkness even then, and it had affected him, affected all of us. With me gone for the longest period of time in a hundred years, he'd been able to detox. In which case it would all certainly happen again—I was still dark. But I was aware of it now. Would that help? I didn't know, and thinking about it made my head hurt. I didn't want to think about it, analyze everything to death. I just wanted to…feel better.

Even if Incy was better off now, standing more on his own ice floe.

I guessed it would eventually become clear. Either things would be okay, or my life would become a much more treacherous atrocity than I could possibly imagine. One or the other. Somehow I'd deal with it, like I'd dealt with everything else—450 years of famines and plagues and floods and wars and crashing economies.

I stared out the window at the busy Boston streets, pleasantly fuzzy from the dreadful wine, wrapped in the warm cocoon of Incy's Caddy. I had uncountable memories of being in a car with Incy, from the very first Model Ts to today's Caddy. Between us, he and I had totaled something like eight or nine cars, prompting multiple newspaper headlines like "Miracle Survivors in Serious Collision." I remembered us driving on the Autobahn in Germany and across a dark, empty desert at night. We'd had fabulous sports cars and old tin buggies with wheels like bicycle tires. Incy and I. So many memories.

My mind conjured River's face, and I drank deeply from the bottle to blot it out. Would any of them be surprised that I had done this, that I was with Incy again? Or would they shake their heads and think that they'd always known I would screw up spectacularly? Would they look for me? Had they looked for me? And Reyn…he'd wanted something from me. And true to form I'd run away from him like a rabbit from a fox.

For less than one second, the merest flash of a blip of time, I imagined the relief of Reyn coming to get me, Reyn storming in, wresting me away from Incy, saving me from—myself.

Then I was furious that I'd had that thought, that I was

so weak I needed someone to save me from myself. Screw that! They didn't know better than I did! Their lives might work for them, but it had been torture for me! I wasn't made for that. It hadn't worked out. I berated myself for picturing Reyn as the strong one, stronger than me. I was plenty strong enough. I could absolutely take care of myself, like I'd done for the past four and a half centuries. I didn't need him or anyone else to remake my life or save me from anything.

I was *fine*.

And I was more than ready to have a good time, after two long months of drudgery and frustration.

"Here we are," Incy said, pulling under the overhang at the Liberty Hotel. We'd stayed here several times before; it was one of Boston's best and spiffiest. The fact that the building had once been the city jail raised its coolness rating to at least an eight. The designer had referenced that in various ways—one of its restaurants was named Clink, for example.

A valet ran up and opened the door for Incy, and a bellhop opened my door.

"Welcome to the Liberty, madam," he said. "May I get your luggage?"

"I don't have any." I swallowed, thinking of what I'd left behind. My amulet. My mother's most precious thing. My family's tarak-sin.

Plus all my ugly work clothes. Good riddance. I had a

safe-deposit box here in Boston with money, passports, etc. See? There are no problems. Only solutions.

"Ah. Very good," he said, trained to not notice that I was wearing a fabulous coat too big for me over dirty jeans and work boots. Smiling, he hurried over to open the heavy hotel door for us.

I stepped through the door and back into my old life.

It was horribly bright. Light hit my eyelids and I pushed my head under my pillow. I was on a big, deliciously comfortable bed, arms and legs out like a throwing star.

Light?

I bolted upright, regretting it immediately as my stomach lurched and my head bobbled on my neck like one of those dashboard dogs.

It was light outside! I must have way overslept! I must have—

I wasn't home. I was at the Liberty, in Boston, with Incy. I blinked groggily at the clock. It was 8:13. I assumed AM. I hadn't slept this late in months. I leaned toward my side table and clawed for the phone, then punched the room-service button. Moving slowly, I piled up my four fluffy down pillows and lay back very carefully.

I ordered a bunch of pastries, a couple of mimosas, and some Alka-Seltzer, then let the phone flop out of my hand onto the bed.

It was astonishing that I was with Incy again, in Boston again. We'd gotten in at around ten last night. Incy had been so cheerful, taking me to the top floor and grandly opening the door to the hotel's biggest suite. Inside, Boz and Katy, vividly alive, and Stratton and Cicely were arguing about something from—I swear to God—*Buffy the Vampire Slayer*.

They had looked up in shock as I followed Incy in, and Katy physically drew back when she saw what I was wearing: olive green jeans with mud-stained knees, a thermal undershirt, and a plaid flannel work shirt.

"Oh my God! She *was* kidnapped!" Katy exclaimed. "Incy, you were right! Look at your face! Nas, were you being held on a work farm?"

"Kind of," I said.

"Good to see you, Nasty!" Hugs and air kisses all around.

"We've missed you!" Katy especially looked genuinely excited to see me. I scanned her carefully but saw nothing of the furious, fed-up Katy of my vision. Also? Totally not in pieces or on fire. So that was good. "But seriously, what are you wearing? Did you come from a costume party?"

"Kind of," I said again, accepting the chocolatini she pressed into my hand.

I had taken a deep sip, which was fabulous, then

grinned at Incy, beaming at me from across the room. Let the party begin!

This part of Boston was great for walking, and after I'd borrowed some clothes and dabbed makeup on my eyes and nose, we'd gone from pub to bar to club to bar. I'd been gone for two months but didn't want to recap the highlights of my work-farm fiasco. Instead they had talked, telling stories about getting kicked off of planes, thrown out of parties, and an unfortunate incident where a heavy hotel table had ended up getting pushed over a balcony in an attempt to hit the swimming pool below. It had missed by only four feet. Boz had lost a thousand dollars on that bet. And Cicely had accidentally spooked a horse in Central Park, causing it to rear, almost overtip its carriage, and race off down a path while the top-hatted driver tried to get it to stop before they ran over someone.

I started off smiling and laughing at some of these stories. Katy in particular was hilarious, and her descriptions of outraged people were sharp, biting, and incredibly funny. But as the night went on, they became less interesting. I didn't perk up again until Boz told me about a citywide art installation in Barcelona. I wished I could have seen it; it sounded crazy and ambitious, statues everywhere. And throughout the whole evening we had drunk and eaten everything we could think of. Everything was available, whether it was locally grown or in season or whatever. I didn't have to prepare any of it or clean up afterward. I loved that.

We'd stumbled home around two-ish, somewhat early — bars actually have a closing time in Boston — but continued to party in our suite of rooms until management came to ask us to keep it down a bit. Good times.

It was just... I had forgotten about the inevitable after-party effects. Now I felt really terrible. Like I had the plague. What I imagine the plague to feel like, having seen its effects. (Quick aside: The Black Death, which killed maybe a third of all Europeans over the course of a century, can nowadays almost always be cured with a course of standard antibiotics. I mean, *antibiotics*. Wiping out the *bubonic plague*. Knowing stuff like that freaks me out, makes me so wish I could go back in time. I'd let the mold grow on the bread, invent penicillin, and make a fortune.)

Plague-victim me couldn't manage getting the door when room service knocked, but he let himself in and set up a cunning little doily-clad breakfast tray on the bed next to me.

"Could you pull the curtains more closed, please?" I asked, reaching for the first mimosa. Mmm. Hair of the attractive, purebred, champagne-drenched dog. Plus vitamin C from the orange juice: We *were* in cold and flu season.

The waiter subdued the morning sun, creating a bliss-ful, dim interior.

I got down half a Danish, the other mimosa, and an Alka-Seltzer chaser. I realized I was exhausted and *had no reason to get up yet*. So I pushed the tray out of the way, punched some pillows into submission, and snuggled down into the cushy, enormous mattress. Cuddling the down duvet around my chin, I thought I had never been more physically comfy in my entire life. Clearly the life I should be living. What. A. Luxury.

"Come on! Rise up, you sleepyhead!"

I felt someone thwacking my back with a pillow. Cau-tiously I pulled my head out from beneath the duvet. The curtains had been pulled wide, and the room was full of bright winter light that was assaulting my eyeballs again.

"Ugh, stop," I mumbled, holding out a hand.

Incy perched on the side of my bed. "It's two o'clock," he said. "In the afternoon."

It was so strange to see him again, after wondering if I would ever see him again in my life. After the huge wall of fear I had built up around him, for whatever reason. He still looked...fine. Clear-eyed, not crazy, and we were on Day Two, so yay. How many times had I woken up in some hotel or some apartment with Incy there? A million? Quite a lot. True, he'd often ended up at someone else's place. Or sometimes I had. But we'd spent a lot of time together in the last hundred years. Much more time than I'd ever spent with any one person in my entire life.

And here we were again.

"I see you've breakfasted," he said, using a quaint phrase to be funny.

"Yes," I said, sitting up and pushing my hair out of my face. "Somewhat."

"Well, you need to get up now." Incy tossed the pillow toward the headboard and stood. "We've got a lot to get done today."

"Like what?" It wouldn't be gathering eggs from hell-chickens or mucking out stables. Thank, thank, thank God.

He kicked at my old clothes on the floor with distaste. "Your clothes are awful, and you can't keep borrowing. Your hair is a disgrace. If you hadn't worn Cicely's Miu Mius last night, I couldn't have been seen in public with you. So let's get you fixed up. Come on! You have seventeen minutes!"

I smiled. Incy was fun. Bright and vivacious. He could be incredibly annoying, but he was also fun. Mr. Excitement. The party began when he walked in the door. He was a catalyst—he made things happen. And I got to be by his side when he did.

"What?" he asked.

"You care about what I wear," I said. The only times Reyn had mentioned my appearance, it hadn't been to compliment it.

"Yeah." Incy sounded indignant. "You're a beautiful girl. You should be draped in satin and velvet. Only the best for my bestie."

I smiled again. It had been such a long time since anyone had called me beautiful. I realized that Incy really did make me feel like beauty was attainable. After having no one impressed with my looks for ages — certainly not at River's Edge — it felt *fantastico*.

I grabbed a leftover pastry and went to the shower. The hot water felt wonderful. I kept one hand outside the door and took bites until the Danish was all gone. Then I just washed off the sugar and stickiness. Very efficient.

Incy had thrown away my clothes by the time I got out, so I went clothes shopping wearing the hotel bathrobe, with my scarf around my neck.

"I'm thinking magenta," the stylist said, pinching her lip in concentration. Once again she ran her hand through my hair, letting it slide through her fingers. "It's in amazingly good shape, considering how you bleached the hell out of it." Then she frowned and rubbed some strands between her thumb and forefinger. "Oh my God, it's not bleached. This is your real color. Wow."

"That's your real color?" Incy got up from his chair and came over. "You're kidding."

"No," I said, remembering when River had done the spell that revealed the real me. Now I was covering me up again. And so what? That was how I felt comfortable, okay? "I guess you haven't seen it."

"Yeah," Incy said, seeming bemused. He touched it, smiled, then sat down again. "I mean, even ancient Romans dyed their hair."

He smirked at me, and I made a face. I wasn't *that* old.

"Anyway, you need a huge change," he directed. "I agree that magenta would be fabulous. And maybe a short razor cut? That would be amazing with your eyes."

I looked at myself in the mirror, seeing the deceptively simple black cashmere sweater, the buttery-soft tan suede pants from Comme des Garçons. I didn't even know how much I'd spent today. My definition-of-perfection Ann Demeulemeester black ankle boots alone had cost three times as much as I'd spent on myself the whole time I'd been gone. I looked sleek and expensive; clothes fit me much better now that I wasn't a scarecrow.

I held out my hands: Incy had bought me a gorgeous Hoorsenbuhs gold-link "friendship" ring, set with emeralds big enough to choke a small dog. It flashed in the salon's lights, and I turned my hand this way and that. Incy saw what I was doing and smiled at me.

Meanwhile the stylist played with my hair, flopping it over, parting it in the middle. I guess waiting for the muse of hairdom to strike with inspiration. I hadn't had a haircut in ages. Even before I'd gone to River's Edge, my shaggy cut had been growing out because I was too dysfunctional to keep it up.

"No, not a razor cut," I said. "Too much maintenance. Can you just tidy up the edges, give it some shape, but keep it long?"

"Sure," said the stylist, while Incy frowned.

"How about something angular, sculptural?" he suggested. "To show off your heart-shaped face, your beautiful eyes?"

I tried to think back, about whether Incy had controlled the way I looked. Had my hair and clothes reflected him, and not me? How would I know? There had barely been a me to reflect. Just the same, I wondered how he would take being crossed.

"Nah," I said lightly. "Something easy that I can wash and go. I don't want to have to blow-dry it and mousse it and futz with it."

The stylist met my gaze in the mirror, a frozen expression on her face as if I'd just suggested we give me a frizzy perm from the eighties. I raised my eyebrows and smiled.

Incy sighed, grinned at me, and held out his hands. "Whatever you want, babe," he said. "It's your hair." Then he turned sideways, put his feet on the chair next to him, and started reading a dog-eared celebrity magazine.

Calm down, I told myself. So you had a few dreams, a few visions. Look at him: He's not trying to control your every move. Just relax.

I looked back into the mirror and met the stylist's eyes. "Not magenta," I said. "But I would do some kind of red."

Like maybe a *magenta-ish* red, for effing example?

"I said some kind of *red*," I said, turning my head to see my new haircut swish. Despite looking like I'd been dipped headfirst in Kool-Aid, the cut was great and did the whole whoosh thing. I was enjoying it while I could, because this effect required blow-drying and moussing and a shine spray and who knew what else? Many hair products had died in the making of this whoosh, and any one of them was too much for me to deal with. Plus, you know, the whole freaking magenta thing. "I said *not* magenta quite clearly."

"It's still fan-*tastic*," said Cicely, standing next to me. I was back in my hotel room, and we were getting ready to go to Den, advertised to me as a "superhot new club."

"It's *magenta*." I tried to recall the undo spell River had done, and of course remembered it as a bunch of magicky-sounding gibberish. "I don't even recognize myself."

"Because you don't look like Hilda the goatherd

anymore?" Katy leaned in next to me and made the OMG face to put on mascara. She caught my gaze and raised her eyebrows. "Honey, you looked like Hilda the goatherd. Now you look fabulous. Like yourself."

I had *bright* magenta hair cut in a crisp bob right at my shoulders, with a few spiky bangs on my forehead. The stylist had layered in the still-too-short pieces, and it all looked on purpose and chic. Around my neck I wore a wide choker made of many thin strands of green and purple Swarovski crystals. I was still paranoid about my neck and had layered a thin silk scarf underneath to be doubly covered up.

I tugged up on my poison green satin boned bustier that emphasized a couple places I had gained weight. I guessed it was supposed to be cut like this, but mainly I was afraid of leaning over to pick something up. I wondered what River—or Reyn—would think of my completely impractical black satin cigarette pants and completely impractical and amazingly uncomfortable needle-heeled Louboutin pumps. Fortunately, neither Reyn nor River was here, and also fortunately, I couldn't care less what they thought. I looked amazing. Really pretty, I decided with surprise. All my bony, hollow places had been filled in with, like, quinoa, at River's, and I couldn't remember my skin looking so clear and glowy. I looked hot and totally fashionable. Huh. I hadn't looked this good in I didn't know how long. The sixties? Late seventies?

"Ladies?" Boz poked his handsome head around the bathroom door. When I'd first met him, I could have only described him as "incredibly handsome and blond." As the decades have rolled past, I could now accurately say, "If Robert Redford and Brad Pitt had a love child, that's Boz." And every time I saw Boz not in big chunks minus all his blood, I was relieved. Those had been some weird, weird dreams. Probably brought on by too much healthy food. Good thing I was cleaning all that out of my system.

"Ready," said Katy, giving herself a last look in the mirror. Over the years my looks have changed as much as I could change them, with every color and length of hair, a big weight range, wide variety of whiteness or tanned-ness. Katy was one of the few immortals I knew who didn't vary too much out of her comfort zone. She had naturally sun-streaked medium brown hair, ivory skin, and brown eyes. She put her hair up or left it down; sometimes she went curly. But that was it. And where my fashion sense (you can put air quotes around that, if you want) had also gone through extremes, from peasant burlap and rough linen to beautiful hand-loomed silk jacquard to torn jeans and kind of trashy to boring and now to slightly cutting-edge high style—Katy had always dressed with very expensive good taste. Not too far out, not frumpy. Just very expensive clothes, beautifully cut and fitted, decade after decade.

Cicely expressed yet another style for immortals: the perpetual teen. Yes, of course most of us look really young; our aging process seems to slow way down when we're about fifteen or sixteen. But then you get the exceptions, like Jess, who literally looked to be in his late fifties. Even River, who was 1,300, looked like she was maybe only in her late thirties, but with silver hair. I get away with a range of about seventeen to barely twenty-one. But Cicely really looked young. With skillful makeup, she still got carded everywhere. With no makeup, she couldn't get into an R-rated movie by herself.

She was smaller than me, more finely boned, with tiny wrists and ankles as befitting a well-born English lady in the late 1800s, which was when she'd been born. Her natural hair was fine, curly, and sunshine blond. It was her clothes that were an issue sometimes. She loved the latest trends, no matter what they were, and shopped in stores meant for teenagers. So she was pretty, really pretty, but almost never elegant, never sophisticated. I mean, not that *I* was. I could get dressed up, but I was still by my very nature kind of a schlump. I just didn't care enough to really work at it. Cicely worked at it but like a teenager would.

The three of us were so different. I hadn't really seen

that before. Still, they were my best girlfriends, and we'd been literally around the world together more than once.

I smiled. "Lay-dees, we look *stunning.*" I took them both by the arm and smiled at us in the mirror. Cicely laughed and kissed my cheek.

"Yes, we do," she agreed.

We took a limo to Den so Incy wouldn't have to drive if he got plastered. Very responsible of us. My stomach was knotted up all the way there, praying the driver wouldn't do anything to upset Incy.

The line to get into Den started at the end of the block and was maybe five people thick. Everyone looked dressed to kill, very un–West Lowing, and I wondered for a second what Meriwether would think of this crowd. Or Dray, for that matter.

The limo dropped us off without incident right at the red carpet that stretched from the club's door to the curb. We got out, and I was pleased by my feet's ability to adjust from sneakers to incredibly high-heeled shoes without making me pitch forward onto my face. Right back on the bicycle, that was me.

Loud, pounding music seeped through the club's closed door. I felt a twinge of excitement, the way I used to, and Incy smiled at me and took my hand. Two large, thick-necked bouncers were there to keep out the serfs and general riffraff. I wondered how they could see, wearing sunglasses at night. They had those coiled-wire ear things that made them look like the CIA. I mean, for what? So they could rush inside if someone heard that a huge sale on drinks was happening at the bar?

One of them nodded stoically at Incy and Boz and stepped aside, undoing the guard barrier. The crowd of people waiting started shouting in protest — who knew how long they'd been on hold, and it was fuh-reezing out here. The bouncer yelled at them to shut up, and then the six of us swept inside. I won't lie: I felt like royalty, or some famous person, getting waved past all those poor line-waiters. It felt fantastic. After two months of being the low wastrel on the totem pole, I loved feeling like I was near the top again.

Inside it took my eyes a minute to adjust to the darkness. The one lit space was the stage, where a gorgeous girl in a red plastic miniskirt was fronting a retro band. The air was full of smoke and scent, loud voices and louder music. The huge bass notes pulsed through my chest like waves. The energy in here was practically crackling, like electricity. Almost like magick.

"I didn't realize how much I missed this!" I yelled into Stratton's ear, going on tiptoe to reach it. He grinned and nodded at me, and I grabbed his jacket tail so I wouldn't lose him, glad that he was tall and as broad as a linebacker as we threaded a path to the way-too-crowded bar.

Half an hour later we had our own table with a curved purple couch around it. I was drinking a whiskey sour, and Katy had demonstrated her ability to tie a cherry stem into a knot using only her tongue.

Good times were here again.

nd the learning curve was quite flat here at Hacienda Liberty. I'd forgotten just how steep the price of good times could be. I woke the next afternoon cotton-mouthed with a splitting, and I do mean splitting, headache. When I raised my head, I half expected to leave large chunks of it on my pillow, like a broken melon.

Sorry. It was a really bad headache.

I looked down at myself: I'd slept in my clothes. I tried not to think about how much they had cost. They would probably dry-clean just fine. At least I'd made it back to the hotel. Wryly I berated myself: Gosh, maybe there's some connection between drinking too much at night and feeling like complete crap the next day! I don't know — what do *you* think?

I crawled out of bed and made it to the bathroom, where I wanted to throw up and couldn't. I wrestled myself out of my clothes, looking at big raw blisters on my feet from those adorable, adorable shoes that I'd managed to dance in for hours. I put on the hotel robe and walked out to the suite's living room.

Stratton, sound asleep, had crammed his large body onto the too-small settee, and I knew it was only a matter of time before he rolled over and crashed onto the floor. Which would be amusing. Cicely was curled up in an armchair, one shoe kicked off, all her makeup gone. She looked like a kid who'd fallen asleep at her parents' party. Their suite was right across the hall, but judging from the bottles littering the floor, we'd continued partying after we'd gotten home, and it had been too far to walk.

I peeked into Incy's room, hoping I wouldn't find anything awful. I didn't. He was asleep in his own bed, one arm thrown over his face. Katy was next to him, but she'd probably just collapsed there — we'd all somehow avoided having romantic relationships with one another over the years, which was amazing and so much smarter than any of us actually was.

I stood quietly, watching Incy sleep. Once in the Metropolitan Museum of Art I had seen an ancient Roman funeral portrait of a young man who had died two thousand years ago. He'd had olive skin and large dark eyes, a straight nose and full mouth. I didn't know whether he had died at the full bloom of his youth or if it was an idealized portrait of an older man who'd wanted to be remembered at the height of his charm. Either way, he had been beautiful in a masculine, classic way, his features so proportionate that not even two thousand years could change a viewer's notion of what beauty was.

Incy looked exactly like him. In fact, when I'd first seen the Fayum mummy painting, I'd gasped and started, as if Incy had played a trick on me by having his own portrait inserted into the museum collection.

I was reminded of that now as I watched him sleep, his face smooth and relaxed.

Incy. He and I knew each other very, very well. We'd seen each other sick, furious, barfing, deliriously happy, bored, drunk, stunned. We'd seen each other at our bests and our worsts, and always stood by each other. Even during his Lala Burkhardt episode. Even during my Evan Piccolo fling, and that one *still* made me wince. God, poor Evan.

Actually, now that I thought about it, I couldn't place when our "bests" had been. When had either one of us been at our best? Hmm. There might be a message here somewhere. I'll let you know if I find it.

I realized anew how incredibly awful I felt and sank into the armchair by his window. I needed Alka-Seltzer, which I believe is one of civilization's greatest gifts. Possibly chelation therapy. I closed my eyes.

I was wondering vaguely how much effort it would take to get hold of some Tylenol when I realized that Incy was propped up in bed on one elbow, watching me the way I had been watching him.

"Hi," I said unenthusiastically.

"What you need is a spa day," he said, sliding out of bed. He stood and stretched, his custom shirt horribly wrinkled. Then he let out a deep breath and smiled, ready to start his day.

"How do you do that?" I asked, keeping my voice down so my head wouldn't implode.

"Do what?" Incy headed for his bathroom.

"You look fabulous." I gestured at his entire being. "You look rested, springing out of bed full of pep and vim. Why don't you look like crap? Why aren't you hungover? You were completely smashed last night. I remember that much, at least."

"Oh, I don't drink as much as it looks," he said airily. He tugged off his shirt and flicked me with it. "Come on, get dressed. We'll take you to get fluffed and primped. You can steam all the toxins out of your delicate little system."

That actually sounded really good, and six hours later I felt like a new woman. I'd been steamed, pummeled, massaged, had hot rocks put on my spine. All with my thin cotton scarf wound around my neck: the eccentric scarf girl. I'd drunk a gallon of coconut water and green tea and eaten a bowl of brown rice with a little vinegar sprinkled on it. It was better than it sounds. My face hadn't been this deeply clean since a very, very bad sunburn in the late seventies that had essentially resulted in my entire face sloughing off.

I'd been mani-ed, pedi-ed, made up, and blow-dried. My hair was whoosh-tastic once again. After Katy zipped me into a black sleeveless turtleneck dress from Armani and I put my Band-Aid-covered feet into hot-pink stiletto pumps, I looked like a short fashion model. With bright, bright freaking magenta hair. God.

That night Incy and Katy and I went to dinner at B&G Oysters, in the South End. There were a dozen fresh entries at the raw bar, and Katy reported that the wine selection was excellent. I felt people looking at me and at first assumed it was my hair, but Incy assured me it was because I was a knockout and they were wondering who I was.

I loved this, I did. I loved going to really good restaurants, instead of, say, Auntie Lou's Diner. I loved wearing beautiful clothes instead of flannel and jeans. I hadn't realized how much I loved it. Over a dessert that made my knees weak, I decided that I truly hadn't appreciated all this before. I'd taken it for granted and gotten, I admitted, to an unhealthy place in my life. But now I knew more about balance. This time around, everything was going to be terrific.

Except for your darkness. God, I hate my subconscious so, so much.

After dinner we were supposed to meet Boz at an art gallery in the trendy SoWa district. Incy hailed a cab, and I tried to quash the instant recoil of fear and dread I felt about Incy + cab.

As Katy climbed in, Incy took my hand and kissed it.

"I was wrong," he said quietly, looking intently into my eyes. "I was wrong, and you showed me that. You have nothing to fear."

There was never a point in pretending not to understand something with Incy. He knew I knew what he was talking about. We always got each other, with words or without.

I nodded and got into the cab, feeling relieved and touched.

The art gallery was less than ten minutes away, and we arrived safely without my darkness overpowering anyone and forcing them to commit heinous acts. You may draw a smiley face here: [   ].

We got out and saw huge, floor-to-ceiling windows showcasing a large gallery full of light, people, and a bunch of art, including some by Lucian Freud, whose work I had always adored. A few people turned around when we came in, but none openly pointed at my hair and laughed behind their hands. The evening was going well so far.

"Ooh, there's Boz!" Katy snagged a glass of red wine off a waiter's tray and made her way through the crowd to where Boz was charming a small crowd of admirers.

"Who's that girl he's talking to?" I asked Incy, when he'd brought me some champagne. "She looks familiar."

Incy glanced over. "There was a picture of her upchucking off a balcony on the front page of *Boston for You* yesterday."

"Oh. Her. The heiress."

"Why else would Boz be talking to her?" Innocencio grinned, and I nodded. No duh.

"He's got to learn to invest his money so it sticks around longer," I said. "There's only so many other people's fortunes you can run through."

"He hasn't seemed to find a limit yet," said Incy. "Shall we mingle?"

"We shall."

Reporters from society magazines were snapping pictures. There were an unbelievable number of beautiful people in this room. I was sure many of them were famous and notable, but I wasn't up on the latest society in Boston, and I didn't recognize anyone except the barfer.

I thought I'd feel like an idiot with my Popsicle hair, but there were so many extreme styles here that I actually blended. A tall, stunning, brick-house-shaped black girl had a short, snow-white afro. She should have been a model with those looks, and I thought very briefly about Brynne. Another Amazon had a mathematically precise haircut that was a deep navy blue on top, black underneath. Someone even told me that they loved *my* hair. That hadn't happened in...decades, I think.

"You really do look sensational, love," Incy said over my shoulder.

I turned around and he offered me a minuscule china plate with an even more minuscule roasted beet napoleon on it and some other tiny nibbly things. We'd just come from dinner, so I limited myself to a couple of plates full. I noticed Incy smiling at me as I rounded up my third or fourth doll-size éclair. I mean, I get the whole precious-food thing. But give me a big honking éclair, know what I'm saying?

"What?" I said.

"You've gotten your appetite back," he said. "Your holiday was good for you."

I smiled and nodded. Was that all it had been, my time at River's Edge? A holiday to recuperate from my life? Now I was back, living my old life again. And I was loving it. Had I really been that unhappy before? Were my friends — was Incy — so awful?

I mean, *Reyn* had killed hundreds of people, if not thousands. My parents had killed people — including my father's brother. River and her brothers had killed *their own parents*. All Incy had done was cripple a cabbie. Which, okay, still bad. I know that. But *relatively*. And possibly triggered by my ancestral darkness, which no one could blame a girl for, could they?

I drank my champagne, mulling over more thoughts than I'd had since I'd left River's. My eyes wandered along with my thoughts, and as if my thinking had manifested him, I saw a tall man with broad shoulders and raggedy, dark blond hair. I stopped breathing as my eyes raked him for details. He was about six feet tall. Could it actually be Reyn? Had he come here to find me? My heart started beating quickly, my pulse buzzing like a blowfly in a bottle.

Then he turned. I held my breath, already moving toward him, thinking of what I would say, how I would explain my absence, how I could laugh all this off.

His face, when I saw it, was such a letdown that I almost stumbled. It was a smooth face, the face of a lawyer or an investment banker. The features were bland, softened; the eyes roundish, blue, and unremarkable. Other women would probably find him good-looking, but he was so far beneath what I'd hoped to see that tears almost came to my eyes.

And when he turned again, chuckling at something someone had said, his back and shoulders looked absolutely nothing like Reyn's. He was altogether too groomed, too civilized, too mannered to be Reyn, or even be in Reyn's world. Reyn had been bashing his way through life for more than four hundred years, and his angular features, tip-tilted eyes, and perpetual look of alert wariness advertised that.

He didn't always look wary.... The champagne coiled warmly in my stomach as I remembered Reyn's face flushed with desire, his mouth coming down on mine as his strong hands molded me to him. Reyn's hot look of determined conquest was nothing like this man's easy sweep of the crowd.

My own face flushed, and it suddenly felt hot in here, crowded and too bright, too loud. I looked for Incy and after a moment saw him standing next to a beautiful girl. She was smiling, wide-eyed, gazing into his dark, dark eyes. She was almost as tall as him and wearing less dress than I was, a strapless mini in deep lilac satin with beading around the top and bottom edges. Incy was leaning close to her, murmuring, and she cast her eyes down as if his words scandalized and tantalized at the same time. Which was probably exactly what they were doing.

As I watched him murmuring into her ear, I saw her eyes glaze over and wondered how much she'd had to drink, and if Incy would take advantage of that. I'd certainly seen him do that before — though usually his own personal charisma was enough to make people drop willingly at his feet. In this room alone, there were probably about thirty people, male and female, who would happily go home with him if he simply asked them.

I almost smiled as I pictured how easily Incy could persuade people to do anything. We'd gotten out of more traffic tickets than I could count, refunds on expired items, hotel rooms when the place was fully booked. He'd been talking people out of their clothes, money, connections, and influence for as long as I had known him.

I straightened, hit by a disturbing thought, and just then the girl slumped. Okay, she'd had too much to drink. As I watched, Incy gracefully guided her down onto a small brocade couch against the wall, and I thought, Good, he isn't going to try to hustle her out of here. He was making the right *choice*, and I was pleased. I smiled as he thoughtfully leaned her head over to rest on the couch's arm, and that was when I saw it: his smile of triumph.

For a couple of seconds I didn't understand. Then a

chill washed over me, as if I were standing beneath a glacier. Noooo…Incy's face. His look of triumph. The girl slumped over, her slight chest moving erratically with uneven breathing. Incy stood, gazing down at the girl. He inhaled deeply. His eyes were bright, his skin glowing. He looked…like we all looked after a circle, at River's Edge: full of life. Full of magick. My breath lodged in my throat like a piece of wood.

It looked like he'd used magick on her, a regular person. Everyone, every*thing*, has power, whether or not they're immortal. Immortals had a lot more. Incy had murmured a spell into this girl's ear and taken hers. I wasn't positive, I had no real proof, but something deep inside me said, Yep. That's what he did.

For a minute I stood there like one of those overpriced statues, my glass half raised to my lips. But current Incy had seemed so different. He'd seemed fine and really not evil. *Was* he as dark as I had once suspected? What was he *doing*? I started toward them and was immediately blocked by a small throng of people surrounding a painting while someone talked about it. I peered through them, seeing Incy glide away from the girl. Was she alive? Had he *killed* her? Increased alarm doused my pleasant alcohol feeling as I tried to squeeze between two suits. What would I do if she were dead? What would I do if magick could save her and I *didn't know enough*?

I finally pushed rudely through the crowd and when I came out on the other side I saw two girls leaning over their friend, shaking her shoulder. The girl on the couch blinked slowly and sat up with difficulty. I slowed my approach. She wasn't dead. Her friends were laughing, teasing her about drinking too much, and she just shook her head and looked confused. I heard her friend say, "Get a taxi, get you into bed, lame-o," and I hoped she would be okay. In fact she was able to stand, and with her friends' help left the gallery on her feet.

I didn't know how she would be tomorrow.

I didn't know how Incy had learned to do that.

I didn't know how I could live with it.

So what would I do now?

hat night, in keeping with my tradition of dreaming about whomever I'm not with, I dreamed about River's Edge. I was standing by the fence that kept deer out of the vegetable garden. I was dressed all in black, with my old motorcycle boots, the ones that had a hiding place in one heel to hold my taraksin. In my dream I felt the heat and weight of my amulet radiating up from my heel to my leg.

I was watching River and Reyn working on River's old red pickup that looked like it was from the early sixties. Maybe it was. River was in the driver's seat, leaning out the window so she could hear Reyn's instructions. Reyn was bent over the open hood, doing manly things with tools. I saw them speak to each other but couldn't hear. I leaned against the fence, striving for nonchalance, and I waited for them to see me, so I could snub them.

The plan was to look marginally surprised when they spoke to me and then be cool and disinterested as they urged me to come back. I would tell them I had better places to be, better people to be with. I would say that I was waiting for my friends to come get me. They would be disappointed, crestfallen.

Then a car would drive up. I'd climb into the darkened backseat, and say, "Adios."

Except they never noticed me. I stood by the fence until my legs ached, until I was achy with standing, and they never turned to see me.

So I'd walked closer, still nonchalant, waiting for their faces to light up, so I could conspicuously not light up in return.

I felt the vibrations of the truck engine trying to turn over, but there was still no sound. I was in a cone of silence, separated from everything.

I went very close to them, dropping all pretense of nonchalance, walking right up. I spoke to them, but no sound came out of my mouth. I tried to grab Reyn's arm, and though I saw my hand reaching out, it never got to him—just kept reaching out endlessly. Now I was shouting, trying to smack my hand on the truck, trying to grab River's shoulder, trying to hit Reyn, but I was silent and alone, affecting no one.

When I woke up, my face was wet, my throat was sore, and all my muscles throbbed as if I'd been standing in a field for hours.

I had no idea what it meant. If you figure it out, drop me a line.

"What girl?" Incy's face was genuinely, sincerely confused.

"The girl from the gallery last night," I said.

"Which gallery?"

"I guess it was probably *the only gallery* we went to," I said. His eyes searched mine. He wasn't used to me questioning anything he did. Until a few months ago, I'd found everything he did pretty funny. Former me was easygoing, nonjudgmental, acquiescent. I'd built up a snarky abrasiveness for outsiders, which had come into full play at River's Edge. But I almost never used it on Innocencio.

"Okay, *what* girl?" Totally perplexed. Complete furrowing of the brow.

We were in my room with the door closed; I hadn't wanted to confront Incy in front of the others. I still felt weirdly like an outsider. After decades of totally belonging with this group, they now seemed like one thing, and I like another. It was only temporary, of course. Probably only in my imagination. But I felt reluctant to shake things up.

It was early evening; we were getting ready to go out to dinner. After I'd woken up this morning in the throes of my dream, the next thing that hit me was that my tarak-sin was still back at River's. I'd never known what its traditional name was—it had always just been my mother's amulet. Now that I knew, I felt even more lost without it. I could try to get it back. I definitely could. But should I? It was dark. It would make my own darkness stronger. I believed that. I longed for it but was still afraid of its power over me. Ugh.

After that, my dismay and horror over what I thought Incy had done last night washed over me like dirty dishwater, and I felt worse. Last night I hadn't had a chance to question him about it—he and Katy had gone to a club right after that. I'd realized how antisocial I felt and had gone back to the hotel. I had no idea what Boz, Cicely, and Stratton had done.

I hadn't fled Boston, though. Hadn't caught the first flight out of there. I was trying to...run less these days. But after thinking about it all afternoon, I'd decided to put some of my emotional progress into motion: to confront someone about an issue, instead of ignoring it or seething silently with anger. Thumbs-up, River!

Not that it was easy. I'd debated confronting Incy all day. On the one hand, I felt I had to; on the other hand, I dreaded the outcome. It wasn't that Incy and I had never argued. We had. And always made up. But for the most part, we let each other do what we wanted to do, without lectures or questions. But maybe that had only been because I'd refused to see what we were actually doing.

I sat down on the boudoir chair in the bathroom and reached for tonight's beautiful Manolo Blahniks: leopard-print peep-toes piped with hot pink. As soon as I started learning magick again, I was going to get a couple of anti-blister spells under my belt, for sure.

I was stalling. I'd rehearsed what to say, but now it all seemed too abrupt. A small, unevolved part of me wanted to just not think about it, not worry about it, pretend nothing was wrong. In the past, that was what I had done. But you know, Eve had eaten the apple from the Tree of Knowledge, blah, blah, blah....

I put on my metaphorical big-girl panties. "Incy. Last night I saw you whispering in a girl's ear—"

He grinned at himself in the mirror and smoothed his hair. "I whispered in many girls' ears last night. Oh, did I tell you who I saw at Carly's? Have you been to Carly's bar? Tiny and squalid and *perfect*—"

"This one was tall, in a lilac strapless dress," I broke in. "You whispered in her ear, and she smiled, and then her eyes glazed over and she slumped onto the couch. When you straightened up, you looked like you'd just drunk an... energy drink or something."

He tilted his head. "Energy drink? They're disgusting. Have you tried one? Why would I drink *that*?"

I took a breath, feeling increasing trepidation about pressing him on this.

"Innocencio." I made my voice gentle. Maybe he just needed help, like I had. And I would save him, and we would laugh about it a hundred years from now. Maybe. "You used magick to take that girl's life force, her *chi*, or whatever. You took it from her so you would be stronger. You sucked energy out of her."

Innocencio looked at me steadily, two pairs of black eyes locked on each other. In the hundred years I'd been looking into those eyes, had I never seen their depths? Part of me felt that our whole relationship had just shifted somehow. The air around us seemed charged, almost electric, and Incy seemed subtly on guard.

"Nas. I don't know what you're talking about." Not a hint of falseness. Solid as a brick, looking at me head-on. I'm a world-class liar, and I can detect bullshit from a hundred yards away. Though I was looking for it now, willing to see it now, I wasn't. It was weird. He frowned. "Wait— you mean the drunk girl?" he asked.

"She wasn't drunk." I stood up and looked at myself in

the mirror, fluffing my cartoon hair with my fingers. Tonight I was wearing a sleeveless Alexander Wang hot-pink satin jumpsuit with a hoodie and a wide leopard-print belt with three buckles. The four-inch heels made me a respectable five foot seven. I looked like a club-goer with too much money. If anyone at River's Edge could see me now…they probably would wonder why they'd ever bothered.

"Okay, no, she wasn't drunk, but the daisy she'd popped wasn't doing her any favors." He leaned closer to the mirror and ran a hand over his chin to see if he needed to shave.

"What do you mean?"

"I was teasing her about staying sober, the better to enjoy my wares, so to speak, and she giggled and said it was too late, that the daisy would be kicking in anytime now. And by George it did, with a vengeance." He shrugged and used one finger to smooth his strong, dark eyebrows. "I moved on to more interesting challenges."

A daisy was a powerful narcotic, popular in clubs. It was round, yellow in the middle and white around the outside, like a daisy. It would have knocked her for a loop, made her act the way she had.

If she had taken it.

I felt in my gut that Incy had used magick on her — in the last two months I'd seen a lot of people in the various throes of magick, and I felt he had. The way that I could now sense a person's energy as he or she approached me or stood outside my room; the way the air felt alive, vibrant in a room where magick had been worked. The way I'd been able to feel the dark smokiness of ancient power drifting off my tarak-sin as if from a stick of incense. All those senses had been awakened, developed, during my short time at River's Edge. And I trusted them.

"Okay, say she took a daisy," I said, putting on moon-drop pearl earrings. The overhead light glinted on my emerald ring as I shut the clasp. Incy leaned against the doorway of the bathroom, humoring me, elegant in his John Varvatos trousers and striped fisherman sweater. "That doesn't explain why *you* looked the way you did. You looked…full of magick, full of power."

Innocencio smiled easily, coming to stand behind me, his hands on my shoulders. We looked at each other in the mirror. "Why, thank you, my dear. I'm flattered. I wish I could take credit for that, but I'm afraid it was probably the whiskey I was knocking back, coupled with the some-what unnecessary heating of that packed gallery. I thought a lot of people were looking kind of glowy and dewy, if you know what I mean."

What a facile explanation. Which I would have totally bought, in the past, if I had even questioned him, which I wouldn't have. I opened my mouth again, and he leaned forward, reaching his hand around my neck to put a finger gently against my lips. "Nas. Are you worried about me?" he asked softly. "The way I was worried about you?" He looked into my eyes, and I could see, absolutely see, the love shining there. "I can't tell you how much that means to me, how much I've missed it. You're worried about me. You don't want me to get into trouble. You want me to be, for lack of a better word, a better man. Right?"

I let out a breath. "Yes. I guess so." I felt confused at the conversation's sudden left turn.

"Thank you." He pressed a kiss on my bare shoulder. "With you by my side, I'm the best I can be. I know I am. And now you're back, to keep me centered. You care about me." He really did look happy at that thought.

"Yes, of course. You know that," I said, feeling like we'd gotten off track somehow. I'd wanted to say —

"Don't worry. Be happy," he said, quoting an old song. He squeezed my shoulders again, looking cheerful, then strode out and threw open my bedroom door. "Is everyone ready?" he bellowed.

I looked at myself in the mirror, not knowing what to think. That hadn't gone the way I'd planned. How had he brushed aside my concerns so easily? I shook my head at the Nas in the mirror. "You don't know anything," I whispered. Then I grabbed my cashmere wrap and headed out into the suite's living room.

The gang was all there; everyone but Stratton was spiffed up. He was wearing an old sweatshirt and a pair of jeans, his thick brown hair untidy and adorable.

"You're not coming with?" I asked.

"Nope," he said. "Game tonight. Play-off. Going to watch it down the street at Paddy's. I'll try to get someone to carry me home. But you guys be good." He grinned and sort of danced sideways toward the door of the suite.

I couldn't help laughing. He was like a big, handsome bear, especially compared to Incy's and Boz's sleekness. It was a relief to be out here with the others, instead of having a difficult conversation with Incy. "Stratton—way American, buddy," I said.

He danced backward out of the suite, and we heard him singing as he went down the hall.

"Since when does he like basketball?" I asked.

"Ye gods, even *I* know it's football," Cicely said, lighting a cigarette.

"It's weird. He's developed a fascination with American football," Boz said. He picked some cookies off the afternoon tea tray and ate one. "I'm worried he's going to want to play it."

"I guess he could," I said. "He could play pretty hard and not worry about injury too much."

"Ruggers," Boz stated, tossing a cookie in the air and catching it expertly. "Whoa, two points! You see that?"

"Yeah, 'cause you only had a couple of centuries to perfect that move," I said drily, and he threw a cookie at me. It fell in my lap, and I ate it.

"Anyway, *rugby*," said Boz. "That's what he should play. None of these pantywaist paddings and mouth guards and so on."

"I can't remember the last time I was this bored," said Incy, heading toward his room. "I'm going to make some calls. Shout when you're ready to go."

"Incy," Cicely said in surprise.

"We're ready *now*," I started to point out, but his door closed. I gave Cicely and Boz a surprised look. "What's with him? Don't we look ready?"

Boz shrugged: It was Incy being capricious once again. I raised my eyebrows and then collapsed on a settee and put my feet up. I'd be walking in these gorgeous leopard-print instruments of torture later — might as well save my feet now. "Who's he calling?"

Cicely finished up the wine in her glass. "Who knows? We ran into some people at Clancy's last week."

I almost started. I'd been in Clancy's several months ago, when I was trying to escape, to disappear. I'd run into a couple old friends there (old — ha ha), and I'd told Beatrice that I was hiding from Incy, as a kind of game. Had they run into her last week? What had she told them? That had been the night our friend Kim had used magick to wipe out a small percentage of Boston's songbird population. It had been…grotesque. Nauseating. A complete misuse of power. Even *I* could see that. It had been the thing that had convinced me to go back to River's Edge the second time.

But speaking of misuse of power…

"Did either of you see Incy with that girl last night, at the gallery?" I asked in a low voice. Incy's door was closed, but I wanted to be careful.

"Which one?" Katy asked. "There are always so many." She pretended to swoon, and we laughed.

"The tall one, in the lilac dress," I said. "I thought I saw—it looked like…like Incy used magick on her."

Cicely's eyebrows rose.

"How?" said Katy.

"To me it looked like he used magick to…take her personal power. I don't know what to call it. But everyone has it, and people can use magick to take it from someone. And then the taker is stronger."

"Yeah, of course," said Boz, and I almost fell out of my chair.

"You know about this?" It had been unwelcome news to me. Was I the only one out of the loop?

"Yeah, you hear about it," said Boz, frowning. "But you need to know what you're doing, and you need to have power yourself. Magickal power. None of us have ever been near being able to do something like that. Enough to get a cab, yeah, or make someone trip." He smiled at a memory. "But for big stuff you'd have to, you know, pay attention and learn things."

"I think Incy has," I whispered, and described what I had seen, and that Incy had told me that the girl had taken a daisy.

Cicely made a pooh-pooh face. "Everyone uses a little magick sometimes."

"Yeah, a *little*," I agreed. "But this is bigger."

"Sounds like a daisy. But you think he used magick on her?" Boz asked, keeping his voice down.

I nodded, not enjoying this conversation. Feeling like a traitor. An uptight busybody. Would they even believe me, given the way I'd ditched them so coldly months ago? I never would have questioned this before. It was a pain, this whole "knowing right from wrong" thing.

Boz sat down and ran his hand through his blond hair, which only made it look more perfectly mussed. He glanced at Incy's shut door, then seemed to exchange a look with Katy. "I admit feeling like...Incy's been going to extremes lately," he said quietly.

A fluttering of alarm ran down my spine. "What do you mean?"

"Here we go again," Cicely muttered.

Boz ignored her. "He just seems more...reckless," he

said uncomfortably. "Like with the cabbie, that night last fall. He's just taking weird risks. Some of them have been really dangerous. Over the edge, even for me." He gave a self-conscious little laugh.

"I told you, you're overreacting," said Cicely, looking irritated. "Incy just likes to have fun. A couple of things have taken a bad turn, but stuff happens. It wasn't his fault."

Boz looked like he wanted to argue with her, and I got the feeling they'd had this conversation before.

"Bad turns like what?" I asked.

Boz shook his head. "It's just—nothing is ever enough. He's always used other people, but now...it's like they're not even real to him."

Boz was the king of users. For *him* to feel that Incy had crossed some line was actually pretty scary.

"There was a thing with a stray dog. He didn't hurt it, but he made it...do things, to be funny. I don't know." Boz looked less and less willing to talk about it. "He seems different, but I can't put my finger on it. Actually, though, he's been a lot better since you've been back." He smiled at me. "Maybe it was just a phase."

"I've been worried, too," Katy almost whispered. "I mean, we're all kind of assholes, but I didn't think we were *crazy*. But there's this place, it's really—"

"You're all being ridiculous." Cicely's voice was cutting.

"Incy's the same as he ever was: out looking for a good time. Like all of us. I don't know what's the matter with you."

"*I* don't know what's the matter with you, *either.*"

I jumped at Incy's voice and turned to see him standing in the doorway of his room. Where the door had been solidly shut the last time I blinked. How had he opened it so quickly and silently? How had he overheard us? His face was stiff, his eyes cold. "I can't believe you're out here talking about me behind my back!" I would have thought he was joking, being intentionally overdramatic, but he looked truly upset.

"What else would we talk about?" I said lightly, pretending not to see his anger. He'd always been a hothead, quick to explode and even quicker to get over it. I knew how to deal with it. "You're the most interesting thing there is."

For a moment he faltered, his face softening, but then his expression got cold again. "But you weren't talking about my good looks, or my charm, or how my face looks the youngest out of all of you," he said mockingly. "You were saying that you were *worried* about me. That I had gone to extremes. What extremes? Why are you all ganging up on me?"

His face looking the youngest...? What on earth? I mean, we all looked young. We all got carded still.

"We're not ganging up on you," Cicely said, shooting me an angry glance.

"What extremes?" Incy asked again. "Give me an example." He'd been sweet, almost tender, with me since I'd been back, but right now he looked pissed and unyielding.

Boz slowly stood, to show that he was several inches taller than Incy. "Just relax, man," he said. "There's no conspiracy. We're friends talking about one of our own."

"Yes, talking *about*," Incy said tightly, his eyes narrowed. "Not *to*. If you're so worried about me, why don't you just talk to me? Why do you have to go behind my back? Why are you so jealous of me?"

"Jealous! What are you *talking* about?" Katy asked.

Incy turned to Katy. "You know what I'm talking about. You guys have been talking about me for *weeks*, saying I'm crazy, I'm dark, I'm doing evil things."

Katy's eyes widened. "No, we haven—"

"Stop! Just stop!" Incy's voice filled the hotel room. If he were a regular person, I would wonder if he was hopped up on something. But a lot of recreational drugs, besides alcohol, don't work well on us. "Look, I'm advancing! You aren't! You're going *nowhere*." He paced the room. "I just want us to be together, like old times. But you guys won't come with me. You're *jealous*." He turned to stare at us, his black eyes lit with fire from within. I sat up a little. Okay, this was weird. Incy was worked up and sounded totally paranoid.

Was he being crazy, dark, doing evil things? Had he been doing dark magick, as I thought, and was that affecting him? His pacing was abrupt, jerky, kind of manic. I'd seen him pitch fits before, when things didn't go his way. He'd thrown things and sworn at strangers and shouted wildly. I'd taken it in stride, even found it amusing sometimes: spoiled Incy. But he'd never been like *this*, paranoid and accusatory. Except in my dreams. My visions. I remembered the chopped-up bodies, the bone-filled fire.

Maybe...was it possible that I had come here to stop those things from happening? That everything had led me here to *help*? Maybe Incy was on the edge, and I was here to pull him back, away from the abyss. Not to get all swell-headed about my karmic influence. But the idea that I was here to help *on purpose* was ever so much more appealing than thinking I'd come here to pointlessly party my brains out. Which of course I had.

"Oh good Lord," I said, sounding bored, trying to keep my tension on the DL. In the past I'd always been able to talk him down, and though this seemed different, I would try. I took another cookie from the tray and nibbled on one edge to give myself a second to think. "I mean, get over yourself, Incy."

He whirled in his pacing. "You!" he said. "I trusted you!"

I raised my eyebrows just a little, implying that he

wasn't worthy of a full eyebrow raise. "Yeah. Of course you do. But listen, not that it's not fascinating to talk about you. I mean, it *is*. I was enjoying it, with or without you. But it's one thing to talk about someone, and it's another thing to listen to someone yap about *themselves*." I popped the rest of the cookie in my mouth and stretched, arching my back over the arm of the settee.

"I love you," he almost whispered. "Why have you turned against me?" His fists swung back and nervously hit the wall behind him, not hard enough to cause damage.

"No one's turned against you," I said. Jeez, this really wasn't like him. He'd always been the opposite, in fact, sure that everyone loved him and wanted to be near his charm.

He looked at me sadly. "You think I'm evil. You think I'm crazy."

Okay, color me officially worried. This was new behavior in someone whose behavior I'd been seeing almost every day for a hundred years. I thought about how River had reached out to me, even at my most obnoxious. How she had been calm and accepting. I had come back to be with Incy, my best friend. I wasn't going to ditch him just because there was something going on with him. I wanted to offer help to him, the way River had offered it to me. I wanted to make a difference in his life, even if I had failed so miserably with Meriwether and Dray. And myself.

Boz, Katy, and Cicely all looked upset and uncomfortable. I got the impression that he'd been doing this while I'd been gone, and without me to handle his outbursts it had gotten to be a real problem.

"We...think you're a little full of yourself, frankly," I said. "Come on—you, evil? The most evil I've ever seen you was when you paired your hippie sandals with that gorgeous sharkskin suit. And crazy?" I tapped my chin with one finger, obviously "thinking." "Okay, yes. I'll buy crazy. You won't eat fruit. You don't like *fruit*. Which everyone in the world likes. I've seen you lick the chocolate off a strawberry and put the strawberry back. You were in French Polynesia, land of the awesome, ever-present fruit, and you ate, like *crackers*. That, yes, suggests a certain lightness of the playing deck. But this—" I waved my arm around. "The drama, the theater? You wish."

Incy was pretty surprised. Oh, I had actually seen him more evil than my example. More evil than I had even realized at the time. But right now I needed to derail his train of thought.

Boz shifted in his chair, watching me. Katy looked like she'd rather be anywhere else. Cicely looked angry.

"However, if you're done with your pity party, I'm hungry." I swung my feet onto the floor and looked up at him. "You done? With the evilness and the whatnot?"

Like he'd flicked a switch, his face lost its sad, angry

look. He blinked several times and scanned the room, as if he was reorienting himself. All I wanted to do now was go lie down with a cold rag on my head. I really needed to figure out what was going on, and if I could do anything. Could I maybe get him up to River's aunt, Louisette, in Canada? Was he even that bad off? I didn't know how much of this to blow off as dramatic Incy and how much to freak out about.

Incy swallowed, looking pale but more like himself. He went over to the suite's wet bar and poured himself a couple fingers of scotch, then tossed it back. Adding alcohol to this volatile situation would be *very helpful*, definitely. Then he turned around again and looked at me. I looked back, an obviously patient look on my face.

"Oh, Nas," he said, coming over to me. He knelt on the ground by my feet and took one of my hands in his. I wanted to recoil at his touch, and that shocked me. He gave a rueful laugh and shook his head slightly. "Thank God you're here. You see how I need you? You're the only one who understands me." I thought I heard Cicely give an angry little cough. Incy's hands were cold and clammy; sweat dampened his forehead and sideburns. He leaned his head down on our hands, on my knees. "I missed you so much. I just do better when you're here. You make me feel human."

"Ew," said Katy.

"You know what I mean," Incy said, raising his head. "Normal. Real."

This was seriously creeping me out. "Glad to hear it," I said briskly. "We aim to please. The sound you're hearing is my stomach rumbling."

He laughed, looking totally like his old self, and rose smoothly from the floor. He took a silk pocket square from the jacket on the back of a chair and gently dabbed his face.

"*Andiamo,*" he said, then swept up his jacket and headed for the door.

Behind him, Boz and Katy met my eyes. I raised my eyebrows at them. They didn't think this was over. And neither did I.

ß ß ß ß ß ß ß ß ß ß ß ß ß ß

eally? *You think* so, dear?" Widow Barker's eyes blinked at me behind her cat's-eye glasses.

I fluttered my hands—all this business talk made my pretty little head hurt. "I cain't even tell you, Miz Barker," I said. "Just between you 'n' me, I'd rather be readin' a magazine by the pool at Beaufort's Motel."

The word *motel* had three syllables with my Southern accent. Mo-tay-el.

"These men, they're always up in arms about something or other," the widow confided, and we shared a laugh. She got up and took the drip coffeepot off the old-fashioned corncob stove. I pushed my cup closer and she filled it with coffee as thick and black as the stuff I was actually interested in: Texas oil.

It was 1956, and southeastern Texas had been gushing with black crude for forty years. Now some people were speculating that the geologic shale vein ran much farther west than had been expected. I'd already been through the California gold rush of 1849; that had turned out very well for me. This time I wanted to be an owner of the resource rather than merely a provider of an adjunct resource.

Which was why I was trying to buy the widow Barker's oil and mineral rights out from under her for a pittance.

Time had not been kind to the widow Barker. The rough stone markers in the yard showed that she had buried two husbands and four sons. I would have thought she had a thing against male people if I hadn't known that the sons had died in World War II; her first husband had run off and drank himself to death; and the second husband had toppled his tractor on the steep hill in the north pasture, just two years earlier.

Now she was living on a tiny government pension, and it showed: Her pink glasses with the rhinestones in the corners were the only new thing in evidence around here.

The small farmhouse hadn't been painted in decades; you could barely see chips of white paint still clinging to the weathered gray clapboards. The stove was, as I mentioned, the kind that you fired up with old corncobs from the feed corn her second husband had farmed for thirty years.

"But why does your cousin think this would be a good place for your mother?" the widow asked, sitting down again at the scrubbed wooden table.

"He just says it would be a lot of land, and she could garden," I said, my tone implying that I thought my cousin was nuts.

"I guess," said the widow, trying not to look out the window at the parched, arid ground that stretched as far as the eye could see. I gave her a limpid smile and took a sip of coffee that was surprisingly good. Her faded eyes turned slightly calculating. "But I always promised my husband—my first husband, that is—that I would never break up the parcel. This land was in his family for generations. His great-granddaddy started this farm before Texas was even a state."

I had no idea if this was true or not, just drank my coffee, looking concerned. "The whole parcel?" I said unenthusiastically. "Oh, I don't know about that. I think Mama would want just the house and enough land for Old Shep to run around a bit. Maybe five acres?"

But the widow Barker had an idea caught in the cogs

of her brain. "That's what my neighbor Edford Spenson said," she told me disapprovingly. "He pestered me all last spring. I told him I wouldn't sell. No, I promised Leland that I wouldn't break up the parcel, and I won't! If you want this property, you have to take all of it."

"But—" My eyes widened in distress beneath my big, black bouffant hairdo. My Texas hairstyle. "Miz Barker, that's almost a thousand acres!"

"No, Miss Whitstone," said the widow. "It's almost *two* thousand acres." She started to look worried—there was probably no way I'd agree to buy two thousand acres.

"Oh goodness," I murmured, taking another Lorna Doone. In fact, county records had shown that her parcel was 1,967 acres, give or take a couple feet. Farmland around here had once gone for as much as sixty-five dollars an acre, but that was before the drought of the last five years.

The widow fidgeted nervously with her paper napkin, her gnarled knuckles stiff with arthritis. She was probably only around sixty, and I marveled that she'd packed a whole life into that brief amount of time, with a beginning, a middle, and now an ending. With no children or grandchildren, no spouse, she was planning to move to Oklahoma and live with her younger sister, also a widow.

"Goodness," I said again, working sums with my fingernail on my own napkin. I inhaled. "Miz Barker—at thirty-seven dollars an acre, that's, oh my goodness. That's seventy-four thousand dollars!"

She tried not to look exhilarated. I imagined that she was picturing herself arriving at her sister's house, several battered suitcases holding all her worldly possessions, and being able to proudly say that she was not here on sufferance, on charity. She had an inheritance, and she could contribute her fair share.

"Edford offered me fifty dollars an acre," she said, which I knew was an outright lie. I could argue her down to probably thirty-five an acre. I took another cookie and dunked it in my coffee. Lorna Doones were dang good.

"Well, you see, Miz Barker, I really only need about five acres," I said again. "Old Shep doesn't hardly get around anymore."

"You could do a lot with two thousand acres," she said. "I'd rather it go to you and your mama instead of Edford or some old oil company who wants to break it all up." Awl kumpneh.

I gave her a weak smile. "My cousin says—" I began, but she cut me off.

"Your cousin is a smart man," she said. "With all kind of business sense, I'm sure. But this is between you and me. Woman to woman. I won't lie to you: This land hasn't been good to me. It needs new blood. It needs you and your mama, come to bring new life to it. I'm ready to sell, ready to live in Greer's Pass, Oklahoma, and never have to mess with this land no more. But it's got to be the whole parcel. And it's got to be fifty dollars an acre!"

She drew herself up, her gray, thinning hair pulled back into an indifferent bun. Her face was wrinkled and leathery from sixty years of the Texas sun. She was definitely gouging me on the land price, but I liked the widow Barker. I grinned at her.

"Miz Barker, I do believe my cousin Sam is goin' to blow a gasket," I said. "But I have money from my daddy, and this is my mama, after all. I'm gonna do it. I'm gonna take your whole parcel—and I'll give you..." I faltered, then reached for my resolve and swallowed visibly. "Forty dollars an acre!"

Widow Barker did the math quickly in her head. Almost $80,000. More than she'd hoped. She held out her hand. I shook it. And that was how I acquired almost two thousand acres of the south-central Texas oil field. I paid $78,000 and change, which was a huge sum in 1956. And I sold it for a truly astronomical amount in 1984. And I never have to worry about money again, for as long as I live, which is saying something. Unless mankind goes back to the barter system. In which case I'll be screwed.

The widow Barker, I assumed, went to Oklahoma with her nest egg and lived out the rest of her days probably feeling a tad guilty about the killing she'd made off the little girl from Louisiana. If she ever knew that oil had been found oil on that property just two years later, I never heard from her about it.

And my "cousin" Sam did in fact blow a gasket.

"Forty dollars an acre!" Incy shouted, slamming his whiskey glass down on the Formica table. "You were supposed to go up to thirty-five, at the most!"

I'd laughed at him, tucking my hair under a rubber swim cap covered with big plastic flowers. It was damn hot here, and the motel pool beckoned. "I have the money; it's still taking candy from a baby, and you know it's worth umpteen times that much."

"Maybe," he said darkly. "If there's oil there."

I shrugged. "Oil, natural gas—this place is loaded with it. You saw the reports. Besides, I liked Widow Barker. We made a deal, woman to woman."

"I should have been there." Incy poured himself another tumbler of whiskey and pushed his cowboy hat farther back on his head. With his dark coloring, he still looked foreign, out of the ordinary here, but he'd gone all out with the clothes and the whole Western persona. I'd forbidden the spurs or the longhorns welded to the front of the car. A girl has limits.

My hand stilled. "Why? Because I don't know how to buy property?" My eyes met his in the mirror.

He paused. "Of course you do," he said. "But you got *taken*. You let that woman gyp you—"

"Innocencio," I said, using his favorite name, the one he would always answer to no matter what his public name was, "I was not gypped. I made a deal. I knew what I was doing. I think it's fine." I let an edge into my voice, which I hardly ever did with him.

He blinked, seeing that he'd pushed me. Then he smiled easily and stood, helping me wrap the towel around my shoulders.

"Okay, Bev. I'll back off. You know I just want to help, right? I mean, I got the parcel right next door for thirty-three an acre. I wanted you to get a good deal, too. You know it's just because you're my best friend. It's you and me. Right?" His eyes twinkled, and the corners of his mouth turned up irresistibly.

I smiled. "I know. But you don't have to worry. You just have to show up at the courthouse to be my witness on Thursday, when we close the deal."

"I'll be there!" he said cheerfully.

"With no spurs," I clarified, and his face fell. And then he had gone out and fleeced the local bar patrons in a long night of poker. I hadn't thought anything of it at the time, but now it seemed to me that he couldn't stand *not* taking advantage of someone, not leaving the person with less than when they'd met. He'd really been sore at me for not cheating the widow out of money after I'd already cheated her out of land she didn't know there was oil on.

"You just don't have the killer instinct," he'd said as we left the courthouse after signing all the papers.

"I have the moneymaking instinct," I said with a smile.

He shrugged. For me, it was about having spent several hundred years having to rely on men; to own property, have a business, work land, be physically safe. Having to depend on a man, even a man you liked or loved, was not a comfortable feeling for me. My father had died when I was ten, my first husband after eighteen months of marriage, and then I'd spent decades being a servant in various households just so I would be protected, not have to suffer all the risks and limits of being a woman on my own.

Hence my drive for money. Here we were in the twenty-first century and, clearly, for some women, relying on men was still a necessity or a choice. But it wouldn't be for me. Ever again.

For Incy, it was about winning, besting someone. Even the people he seduced were about the challenge, not about love or like or even just chemical attraction.

We were both about control, but in different ways and for different reasons.

"Oh no," said Katy. "Let's not."

Incy glanced over at her. After his outburst in the hotel room, the idea of going out in public with him had seemed ill-fated at best. But I needed time to figure this out, figure him out. I needed to know more about what he'd been doing. In the end I'd decided that I'd already been in mortifying scenes with Incy, and if this evening went south, loudly, it wouldn't be the first time.

I wasn't thrilled with him driving, but he was sober, if a bit off-kilter, and I admit I didn't want to risk him being in a cab. Not that cabs automatically set him off. But I just had a feeling. Not a strong enough feeling to write him off, leave again. Not yet. I still wanted to work this through, to help him. Instead of seeing him as hopelessly lost, I saw him as flawed and uncomprehending, the way River no doubt saw me.

So we'd gone out to dinner and it had been fine—we'd practically closed the restaurant, with waiters not living up to their name as we lingered over drinks and dessert and more drinks and then more dessert. Incy had been his old self, charming, even sweet, and blisteringly funny. There had been much fun and laughter. I'd felt better by the time we were done, with Incy back to normal. And Cicely had loosened up after being mad at Boz and me back at the hotel.

But now we were debating going to Incy's new favorite bar, a place on the edge of town called Miss Edna's.

"Can't we go to Den again?" Katy asked.

"Don't be a stick-in-the-mud," Incy said with a new snide edge in his voice. "Strat called. He's meeting us there after his sports experience is over."

Katy sighed and looked out the Caddy's window. I was in the front seat with Incy; Katy, Cicely, and Boz were in the back.

"It's just not that fun, man," said Boz, sounding tired. He pinched the bridge of his nose, then straightened up. "Hey, let's go to the bar at the top of the McAllister Building! It has great views, lots of Boston's dumbest and richest, *and* a jazz combo."

"That sounds fab," I said. A jazz combo > another bass-pounding club.

"No," said Incy stubbornly. "We can go there anytime. I want to go to Edna's. I want Nasty to see it."

"Oh, that'll go over well," Boz muttered. I glanced back at him and he rolled his eyes at me.

"What's Edna's?" I asked.

Incy smiled and patted my hand. "It's a really special place," he said. "You're going to love it. I've been dying to take you there."

"So to speak," I said, and he laughed.

"And Strat's meeting us there," he repeated.

"It's really interesting," said Cicely. "It's a whole new experience."

"Maybe you could drop me off at the hotel," Katy said.

"No!" Incy snapped, stepping on the gas. "You're so ungrateful! I found this amazing place and you want to crap on everything I do! You just want to tear me down! You can't stand that I'm better than you!"

Not again. I gave Boz a WTF expression. He answered with a pained one. Cicely was looking bored, examining her fingernail polish.

"Better than me!" Katy began angrily. "At what? Pissing standing up? Listen, you *wanker*—"

"And here we are." Innocencio slammed on the brakes and cut the lights before I even got an impression of our surroundings.

"Where's here?" I asked. "Incy, where are we?" I looked out the car window and saw that we were apparently in a movie set of a "bad neighborhood." Yes, I would prefer to avoid bad neighborhoods. If I got shot or knifed, I wouldn't die, but it would still hurt just as much as for humans, and it would be damn traumatic. We're not superheroes. We don't have Spidey strength, and we do have all the normal pain receptors. We can still get mugged and robbed and assaulted in various harrowing ways.

Incy smiled at me and took the keys out of the ignition. "A little place I know in Winchley."

Winchley. A long time ago it had been a thriving middle-class community with shops on the first floors of the buildings, and apartments above. I had no idea what street we were on, but when I thought of Winchley, I pictured a sunny day, a straw-strewn cobbled street, horses and carriages and street vendors. That had been back in...like, 1890 or so.

I looked around. Winchley had fallen on hard times. Some neighborhoods look worse than they really are, and some neighborhoods are worse than they look. This was a neighborhood that would get a truth-in-advertising stamp. We were surrounded by dark, brownstone-type three- and four-story buildings, many of which looked burned out or were boarded up with graffiti sprayed over the plywood. Chain-link fences crossed empty lots full of trash, and several sections of fence had been knocked down. Even the streetlights had been broken or shot out. In the darkness, I saw the occasional glowing tip of a cigarette.

"What are we *doing* here?" I asked.

"We're visiting Miss Edna," Incy said. He popped the lock on his door and slid out.

"This bites," Katy said.

Cicely made a face at her. "Then stay in the car."

Katy snorted. "And be in it when it's carjacked? I don't think so."

"Come on!" Incy said, bouncing impatiently on his feet.

West Lowing crossed my mind like a shooting star. People didn't even lock their cars at night. Everyone knew everybody else. One day I'd been at work and saw a car parked outside. There was a GPS inside it and an iPod mounted on the dashboard. The windows were rolled down, no one was around, and I made a bet with myself that the car would be about a pound lighter when its owner came back. But though at least twenty people walked by, and a bunch of cars passed it, when the owner came back, all her stuff was still there. It had been weird.

My car door opened and Incy stood there, holding out his hand. Incy had always been a roller coaster, swinging from bliss to anger to sadness with the ease of a pendulum. This felt different. More...malevolent. Not just cheerfully selfish and thoughtless but controlling and dark. Had he changed so much since I'd been gone? Had he always been like this and I'd chosen not to see it? For the first time it occurred to me that my desire to help him was naive, even self-serving. As I knew very well, one had to want to be helped. Though Incy had said that he was glad I was back, to help him be a better man—still, we all know that I'm not one thousandth as wise and patient and giving as River.

"Are you going to be a buzz kill, too?" Incy asked me, then laughed. "Not Nastasya! Nastasya can keep up with me!" He gave me a loving look. "You and I are a pair. Bread and butter."

I used to think so, too, without question. Now, not so much. At all.

I got out of the car.

Cicely was already standing by Incy, her hands shoved in the pockets of her fur coat. It was starting to snow, and a deep, bitter cold had fallen on the city. This had been the coldest and snowiest Massachusetts winter I could remember. Katy and Boz, both looking like they'd just bitten a lemon, got out, too. Incy clicked the car locks and then quickly waved his hand, muttering something.

My eyes widened. "Incy. Are you doing magick?"

Innocencio laughed. "Just a tiny thing. We want the car to be here when we come back, right?" Without waiting for a reaction, he swiftly headed down a dark alley. Of course. God forbid we should go have fun without being in a horrible neighborhood replete with a dark alley.

"Nastasya, come on," said Cicely. "You're going to love this."

I had almost always loved the stuff Incy came up with. He'd shown me more good times over the past century than I'd had in the three centuries before that. Why was I hesitating?

Maybe because you don't have your head in the freaking sand anymore, said my snide subconscious. *Oh, and who asked you?* I said back just as snidely, and hurried to catch up with Incy and Cicely.

I made it to the end of the alley without getting accosted. We arrived at a tall brick warehouse that had one lightbulb trying to light a gray metal door and not succeeding. I heard no music, felt no heavy bass vibrating through the walls or the ground.

"Oh jeez, is this, like, rock climbing or something?" I asked.

Cicely sighed. "Yes. We're all about physical fitness."

There was a small black keypad by the door — you could hardly see it. Incy punched in a code, and the metal door clicked and swung open.

Inside was a tall, tall, tall, narrow black-painted stairway and nothing else. Pink lights glowed at the top of it. Now I heard music tumbling down the steps toward us.

"Is this a brothel?" I asked. I wasn't judging. I had made a fortune with my brothel during the California gold rush, but you know, come *on*. Why were we here?

"No." Incy gave a secretive smile. "Not really." He started up the stairs.

"Not *really*?" My eyebrows rose.

"It's *not*," said Cicely, and followed Incy.

It was on the first step that I felt it: darkness. I stopped, one foot on, one foot off. Incy was sprinting up the stairs. Cicely had followed him, leaving a jet stream of Dreams by Anna Sui in her wake. Boz and Katy almost ran into me as I paused, quieting my senses.

I looked up the staircase. Tendrils of darkness—dark magick—were coiling down toward me in the dim light. I glanced back at Boz and Katy.

"What?" Katy asked. "Let's just get it over with."

"What is this place?" I asked again.

Boz rolled his shoulders. "This stupid place Incy found. I don't even get it. It's incredibly boring."

"Well, let's just go get a drink at least," said Katy, motioning for me to get a move on.

Dark magick beckoned to me, whispered for me to come up, come up....

"So...do you guys feel that?" I asked casually.

"Feel what?" Boz looked around.

"Uh, the um...darkness?"

Katy frowned. "Yeah. It's not lit in here." The "duh" was implied.

"I feel the coldness and the likeliness for my cashmere overcoat to pick up fungus or worse," Boz said.

I nodded, took a deep breath, and started to climb the steps, feeling that this place held the clues of what was going on with Incy. This was the thing that was different about him. This was what had affected him and had not yet affected me.

What awaited me at the top? With each step I felt the weight of darkness, of Terävä, of people making choices for power. The air around me buzzed with magick that felt uncontained, uncontrolled. Two months before, I probably wouldn't have felt it, the way Boz and Katy seemed to not feel it now. I'd learned a few small-scale protection spells, and I said them now under my breath, over and over. Had no idea if they would work.

The stairs ended with a huge room lit by a few pink lights here and there. A long, beautifully carved wooden bar ran along forty feet of one bare brick wall. The rest of the room was open except for thick support columns. The ceiling was about sixteen feet high, the wooden floorboards black with age. There were few windows. There was a malty, hoppy scent in the air, as if this place had once been a brewery.

"I'm getting a drink," said Katy. "You want anything?"

"God yes," I said, feeling surrounded, almost smothered. "Anything."

Katy and Boz went to the bar and I stayed still, looking around, trying to control my breathing. Fear scratched my skin like insects' legs, but I tried to keep focused. I didn't see either Incy or Cicely. Though it was a large, open room, it was strewn with little collections of furniture — couches and chairs grouped around small, low tables. The couches were run-down and brocade, old-fashioned, giving the whole place a weird 1930s vibe, in addition to the dark magick almost choking me.

Folding screens of different designs made semiprivate

alcoves where clusters of two, three, or more people seemed twined together. When I looked more closely, I saw that no one actually seemed to be doing the wild thing. Clothes were on, movements were slow, voices were low murmurs. Not a brothel. Then...an opium den? Did they even exist anymore, outside of Asia?

"Here. They don't water their liquor down, at least." Katy pressed a short glass into my hand and I almost gulped it, my throat burning a little as the whiskey and soda went down.

"What are the people doing?" I asked, not sure I wanted to know.

Boz sighed. "It's that thing Incy probably did at the gallery. People, regular people, come here, and immortals sort of feed on them, for lack of a better word."

"There's no better word." Katy sounded disgusted and took a big swig of her gin and tonic.

I looked at Boz. "You're kidding. A whole place, for that? And regular people come here willingly? You told me Incy didn't know how to do that."

"I didn't think he did," said Boz. "I knew he liked coming here, but after a few times I didn't see the point of it. I don't know how to suck up someone's energy—it's not like they were handing out lessons. I don't know who taught Incy." His blue eyes scanned the room, and he gave a sardonic laugh. "I mean, take someone's money, her fortune? Yes. Even her innocence. Even her happiness. Call me a scoundrel. I'm happy to rob anyone of basically anything...except their energy. Their will."

"As soon as you mentioned the girl in the gallery, I thought, oh God, Incy learned how," Katy said. She shook her head and drank.

This was the answer to my doubts about Innocencio.

"Hello." A girl stood before us. She looked young but was, I hoped, over eighteen. Again I got the sense that this place was a throwback in time; her dark hair was arranged in careful waves and held off her face by a clip with a white flower on it. Her dress was dark green velvet, cut into a deep V in front and held at the waist by a black, beaded belt. "I'm Tracy."

Boz looked her up and down and sipped his drink.

"Hi," Katy said shortly, and looked away.

Tracy focused on me. "You're new here. I haven't seen you before."

"You are correct, sir," I said, and sipped my drink.

Tracy's sweet, old-fashioned face gave me a gentle smile. "I'm not immortal."

My eyes flared. "Oh-kaaaay?"

"But you are."

I almost choked on my drink and gave an awkward cough. Good Lord. "Oh my God, can you see me? I thought I was wearing my invisibility cloak." Yes, I'm suave. I'm mysterious. My name is Crowe—Nastasya Crowe.

Tracy looked at me with affectionate pity. "You feel alive. Regular people feel dead."

Okay, welcome to Creepy Territory. Here's your map.

"I have new batteries in." I tried to take a drink, but my glass was empty, and the ice slid down and hit my nose. That happens to us suave people. I wiped it off with the back of my hand.

Tracy reached out and took my hand. "Do you want me?"

My eyes widened again, and I glanced at Boz and Katy. They had gone, deserted me to this girl, this automaton girl.

Tracy's soft hand was stroking my arm. Her eyes were a beautiful green, like her dress. Her hair was soft and smelled like forget-me-nots. Her lips were soft and pink and smiling at me. She was...so adorable. And just like that, she had offered up her life, her power, for me to take if I wanted it.

She started to lead me to an empty couch. Could she actually be this stupid? Yes, Boz had told me what people did here, but confronted with the reality, I was still shocked. Almost without realizing it, I sank down on a soft peach-colored sofa with thick, rolled arms.

Tracy tucked one knee under her and then she was leaning against me, surrounding me with the scent of flowers. I began to pray that Katy hadn't put anything in my drink. I could trust Katy, right? Ha ha ha ha.

"What are you doing?" I murmured against Tracy's hair.

"Take me," she breathed. "Make me yours."

I had to hear her say it. I just couldn't believe that she would offer her life force to an immortal like this. "What are you talking about?" I sounded a bit more alert, and Tracy sat up and looked at me.

"You...put your hands on me," she said. "And, you know, sort of *take* me. Take my energy."

I sat up and put my empty glass on the small table.

"And then *you* feel lovely." Her coaxing voice was back. "And I do, too." She leaned against me again and put her hand around my waist. "You feel...very alive. So alive. I like the way you feel."

This place *was* a brothel—a dark brothel where immortals came and fed off regular people. Like vampires, if they existed. And these people, these astonishingly stupid and self-destructive people, were offering themselves up. They knew about us and seemed totally down with the whole immortal gig. But how, or why? And Incy liked to come here. And Incy had learned how.

"How could you possibly feel lovely?" I asked.

Tracy blinked at me. "I just do. It makes you feel dreamy and floaty. And sometimes I need to conk out afterward. One time I slept for three days."

"Tracy—you—" I shook my head. "You know this can kill you, right? Someone could literally channel enough of your life force to actually kill you. Leave you a vegetable, or worse."

"No," she said, looking disbelieving.

"Yes," I assured her. "That's how most immortals make magick: They suck it out of something else. And it can kill something, leave it dead. It's abhorrent, frankly."

"No." Tracy shook her head.

"Yes. Really," I said. Now I could see clearly what was happening. The humans here looked dazed, dissolute. The immortals looked fabulous, bursting with life and energy. And that wasn't all. Besides all the life-sucking, there was big magick being made here. Dark magick. I felt it in the air, practically smelled it, like ozone before a storm. This was...a really dangerous place. A really dark, evil, dangerous, bad place. And I had to get out of here.

I hadn't seen Incy since he'd come upstairs. Katy and Boz were leaning against a column, not talking to anyone. I was a bit surprised that they hadn't leaped into this wholeheartedly. Not that they were awful people, but they were just—unseeing. Unknowing. Not worried about consequences. Like we all were. As Boz had said, he was willing to rob anyone of anything. And had done so. He'd ruined people, broken hearts. Like Incy had.

And the thing that sobered me right up, that pierced

me to the core was the knowledge that two months ago, this would have been...very interesting to me. I wouldn't have known how to do it, but I would have been willing to learn. I don't think it would have bothered me to rape these people's energy, take advantage of their stupidity. I would have thought they deserved it, since they were literally asking for it. It wouldn't have given me a single sleepless night.

It was revolting that I had been like that. Shameful. Disgraceful, in the old-time sense of the word. And what was even worse? That I could now see myself so wretchedly clearly. I had changed, I recognized bitterly. I hated that I could see myself as I was. What a terrible thing to know. I would never be able to not know it, to forget it.

I didn't see how I could ever forgive River for that.

CHAPTER 22

aving a good time, love?" Incy leaned over the back of my couch. His eyes were bright, his face flushed and happy. Earlier he'd seemed increasingly agitated, almost jumpy. Now as he sank down next to me, he seemed very, very calm, very centered.

He'd been feeding on someone. Maybe more than one. I found it so...reprehensible. And I'm not even a good person. I'm a loser and a waste, and *I* found it reprehensible.

"*Good* is a strong word," I said, wishing I had another drink.

Incy looked taken aback. "I see you've met the lovely Tracy."

"Yes."

Tracy looked thrilled to see Incy and immediately abandoned unfun me to wind around him. He smiled at her and stroked her hair, and she almost purred.

"Tracy is a very giving girl," said Incy, and Tracy's eyes gleamed. He looked at me. "You really should try her. I'm sure they taught you how, at the witch school."

"Witch school?" He'd called it a farm earlier. As if he hadn't known what it was.

"I'm sure they taught you all kinds of things," he said, and I recognized the seductive tone he used on people. He was now using it on me. I had, after a hundred years, become someone he needed to subvert and seduce. Inside my chest, I felt my hard little heart crack right in two.

"How to gather eggs," I said woodenly.

Incy laughed, stroking the back of Tracy's neck. "They have more private rooms, in the back. Why don't the three of us go there? Tracy would probably like to be with both of us."

Tracy's face lit up as if she'd just found a hundred dollars in the pocket of an old pair of jeans. "Yes! I would."

I swallowed. "I just...this isn't for me, Incy." I was stunned by the thoughts battering my brain: I didn't *belong* here, not anymore. I didn't *belong* with Innocencio and the others. I thought I'd been overreacting before, when I'd run away. I thought I'd just had a brain attack, then had continued lying to myself at River's Edge. Coming back here was supposed to feel like coming home, like I was putting myself back into a world I knew how to navigate, how to do well in.

But I felt like a weed in a hothouse here, too.

I didn't belong anywhere. With anyone. *Oh goddess.*

"Don't be silly." Incy gave a little laugh. "It will be perfect for you. You'll love it. And darling, when you see how you feel..." There was so much love in his eyes. "Remember when you introduced me to a Hansen's Sno-Bliz in New Orleans, and it changed my life? This is like that, only more so. This is what I want to give to you."

I looked at Incy and Tracy, sitting closely on the couch. They were both unnaturally beautiful, seductive, alluring. Incy had talked me into a million different things over the decades—including coming back to Boston—and I hadn't balked and very rarely regretted anything. I forced myself to consider whether this was another of those times, whether I was being narrow-minded and uncharacteristically knee-jerk moralistic.

But I couldn't bring myself to do this. It was bad; it was wrong; it was unclean. I recognized that. I felt it. Going against those feelings would be unbearable. Another thing to blame River for.

I gave an uneasy smile. "It's tempting...." Oh God, I was such a coward! Such a freaking spineless jellyfish of a *coward*! I was still trying to *placate* Incy, to go along. But I was done with lying to everyone. Done with lying to myself. My heart sped up. I swallowed and took a deep breath. "No, Incy. It isn't tempting. It isn't. It's disgusting."

Tracy looked offended. Incy's face was very still, his eyes on mine.

Might as well jump completely under the bus. "It's repulsive for Tracy, or any of these others, to offer their energy to us. They're crazy and suicidal and lying to themselves. For immortals to take them up on their ridiculous, wrong-headed offer is, well, *wrong*. As much as my moral compass spins like a game dial, even I can see that this is not the path to skip down. It's bad. I would feel...like something I would scrape off a shoe."

"Yo!"

We were all startled by Stratton's sudden appearance. He took a slurp of the foam on his glass of stout and looked at us. "And what a delectable little treat you have here." Stratton looked at Tracy, who blinked leaf green eyes at him.

"She is delectable," Incy agreed, and Tracy looked pleased. "But Nastasya doesn't agree. Nastasya thinks Tracy is disgusting and repulsive."

Tracy looked at me reprovingly.

"I said *what goes on here* is disgusting and repulsive," I clarified. "Not Tracy herself."

"No," said Incy. "Tracy herself you called stupid and crazy and suicidal."

Tracy's eyes narrowed at me.

Stratton looked thoughtful, as if trying to figure out whether "disgusting and repulsive" could be seen as a good thing. Finally he looked up, his mind clear. "Naahhh." He sipped his beer, completely at ease.

"You're overreacting, Nas," Incy said, still cajoling. "Those puritans brainwashed you." He laughed. "Trust me — this is what you need. Look, try it once. Like bungee jumping. You'll advance very quickly."

He meant advance magickally. What had he been getting into? And for how long? Since London? Earlier?

Somehow, two months ago, I'd had the dumb animal instinct to get away from him, to try to get to a place of safety. But it had been too hard. My inadequacy and my darkness had scared me. Now, here, my blooming darkness would be an asset, a strength. But now I knew too much to let it.

I couldn't believe I was in this position. I don't think I've ever gone against the crowd in my whole life. Never stood up for anything. I always just went with what was going on, what the most powerful people were saying and doing.

My stomach turned at the thought. Sickened, I realized I had to deal with four hundred years of regrets. I would not survive this.

I stood up, feeling like my skin was splitting. My heart had already broken, and it now lay in a heap of tiny, sharp shards like animal teeth in the pit of my stomach. I felt…obliterated. If I'd been a shell when I went to River's, I was now a grotesque, crumpled piece of florist's foam, the kind that dissolves when you press on it the slightest bit.

"I'm going to go," I said shakily. I pushed my arms into my cashmere Jil Sander coat. "I'll see you guys later."

They looked at me as if I'd started talking in ancient Greek, and said nothing as I turned and headed toward the door. I hadn't seen Cicely since we'd arrived. Maybe she was in one of the private rooms in the back. I met Boz's and Katy's eyes as I left the big room behind. Of course I had no ride, no way to get out of this hellhole. I pulled out my brand-new cell phone and clumsily tapped in a search for taxi companies as I trudged down the stairs. My soul felt lighter with every step, but I wasn't fooled; I had no home, no place to go. I had no *me*, actually.

"Nastasya! Wait! Wait!"

I turned to see Incy hurrying down the stairs.

"I'm going to go, Incy," I said. "This isn't working."

For one second, fear blazed in his eyes like a bon-fire; then it was gone, and I wasn't even positive I'd seen it.

"Nas." He gripped the collar of my coat and leaned down to put his face close to mine. Alarms went off, but I tried to keep my face blank. This whole thing had been such a mistake. I had totally and completely screwed myself, but good. Incy was uninterested in being helped or saved. That had never been what he wanted from me. "Nas," he said again, gently. "I'm sorry. I truly thought this would be fabulous and that you would love it."

And what did that say about me? Ick.

"But if you don't, that's fine," he went on. "We don't have to stay. Boz and Katy want to leave, too. You three have turned into a bunch of party poopers." His voice was slightly bitter, but he forced a laugh. "Stratton and Cicely are going to stay. They understand."

He seemed to catch himself then, realizing that he was digging himself in deeper. He shook his head and smoothed my collar down, tucking my scarf around my neck.

"I *understand*, Incy," I said. "I just think it's repugnant. It's *rape*. Those idiots in there don't know what they're doing, how dangerous it is. You're taking advantage of them." I looked at him earnestly. "This isn't you, Incy. It isn't us."

His lovely face twisted quickly into a cruel sneer that

made me step back against the stair railing. Then Boz and Katy started coming down, and he got himself under control.

"Yay," said Katy. "Let's go somewhere else."

"Bars will all be closed," said Boz, and then caught on that Incy and I were having a moment.

Incy flashed a smile. "Yeah. But that's okay. We can go do something else. Okay, Nas? Nas is back!" He put his arm around my shoulder and kissed my cheek. "Back forever! It's you and me, babe! You'll see. A few more days and you and I will be like bread 'n' butter again."

Bleakness settled over me like a quilt.

Outside it was still breathtakingly cold. The four of us walked briskly to Incy's car, which hadn't been touched, thanks to his spell. I glanced up at the sky, its stars almost blotted out by the city's lights and the striated clouds that moved quickly from southwest to northeast. I could just make out enough to guess that it was about two in the morning.

I felt very, very old.

A piercing sense of regret and loss swept over me. With despair I realized that I would give anything to not be here, to wake up tomorrow in my hard little bed at River's Edge. I wanted to break down in huge, racking sobs. Why had I done this?

Oh, right. That's right. Because I always, *unfailingly*,

screwed things up. I always knifed myself in the back. I was afraid of being happy because no one can be happy forever, and I couldn't bear the fear of its inevitable loss.

I climbed into Incy's frigid car in numb misery. Boz and Katy got into the backseat; doors slammed and Incy started the engine. I gazed out the window, imagining that I could see River's face right in front of me. Her eyes with their wisdom, their love and forgiveness. Their understanding. That's all she had ever offered me. I'd thrown it back at her—not once but twice.

And Reyn. I'd pushed him away, even as I'd hypocritically lusted after him. Despite his past, he was sincerely trying so hard to be good. And here I was with Incy, bread 'n' butter. The thought turned my stomach, the alcohol solidifying into a knot of pain. Incy had a bad past, and clearly had zero interest in being good. How had I not known this? Maybe it had been creeping up so slowly for years that I'd been able to avoid admitting it to myself. Or maybe it had happened all at once, in the last two months. I hoped I could talk to Boz about it, the next time I was really sure that Incy couldn't overhear us.

I leaned my head against the cold window, knowing that I had to plan a new life for myself. Which was about as bleak a thought as I could possibly have.

"Nasty!" Incy's voice was insistent.

My head jerked upright. "What?" I glanced around, saw that we were making our way out of Winchley. Incy was staring at me, looking upset.

"I asked you why you thought Miss Edna's was about rape. The people there are *offering* it. If they say yes, it's not rape, is it?"

"It still is," I said, wanting to go back to the hotel, get in my shower, curl up on the floor, and cry for a couple days with hot water sluicing down on me. "They don't understand what they're doing."

"Some of them might not, I grant you," said Incy, eminently reasonable. "But some of them truly do understand and want to do it anyway. It's kind of like hypnosis. While you're joined, you can instill a sense of peace and well-being in them. They feel high afterward."

"It could kill them," I said.

"It never does," said Incy. "We're always very careful."

"Who taught you how to do that?" The car's powerful heater had come on, but I was still trembling.

"Miss Edna," said Incy, turning down another street.

"Are we headed back uptown?" Boz asked. "Where are we?"

"We're in my *car*," said Incy with exaggerated patience. "It never does kill them. It makes them feel fabulous, and they offer it up freely. How is that rape?"

I was sick of this discussion, so sick of Incy, so anxious

to be out of this car and alone somewhere so I could let some of this emotion out. As of tomorrow, I was going to start completely suppressing all emotion again. There was no other way.

"It's statutory rape," I said stubbornly, leaning my head against the window again. "It's just wrong."

"Wrong!" said Incy, astonished. "Wrong for *who*?"

"Wrong *in general*," I said, feeling sobs start to thicken in my chest, like storm clouds. "It turns out that there actually is a wrong and a right, and it makes a difference which side your decision falls on."

Incy took his eyes off the road to stare at me in disbelief. "What are you *talking* about?"

"Some things are right to do; some things are wrong." I actually had to explain this.

"Like *you* would know!" Incy said, unconsciously mimicking the words Dray had shouted at me. I was detecting a theme here. "You, who stole from people for *decades*! You, who've left people behind to *die* while you escaped! This is *me* you're lecturing from your pulpit, Nas. Me. I've seen you do stuff that would make a cockroach give you a high five! What about that train wreck in India? How many people did you save then? Oh, wait—you were too busy picking their valuables up out of the grass, stuffing them into your pockets!"

"That was then!" I said, burning with the knowledge

of how true it all was. Incy could go on for days about the many awful things I'd done. I'd never be able to remember them all, even if I tried for the rest of my life.

Incy laughed shortly, derisively.

Some scathing, defensive retorts came to my lips, but I bit them back. It was pointless to remind him of his own crimes. He was right. I was no one to judge.

"That was then," I said again lamely. "But I know right from wrong *now*, and I can't unknow it." I could barely speak, full of revulsion for myself, my past. In desperation I closed my eyes. Immediately I saw Reyn's face, harsh and forbidding, then intent and focused, then flushed with desire as we fused our present and our past with just a kiss.

I'd thrown him away like an old apple core.

"I don't know about all that," said Boz, "and this is all interminably boring. But I would definitely rather hang out at a different bar."

"Me too," said Katy.

"Me too." My voice sounded as broken as I felt.

There was silence for a while, though Incy was muttering angrily under his breath. Probably cursing us out as ungrateful traitors. Inside I was writhing in pain, my thoughts ricocheting in panicked hysteria. I was lost; I was alone. I had nothing and no one to help me. Not anymore.

When Incy spoke, his voice was mild, almost disinterested.

"I'm really sorry to hear you all say that," he said, and flicked his hand sideways, as though shaking off water.

And suddenly I was drowning in darkness.

CHAPTER 23

 couldn't move. My hands, my feet—all of me weighed a thousand pounds. I could still feel everything, but even my utmost, straining, panicked efforts couldn't move anything except my eyes.

The world looked like it was smeared with Vaseline. Edges were blurry and indistinct. Lights outside the car were fuzzy halos. Incy seemed to be talking to me from very far away.

I tried to scream, tried to summon an immense noise from deep in my belly, but I was aware of only a high-pitched keening sound. Again I tried to move my arms, my legs, but gravity was much too strong. And of course this reminded me of some of the worst times in my life: The night my parents died, my father's steward hid me in a neighbor's wagon, beneath a mound of hay. I hadn't moved or made a sound for many long hours, out of shock, trauma, the fear of being found. Even when I breathed in warm hay dust, I fought the coughing down. I kept my eyes squeezed tightly shut, as if the world couldn't see me if I couldn't see it. Covered by the heavy weight of suffocating hay, I'd had hours to vividly relive the deaths of my parents, my brothers and sisters. Over and over I had seen Eydís's head topple off her shoulders and fall to the ground.

Other times, during raids by the Butcher of Winter or other tribes, I'd hidden up in trees, down in root cellars, in the special hidey-holes I'd made sure to have until the late sixteen hundreds, when raiders weren't part of my world anymore. For hours I'd clung to tree branches, my skirts tucked up under me, trying not to shake a single leaf, knock loose a single acorn or pinecone. I'd stayed silent and still until my muscles screamed in agony, until I was shaking with cold and my jaw ached from keeping my teeth clenched. When I'd finally been able to move, long after they'd gone, my body had been so stiff that I couldn't climb down. I'd fallen, hitting several branches and then landing so heavily on my shoulder that my collarbone had snapped.

Later I'd found a neighbor who'd hidden in a hay rack, which had been torched with him in it. Another neighbor had hidden in a barrel that had been axed open as the raiders looked for ale. The neighbor had been axed open, too. I'd been the lucky one, for I was still alive, broken collarbone or no.

All my memories of having to be still, silent, all those memories that were associated with terror and pain and dread—they came back and whirled around me like tumbleweeds of barbed wire, like shrieking banshees, as I sat petrified and immobilized in Incy's car. Oh goddess, help me. Oh God oh God oh God...

Next to me, Incy laughed. He swiveled to look at Boz and Katy in the backseat.

"There! All of you are nicely cocooned, right?" He laughed again. "Even better, you've *shut up*. No more of your whining and yapping and self-righteous mewling. Fantastic!" He turned to me. "See what I can do when others give me their power? I become very, very powerful myself."

Muffled sounds came from the backseat. Incy had obviously put some kind of binding spell on all of us. How did he know how to do that? I wondered with rising hysteria. Had the mysterious Miss Edna taught him this, too? I tried to grit my teeth, to lift one finger using all my strength, and screamed inside when nothing happened.

Incy let out a sigh. We'd left the main streets and were now on a smaller road that wasn't lit. Holy Mother, where was he taking us? This couldn't be happening. In all my fears of Incy I'd never imagined things coming to this, never truly believed that he would turn on me, hurt me.

I tried to say, "Incy, you love me!" but it was like being encased in firm jelly and I couldn't get out any sound, couldn't move my jaw.

"You know, I really tried, Nasty," Incy said. "I *really* tried. This is all your fault. You brought this on yourself, and you know it. This isn't how I wanted it. I didn't want you dead. I wanted you by my side, bread 'n' butter, like the old days. The two of us, ruling equally."

My eyes widened. Ruling? Ruling *what*? Wait—dead? Dead?

Incy reached across and took my hand, which felt like it had been dipped in Novocain—I could sense it, but it was numb.

"I've tried so hard, for so long," he said. "I did everything you wanted. I was there for you. I supported whatever you wanted to do. But it was never enough, was it? You should have been thanking me. You should have been grateful. Instead you just left, with no word. *With no word!*" He shouted the last part, painfully loud inside the car, and slammed his hands on the steering wheel. "You *left* me!" he shouted. "How dare you! How *dare* you! You ran away! I had to *ask* people! No one knew where you were! Do you know how *humiliating* that was? Everyone was surprised that I, your other *half*, didn't know where you were!"

I *had* thought of him as my best friend, my other half. It had seemed like a good thing. Now I saw it as I was a building, and he was poison ivy covering the building, blocking the windows, creeping inside. Again I struggled, my arms trying to push against ropes that weren't there. Maybe his spell had lessened, or he hadn't done it right, or it would wear off.... No. I tried to scream and barely got a tiny *unnhh* sound out. I was drowning, drowning in a cocoon of dark magick.

"And *you*," Incy went on, pointing his finger at me, as he had done in the hotel room. Had that been tonight? Just *tonight*, earlier? "You have all this lovely power. Did you offer to share it with me? No. You ran away and gave it to strangers! You threw it all at those laughable puritans! And they don't even care about you! Not like I do!"

I discovered my eyes were still capable of tears. They had cared about me, at River's Edge. They had. I'd given them nothing in return. Had I ever even said thank you? Once? I couldn't remember. My eyes burned. All of Solis's words about consequences, about cause and effect, came tumbling into my brain. This was the universe dropping an anvil on my head and shouting, "You made the wrong effing choices, you colossal *idiot!*" Because none of the previous hints had worked.

Incy wanted my power. He wanted more power than a regular person could give. Just like in my dreams, my visions.

Why was I — why was I *wasting time wallowing in self-pity?* My brain suddenly cleared, my shrieking panic temporarily held off. I would deal with the unending regret and despair later. Right now I had to save my ass, if only so I could go to River's Edge, apologize for being me, and then hide in a cave for the rest of eternity.

I concentrated. I focused on dampening the white-knuckled terror rising in me. Think, Nastasya, *think.* I remembered all the boring meditation lessons foisted on me. I inhaled slowly, one, two, three, four. Those four seconds felt endless. Adrenaline lit my brain as I exhaled slowly, one, two, three, four. And again. Pull the air into your belly, Anne had said. Inhale and exhale only through your nose. Breathe in calmness, breathe out external distractions. Breathe. And again.

My jaw felt looser. "I don't have any power," I managed to mumble almost incoherently.

Incy laughed, throwing his head back. Then his face contorted and he swung at me. I couldn't move, couldn't duck. He slammed his fist into the seat right by my head, making my head bounce. "Don't lie to me!" he screamed in my face. "You keep lying to me!" His face was ugly, splotched with red. Suddenly he leaned over and yanked on the scarf around my neck. I felt so enveloped that I was shocked when he managed to touch me. He tugged on it several times and got it off my neck. Rolling down his window, he threw it out into the night. My *scarf*, my protection...now I was completely bat-shit freaking.

Oh God. *Breathe*. Breathe. Slowly. In, two, three, four.

Incy was driving crazily, speeding down the dark road. The car kept slipping on the falling snow. If we wrecked, Boz, Katy, and I would be trapped, unable to move. If he flipped the car and the gas tank exploded, we would burn and burn, with so much pain that we would lose our minds. But *not die*.

Incy roughly pushed his hand beneath my collar, his fingers easily finding my scar with its raised edges. "Do you think I'm stupid?" he shouted. "I know who you are! I know *what* you are! Did you think I couldn't add it all up? I'm! Not! *Stupid!*" He banged on the steering wheel with each word, and the car zigzagged, making my stomach roil.

He *knew*? About my family, my heritage? How? For how long? Had he stayed with me only to try to benefit from it? The thought was crushing, deepening my sadness and disillusionment about all that Incy and I had been to each other. So Incy knew I was the only heir to the House of Úlfur the Wolf. My power was supposedly immense and ancient. Incy was going to take it from me.

"You're a selfish *bitch*!" Incy said. "But I welcomed you back with open arms. You didn't deserve it, not after what you did. But I took you back." He looked at me with a cold malevolence, and the car skidded again.

I'd never felt so powerless, which was ironic, since he was doing this to get my power. I had no doubt he had already mapped out how. Innocencio was going to wrest my family's power from me, and unlike me, he had plans for it. Look at what he was able to do just by stealing power from regular people. What would he do with a power so big, so strong? *I'd* done nothing with it besides try to flip Nell out. I had done *nothing* with my legacy, my potential, my heritage. Now I was about to lose any chance to.

I had to get out of this, had to come to terms with who I was and what I could do, or I would never do anything else again. This knowledge settled on me like a shroud, and I almost wept with desperation.

Is there a manual somewhere that lists abandoned warehouses suitable for crazed maniacs to take victims to? On TV, in movies and books, there always seems to be one handy where the axe murderer of the week can hole up and do his dastardly deeds.

Incy apparently had that manual. His was, I think, on

the very outskirts of Boston, past Quincy, on a spit of industrial land that jutted out into the ocean. He pulled the Caddy onto a loading dock and got out, leaving the car's headlights on. As soon as he left the car, I struggled again, trying to squirm, then relax, then squirm again to break free of this goddamn holding spell. I didn't know how Boz and Katy were doing. I hadn't heard anything from them, and I couldn't turn to check.

I watched as Incy jumped up on a platform and pulled open a metal sliding door that led into a vast darkness. Looking excited and determined, he came back to the car and yanked open the side door.

"You first," he said grimly. I heard rustling sounds and felt someone's legs hit the back of my seat. It wasn't until Incy had hauled Boz out onto the gravel and dragged him past me that I could see him. Boz's face was white and wet with sweat. His eyes were half closed, unfocused, his mouth hanging open slackly. Incy put his shoulder under one of Boz's arms and walked him up the cement ramp to the open door. Boz's feet scrabbled clumsily on the ground; an onlooker might assume he was completely wasted. Incy pulled Boz into the warehouse, right into the darkness, and my throat ached with sobs. Incy had brought us here to die. I didn't know why he was going to include Boz and Katy in this scene—it was aimed at me. But their deaths would be on my hands as well.

My brain was locked in a dull panic. I was trying to remember any magickal thing I'd ever been taught, from how to keep flies away to how to help onions grow, hoping that something useful would hit me. My thoughts were random, disorganized, pinging slowly from one side to another like atoms in a supercooled matrix. I heard a quiet huffing sound from the backseat, as if Katy was trying to cry or was having trouble breathing.

Innocencio was gone for ages, I don't know how long, and then he came back for Katy.

He grabbed her and pulled her out of the car, handling her more easily than Boz. She slumped like a stringless puppet over his arm, looking unconscious, bloodless. It occurred to me that Incy was probably drawing power from Boz and Katy right now. And it was hurting them. Maybe even killing them. He was using them to keep us all bound, so that he'd be able to get my much greater store of power.

Eventually he came back for me, his third hostage. I wanted to kick him, punch him, scream like a harpy, but the little I'd said before had taken herculean effort. Think, Nas. I had to harness whatever mental and magickal energy I had for the brilliant escape plan that I was sure was going to pop, fully formed, into my fogged brain at any second.

"*Tsk, tsk.*" Incy looked regretful as he opened my car

door. I was encased in a magickal spider's web, a deadened cocoon of numb helplessness. He unclipped my seat belt and pulled me out of the car as if I was deadweight.

"Incy," I murmured, struggling to get my feet under me as he hauled me up the ramp.

He frowned down at me. "Shut up. You've had your chance. Now you're going to do what *I* want." My legs felt like blades of grass, unable to support my weight, unresponsive to my hazy commands. At the warehouse door, dank, chilly air wafted out, and with it came an unmistakable impression of corruption and malignancy. Dark magick had been worked here before. Foul, inhuman deeds had taken place. Passing through the doorway reignited my panic, as if crossing the threshold removed my last bit of hope.

Incy let go of me and I fell heavily to the cold, dusty concrete floor. A dull, radiating pain started in my shoulder and snaked around to my chest, making it painful to breathe. He pulled on some rusty chains, and the loading door creaked and groaned, then crashed down like an old-fashioned portcullis. Dust entered my nose and mouth and I wanted to sneeze, but even those muscles seemed incapable of getting organized, and I was left with a nagging irritation in my sinuses.

"I'm sorry we're ending this way," Incy said conversationally as he grabbed me under the arms to half drag, half carry me to a wire cage. "It didn't have to be like this. It could have been you and me. Bread and butter. Sharing your power." He got me inside the cage—it was an elevator. He pushed the button and the cage rose unsteadily, with screeching cables and grinding gears. It stopped with a heavy jolt that made me lose my balance again, and I toppled against its wire-grate side. Incy pulled the gate open and looped one arm around my waist. We were up on a balcony that ran around three sides of the building, overlooking the main warehouse floor. Ragged-edged shafts of moonlight fell through holes in the rusted metal ceiling and streamed through the broken panes of windows placed high up on the walls. It was freezing in here, as cold as it was out in the open. The air itself was tainted. This place was soiled and unclean, filling me with a creeping revulsion with every breath. Incy had known of this place. What had he done here?

Think, Nastasya, think. You're so powerful—show us. Think of a spell, any spell, that you could use. Think of *something*, for God's sake. Oh, River, *help me.* I'm so sorry. I'm so sorry!

Incy pulled me along, an unwieldy and clumsy baggage. Our feet kicked up dust that filled my nose and mouth, and I would have given a lot to be able to spit, to sneeze. Candlelight flickered ahead; as we got closer I saw the dark, slumped forms of Boz and Katy kneeling on the floor, their hands behind them, chained to two rough wooden support posts some eight feet apart.

I stumbled, seeing their gray faces, hair streaked with sweat. Their chests moved with rapid, jerky breaths. They neither looked up nor gave any impression that they knew we were here. Lightning-fast images of the two of them through the years flashed through my brain. Boz, dressed in a white linen suit, laughing and drinking champagne; Katy, in black from head to toe, holding one finger to her lips as she helped me break into a wall safe. I saw Boz's white, wolfy smile as his eyes lit on a new mark; saw Katy's brown eyes gleam as she whirled at a dance, her skirts swinging around her.

"Here. Join your friends. The three of you can sit here and think about what hypocrites you are." Incy roughly dragged me to a post across from them and pushed me toward it. My injured shoulder slammed against it, making me gasp thickly as fresh pain exploded across my collar-bone and back. I slid down, ending on my side almost face-first on the filthy wooden floor. Boz blearily tried to look at me, but after a moment his head dropped again.

"You've done this, not me," said Incy, like he was talk-ing about a stain on my clothes. He pulled out a length of chain and grabbed my shoulders, propping me up against the post, which was maybe twelve inches square, unfin-ished, studded with old nails and staples, thorny with splinters. As soon as the chain touched my skin, I recoiled as if it was electrified. The chain was spelled. It was anti-magick, anti-life. I hadn't known something like that existed.

Incy wrapped the chain several times around my wrists, and I heard the click of a lock. I felt dizzy, light-headed, the cold chain burning against me. I couldn't get two thoughts to line up together in my brain. I saw what was happening in front of me, around me, heard Incy talking, the muffled gagging sounds Boz and Katy were making. But it all seemed surreal, as if I were watching a horror movie out of the corner of my eye. My shoulder was still a throbbing pain, and now I became aware of the ache of pulled muscles, starting at my elbows, felt the bare, splintery wood of the post rubbing against my wrists.

"None of this had to happen." Incy waved a hand around the warehouse, then leaned down in front of me. Even through my haze I saw a yellow glint deep behind the blackness of his eyes. Why hadn't I seen that yester-day? The day before? Last summer?

"Here's your chance," said Incy. "Give me your power, and all this can stop right now. You aren't using it. If you give it to me, I'll let Boz and Katy go." He looked at me. I imagined shooting him the bird. I wished I knew a spell that would let me control one finger on one hand.

I swallowed, almost gagging on the simple action. "Bite me," I managed thickly.

His mercurial face changed again, and then he was raging, shouting, stamping his feet, making billows of unbearably itchy dust swirl around us. He swung a thick length of chain, whipping it right next to my head, so close that I felt it brush my hair, and all I could do was blink.

"I hate you for making me do this!" he screamed, an inch from my nose. "For what you're making me do to *them*!" He lashed out with the chain again, hitting Boz's post, where it gouged out a chunk of wood.

Incy was incensed, out of control, shrieking and spewing and kicking things. He picked up a hunk of metal and hurled it across the warehouse, where it hit a brittle old window, making it explode.

There was no reason to think he would let us live. I knew this with cold certainty, fear forming pointless, stinging tears in my eyes. He was going to kill us and take our power. No one would miss us. We were old hands at disappearing. People would assume we'd taken other names, gone to other cities. Who would care, anyway? The three of us had left a wake of disappointed friends, hurt and embittered acquaintances. We were losers, and losing us would bother no one.

After everything I had been through, the dozens of

times I had cheated death, I would actually die, tonight. I hadn't, 450 years ago. Tonight I finally would. I was already shaking with cold, and now fresh fear sent a new surge of adrenaline into my heart. I felt jittery, hopped-up and yet immobile, as if I'd drunk a hundred cups of espresso and then gotten sewn into a mummy costume.

Even as Incy ranted, working himself up, I kept picturing River's face, how she had looked at me with kindness and understanding. I saw Reyn, remembering how angry he made me, how much I'd wanted him, how much I didn't know about him, how much I should try to understand. Reyn had been there, the day my first life had ended. He had been here in my present, as I'd tried to become yet another new me. I would never see him again. The idea was shocking.

Incy stopped suddenly, standing taut and furious in front of Boz. Boz blearily raised his head and blinked, his eyes unfocused. He was so handsome, even pretty. I'd known him for ninety years or so, seen his looks change through the ages. He'd always been the most handsome man in any room, not in a supermasculine way, and not in a fallen-angel way like Incy. Just blond and fine-featured and twinkly-eyed. Now he was in a stupor, his mouth open, hair mussed and streaked with dirt and nervous sweat. He was bent far forward, putting a painful strain on his shoulders, his hands chained behind the post.

He slowly licked his lips, seemed to struggle for a minute.

"Don't do it, man." The words were barely decipherable, his voice sounding clotted in his throat.

"Boz." Incy looked regretful as he knelt next to him. "I'm sorry. I really wanted Nas, but you got in the way."

Great. That wouldn't haunt me forever. As short as my forever would be.

Gently, Incy reached out and put both his hands on Boz's face, framing it with his fingers.

"Give me your power, Boz, old man," Incy whispered.

Boz struggled to swallow, weakly formed the words: "Fu...ck...you."

Incy's fingers tightened on Boz's face. "Give me your power." His voice was low and deadly.

"No." I saw Boz's mouth move, but couldn't actually hear him. But Incy did. He began to chant, slowly and softly at first, then building in strength and volume. I couldn't make out any of the words, but even from ten feet away I could feel their vindictiveness, their hatred. My skin prickled as I felt bits of dark magick coalescing, creeping up through the floorboards like insects drawn out by the scent of refuse. It sank down through the holes in the roof, the broken windows, dark wisps of evil and despair coiling through the air like cold, oily smoke.

A regular person would have felt nothing, sensed

nothing. But all the hairs on my arms were on end, and I writhed inside as darkness rose.

"Stop," I whispered, so softly I could barely hear myself. I tried to clear my throat. "Stop." Incy ignored me. His chanting continued. He had been practicing this, planning this, for a long time. Probably since right after I'd disappeared. Maybe even before.

Katy watched the scene dully, her reactions cocooned as well. Did she understand what was happening? I suddenly felt that as much as I had hung out with Katy, traveled with her, practically lived with her at times, I actually didn't know her all that well. I couldn't tell what she was thinking, what she would do if she could.

Incy's smooth tenor became stronger, harsher, his words sounding like bullets, like whips, filled with evil intent. Suddenly Boz seemed to awaken and started to struggle. His shoulders jerked; I heard his chains rattling and grinding against the wood column. His eyes flared, staring at Incy with disbelief.

"Stop!" I said, spitting out the word like a lump of clay. Once more I tried to free myself, with no result.

A sound tore from Boz's throat, an unintelligible animal sound of pain and fear. "Okay! Okay! Yes! Take it!" he cried, sobbing. "Take it! But stop!"

Incy smiled cruelly and kept singing.

Boz started screaming, the sound deadened and choppy.

His eyes bugged out, the pupils filling the blue irises like a black oil stain. Horror filled me as I saw true evil stripping Boz away from himself. I remembered the sight of Reyn's brother being flayed by my mother, during the siege. Her words had been dark and terrible like this, her face almost unrecognizable. She'd raised her hand, snapped it out at the raider, and her amulet had seemed to glow with a frightening power. The raider's skin had burst from him, shredding through his clothes and leather armor, his chain-mail shirt. I'd watched dumbstruck as he'd stood there like an anatomical statue, raw muscle and sinew and bone, his eyes huge and surprised without their lids, without brows. It hadn't killed him, of course. Sigmundur had leaped forward and severed the raider's naked head, and that had killed him.

My mother's power had been as dark as this, as evil, though she was trying to save us, her children.

"Stop!" I said, the word sounding like a sob, and even that sapped my strength, made me feel like collapsing in the dust and passing out for a hundred years.

Still Incy chanted, his voice victorious now, his face flushing with triumph and life, eyes glittering. The air felt polluted, defiled, as if I were breathing illness, breathing in wretchedness and despair.

Incy's voice rose in a crescendo of exhilaration. His hands pressed against Boz's face so hard that the skin glowed white around his fingertips. Tears ran out of my eyes and down my cheeks.

Boz's back arched. His voice was raw and strangled. Katy slowly turned her head toward him, watching him uncomprehendingly. Incy shouted his last few words, then jumped up, arms raised, standing like a matador who'd just killed a bull for the crowd.

Boz's voice broke off abruptly. Just ten feet away from me, his face...crumpled inward on itself, as if deflated. I gasped, my stomach heaving at the sight. Boz's shoulders folded in, his head sinking onto his chest in a grotesque, unnatural way. His skin was gray and powdery, withered and wrinkled beyond recognition. His body slumped forward, held only by the chains binding his reedy, stringlike hands. It was as if Incy had sucked Boz's actual soul out, leaving a desiccated, inhuman husk, a repulsive, empty skin that had once been my friend. Everything that Boz was, everything he had been, everything he had done in his life — it was all gone, forever.

I'd never seen an immortal die without having his head cut off. It was stunning, for some reason hitting me so much harder than the odd occasion when I'd seen a human die. I hadn't known it could be like this. Incy had known.

The air crackled with magick and darkness. It felt sharp, barbed, painful, and disgusting all at once, all around me. I tried not to breathe in the foulness, almost retching from its noxiousness. Incy was laughing, dancing around, so full of Boz's life and energy that he couldn't stand still.

"I am invincible!" Incy shouted, whirling and leaping near Katy and me. "I am *invincible!*"

I tried not to throw up with revulsion and dread. I looked over at Katy and behind her dull stillness I saw terror and comprehension. She knew beautiful, selfish, silly Boz was dead, knew that something unspeakable had just happened. And would happen to her and to me. Either way, one of us would have to watch it again.

She started crying then. Her shoulders, pulled back so painfully and awkwardly, shook. She choked on her tears, gagging like I was, and at one point seemed to pass out. Then her head rose again, tears streaking the dirt on her face. Her mouth opened but closed without saying anything. I'd seen her drunk before, and sick; laughing hysterically, crying with shared emotion as people all around us whooped in the streets on V-Day. I'd never seen her like this, disheveled, dirty, dopey, well past fear, well past terror. I wished I could comfort her.

Still Incy danced around us, vibrant with power, alive with Terävä magick, laughing maniacally, rubbing his hands together.

Finally he whirled to a stop in front of me, looking

unholy with a terrible, unnatural beauty. "Nastasya—you're next. Give me your power, like ol' Boz here, and Katy won't have to buy the farm. Deal?"

I stared at him. Did he mean it? Could I save her? But...what would he do with my power? Nothing good. What a choice. What would River want me to do?

ew Year's Eve felt like hundreds of years ago. I had danced in a circle with everyone at River's Edge, danced around a fire and felt magick rise in me like a fountain, like a sunrise. I had tried to cast darkness out of me.

Afterward Reyn had waited for me. In the snowy woods I had reached for him and he had kissed me. He'd been so warm, so strong. He'd told me what he wanted—me—and asked if I wanted him, too. I'd been an idiot, a scared idiot. I had learned so much there, but it had come at me like unrelated bits and pieces: crystals here, herbs there, stars, names for things, spellcraft, oils, and moon phases. I'd been so stupid that none of it had fit together; none of the pieces had been made into a stained-glass window of understanding. If I could try one more time...

"What do you say, my love?" Incy's face was glowing, as perfect and eternal as that painting I'd seen in the Met, full of stolen life and energy.

His voice snapped me back to the appalling present, with my muscles seizing and cramping, my brain lit and frantic, this unnerving binding spell wrapping me tightly in victim cords. I stared up at Incy, focused on his face. A word floated into my consciousness, indistinctly at first and then forming more completely: *fjordaz*. Fyore-dish. It was an ancient word for what Incy was stealing— somehow, instantly, I knew that. He'd taken Boz's *fjordaz*.

Where had I heard that before? My mother? Yes. It had been a word in the song she sang to call her power to her. I remembered her strong, lovely voice singing, and the word *fjordaz* being woven in. Was she calling on her own power? Trying to subvert someone else's? I closed my eyes, trying to think.

"Fine!" Incy shouted. My eyes popped open as he pulled out an old sword, its blade inscribed with symbols that made my flesh crawl. The metal glinted in the candlelight as Incy hefted it. "Did you know there's more than one way to skin a cat?"

My brain struggled to follow his thoughts.

"With Boz, I actually ripped his power away while he was alive, just to see if I could." Incy smiled, showing teeth. "And it was incredible. I hope it was good for you." He did a few dance steps, tapping the sword on the ground like a cane. "But if I just whack Katy's head off, I'll be able to grab her power out of the air. So, easier, eh?"

"Wait!" I got out. I'd been kneeling all this time on the cold floor, and my knees burned and throbbed with pain. "Wait!"

"Wait? You want to think about it? No." Incy bounded over to Katy and raised the sword above her head. She blinked several times, looking up at him, and I saw her try to move, try to stand. It all seemed surreal, a bleary recollection of a nightmare that I would soon wake from.

"No!" I couldn't shriek, but I made my voice as loud as I could. It was garbled, like I was yelling through a tunnel of felt. "No, Incy, wait!"

Katy was gagging, unable to sob. Her eyes were wide, still disbelieving.

Incy looked at me. "You are making me do this," he said clearly, and brought the sword down.

"Katy!" I choked out, even as I heard the unexpectedly loud *thwack*. Everything in me bolted forward until the deadly chains yanked me back. Katy's inarticulate shriek stopped.

My mouth hung open as I saw Katy's head drop to the floor and roll slightly, facing me. Her eyes looked at me, slowly blinked once, and then glazed over, like scum forming on old milk. A gush of blood, vivid red, erupted from her neck and pulsed outward several times with her heartbeats. In a split second I was back to the night when my entire family was slaughtered. There had been so much blood then, too. I had walked through it, my felted wool slippers squishing in the soaked carpet. Now I stared as Katy's blood, red and shining on the old warehouse floor, flowed toward me, making rivulets through the dust. The heavy, coppery smell hit my nose, filled my mouth.

My guts heaved. I leaned sideways and hurled, my stomach convulsing over and over. The drinks I'd consumed just hours ago burned with bile at the back of my throat.

Incy had been chanting during this, but now he stepped back quickly to avoid getting the spreading blood on his shoes. He was breathing hard, little puffs of smoke visible in the weak moonlight. His eyes shone when he looked at me, and he seemed amazed, impressed, giddy that he had actually done such a heinous, ruinous thing.

"Are you happy now?" he asked. Blood dripped off the sword that dangled from one hand. "You see what you made me do? That's *your* fault!" He gestured at Katy. "She didn't have to die! *You* could have saved her! But *your* selfishness killed her!" His words would have stung even more if he hadn't looked so exhilarated.

That was when my hatred of him began to override his binding spell, just a bit.

"I hate you!" I said, my tongue still feeling thick but my voice stronger than before. Incy reeled back in shock, whether from my words or my ability to say them, I didn't know. But it was pouring out of me now, the way Katy's blood had poured out of her.

"I hate you! I hate everything about you! You're crazy! Evil! Drunk on power!" I was going to die anyway—might as well let it rip. I put all the coldness and loathing into my voice that I could summon.

Incy's face contorted with rage. "*Shut up!* You're the dark one! *You're* evil, all the way down to your shriveled little soul!"

"I used to think so. Used to fear it," I spit. Speaking was still difficult, not fluid, and required effort, but I could get words out. "Everything was going wrong, and I thought it was *me*! But it *wasn't*! *I'm* fine! It was *you*, all along! *You're* the dark one!" I wanted to sob with relief at that realization—assuming it was true—but since I was about to die, there wasn't much point.

"Shut up!" Incy yelled again, waving the bloody sword at me. "You don't know what you're saying! You love me! I've done everything for you!"

I gaped. "*Love* you? Are you *insane?* Look around! Look what you've done! Look what you're doing to *me!*" My chains rattled and scraped against my post. I felt the sharp sting of wooden splinters digging into my wrists.

Incy did look around, and a moment of confusion crossed his dark, handsome face.

I shook my head. "I can hardly imagine the Incy of the past, my friend," I said. "Every memory I have of you is spoiled, uglier than I remembered. I want to *erase* you from my past, erase every single thing about you." I spoke these true, hurtful words more calmly, and it pushed Incy over the edge.

Two bright blotches of anger rose on his face. "You don't mean that!"

I nodded, my head feeling like it weighed about fifty pounds. "Oh, trust me, I do, Incy."

"Yeah?" With an enraged bellow, he leaped at me, swinging the sword. I could barely flinch the slightest bit, snapped my eyes shut for the blow. Instead the sword hit my post with great force, shaking it, sending stinging reverberations through my hands.

It took him a second to dislodge the sharp blade, and I wished so much that I could swing my feet out and knock him down. I pictured hitting him, over and over, pictured picking up the sword....

He got the blade free, stepped back, and pointed it

right at my face. He held the tip, still slick with Katy's blood, a few inches from my eyes. "You hate me, huh? Then I won't even *pretend* to feel guilty about taking your power."

My chin lifted. "You can't have it! I won't let you."

Incy giggled, his laugh becoming disturbing, high-pitched. "Like you can stop me."

"I can!" I bluffed, but Incy wasn't fooled.

He pointed his finger at me and said a few words, and with the next breath I sagged heavily, barely able to move even my eyes. He'd strengthened the binding spell, and I wanted to howl with frustration and rage. My eyes stung with tears again and I couldn't believe that he would win this way, that I couldn't fix this.

"It would be better if you were *giving* me your power," Incy said conversationally. Using his hand, he stooped over and began to trace Katy's blood into the shape of a big circle around us. Apparently taking my power required more of a setup, more preparation than for Boz or Katy or a regular person. The horrible tang of blood, plus the stench of alcohol and vomit, made my stomach heave again. "But I'm sure I can take it, even against your wishes. In fact, it will be an interesting challenge."

I wanted to scream, but my jaw felt rubbery and too big for my face.

Before Incy closed the circle, he put four large chunks

of hematite at the four corners of the compass. Then he took more blood and drew a large, upside-down star in the middle of the circle, making a pentacle. I'd seen Anne use one in healing rituals. Like everything else, it wasn't dark in and of itself. Everything can go both ways, light and dark. It depends on the user's intention.

Next Incy set up eight black candles and four purple candles and lit them all with a regular silver cigarette lighter. The additional candles made the whole tableau even more sickening: Katy's blood was now a brighter red, Boz's crumpled, dried-apple face looked faintly greenish. The lights cast deep shadows into the corners of the huge warehouse. I wished a traffic chopper would go by overhead; the crew could report a suspected vandalism, and the cops would come....

"All that lovely power," Incy was crooning. "Nas's lovely, lovely power. Mine, all mine. I'll be so strong. Miss Edna will be amazed. Miss Edna might even be scared." He cackled.

"Who's Miss Edna?" My tongue was swollen in my mouth, reluctant to form words. I felt both hyperaware and still cocooned. Each second was taking forever to get through, but I couldn't move, couldn't even feel my hands anymore.

"It will be delicious." Incy's voice was singsongy, childish. "Delicious and nutritious." He straightened and looked at me. "Miss Edna. Miss Edna is...very old. Very power-ful. But not as old and powerful as her master." He waved a hand around. "In fact, this warehouse belongs to her master."

Holy shit. "Her *master*?" Did we even have stuff like that?

Incy giggled again and went back to preparing his dark spell.

"Who's her master?" My tongue still felt thick; it was still hard to speak.

Frowning, Incy shook a finger at me. "None of your concern! Now shut up!"

A master?

"I will be so strong, so strong," Incy sang. He stopped at each piece of hematite and said words over it, words that sounded full of oozing greed and perverted desire.

I would be dead soon. That was an odd realization. There were times during my 459 years that I had wished I were dead, definitely. But it was only now—this year, this month, this *day*—that I even knew what it meant to be alive. That I even had a purpose in living. I had seen the future as a huge, gaping maw of time, stretching pointlessly, endlessly forward. Now my entire future would be wrapped up within the next hour. It was...so unexpected.

If only River—

Then a thought slammed into my head, ripping through

the fog. River was incredibly strong because she was of the Genoa house of immortals. Also because she was really old and had studied magick deeply for centuries. But a lot of it was *just being born into that house*. I had been born into the Iceland house of immortals. I was just like River. Potentially *just as strong* as River. Of course, I was completely untrained, completely lacking in knowledge, and a total ignorant screwup besides. But. I was the sole survivor of the House of Úlfur the Wolf. My power was why Incy had wanted me in the first place. If *he* could access my power, *why couldn't I?*

The idea was stunning, as if I'd just had champagne thrown in my face. Thoughts started firing with organized clarity for the first time since Incy had kidnapped me. With great effort I put aside my grief and disgust over Boz's and Katy's deaths, and instead I looked at Incy. He was going from candle to candle, singing a short verse over each one. He looked solemn and self-important and deeply happy. Uncharacteristically focused and determined. He'd never wanted anything this much in his entire life.

I was strong. *Super*strong. Unnaturally strong. I thought back to Helgar. I'd worked for her as a housemaid in Reykjavik when I was in my early twenties and already a widow. It had been Helgar who had recognized me as immortal, and told me so, to my astonishment. She had told me about

354

our magick, how we were born in darkness and lived in darkness, and that was how it was. That had been my truth for four and a half centuries. Now, at this advanced age, I was clinging to a new truth: that we can *choose* to be light or dark, good or evil. It was such an astonishing truth, with so many implications. I wanted to have days just to think about it instead of just minutes to regret being so long unenlightened.

Helgar had described our magick as a black snake, coiled inside us always. When we made magick, we opened our mouths and called on the snake.

I knew only a few basic spells, and I couldn't even remember them. My black snake was sleeping.

Incy closed the circle, looked at me intently, then knelt in the center. He put his hands over his eyes and started to chant.

I am superstrong. I have huge power, like River.

I opened my mouth.

That was the extent of my plan. I let my eyes unfocus and thought about my power, the few tiny spells I knew, the classes I'd taken. I thought about my moonstone and realized with shock that it was in my pants pocket. I'd put it in there automatically out of habit. I thought about my moonstone, how much I loved it, how it felt like a part of me.

Okay, black snake, I thought for the first time in my

life. Calling you now. Then I thought, Black snake, yuck. Make it a white snake. No. It was my power, and it was going to be...a dove, a white dove for me, dammit. Okay, white dove, white dove, white dove...come to me.

I closed my eyes and saw Reyn's face scowling at me. *Don't be a pansy-ass,* he seemed to be saying. *Just summon it already! Quit relying on everyone else to do stuff for you!*

Incy now crossed his hands in front of his mouth. The timbre of his song changed. The air felt colder to me, more malevolent. Once again I was aware of dark magick seeping through the floorboards like foul, chitinous creatures, coming in the broken windows like an ill wind, slipping down through the rusted holes in the roof along with the innocent moonlight.

Hvítr dúfa. White dove, in the language of my birthplace, the language of my parents. *Hvítr dúfa,* come to me. Would it work if I wasn't calling it a black snake? I didn't know. I just knew that if I pictured a black snake coming out of my mouth, I would hurl again.

Hvítr dúfa... come to me.

My thoughts broke up as if static was interfering. Incy's song was growing louder. What had I been doing? Why was I so cold? There was darkness everywhere, coming closer to me like waves, licking around the edges of the circle.

Oh, *hvítr dúfa.* Think, Nas, keep it together. I started murmuring anything, whatever came into my mind. I hoped it was the chant I used to call my power, but I had no idea at this point. I was exhausted, my cobbled-together energy seeping from me.

I had my moonstone. My mother had had a moonstone. I forced myself to keep making sound, keep the image of a strong white dove in my head, but it was fading in and out and I wanted to cry.

The black fingers of darkness were getting closer, closer. Soon they would be tapping at my feet, my head, my hands, scratching me, worming their way under my skin. Soon I would feel them sidle up to my brain and begin to edge inside, begin to pry their way into my thoughts, my soul.

Once again I sang to call on my ancestral power. I let go of my physical pain, my emotional anguish. *I was power.* Breathe in, two, three, four.... *Hvítr dúfa...* my dove. My dove. My white dove of power. My heritage, my birthright. My mother. My father. Iceland. Was I imagining things, or was my moonstone getting warmer? I kept murmuring, singing under my breath, keeping one eye on Incy. He was standing now, his arms out to his sides. His voice was strong, its smooth clarity debased by the evil intent of his song. The words were foul and ancient, had been used to wreak death and destruction for millennia. With barely controlled panic I felt the darkness around me gelling, thickening.

Incy was reaching a crescendo. His face was covered with sweat, his eyes were wild and unseeing, but his joy was evident. He raised his hands to the ceiling and slowly turned in a circle.

His spell touched me like glacial air off an arctic ocean. I shook with cold and closed my eyes, breathing out my chant of power, feeling that I would never be warm again. I was a conduit, a vessel to be filled by my family's heritage. I wasn't taking power from Incy, from the wooden floor, the night air. I was channeling it, letting it move through me. I would not give up. I wouldn't let him win without a fight. I wouldn't let him or anyone else take what was mine. My power would be mine forever. The cold was creeping over me like strangling vines. When I opened my eyes, my vision was blurring. Soon the darkness of Incy's mind would slide down my throat, go into my ears, my eyes, and it would all be over.

Haft, haft, efta gordil, efta alleg, I sang. The words had been ancient before my parents were born, crafted by some Old Ones at the beginning of magick. *Hvítr dúfa, eilil dag…myn hroja, myn gulfta…*my white dove. I pictured it, pictured every feather, its eyes black like mine. It was *my* power. *I* controlled it. My power was boundless! It was in the wings of my dove, so strong and light, in the white feathers, fanned out like the sun's rays. My dove was coming at my call, as its different incarnations had come at the calls of my ancestors for centuries. It was so much stronger than Incy's patchwork, stolen *fjordaz*. This was *mine*, down to my bones, my blood.

Incy was shouting now, turning around and around. With each revolution, the dreadful coil around my neck grew tighter. I was going to faint. Suddenly Incy stamped his foot and stopped still. He brought his arms down hard, as if silencing an orchestra.

My vision faded. I could no longer see. A garrote of dark magick squeezed my throat....

Hvítr dúfa, *I release you! I release you!* In my mind I pictured throwing my hands in the air, releasing the power of my clan...and then, to my shock, a huge surge of power shot through me, electrifying every cell in my body! My back arched violently, yanking my hands hard against the rough wooden post. As if I'd been hit by lightning, my hair stood on end, my skin burned and felt like it would split. My nose filled with blood, and a piercing pain in my ears made me cry out. I felt something leave me, something huge and tangible, as if I'd conjured an immense dust devil that was spinning away from me to do my bidding.

In a split second Incy's binding spell was broken: I was wide awake and shimmering with generation upon generation of immortal power. The chain binding my hands burst free, sending ruined metal everywhere.

Six feet away, Incy's circle exploded. The candles snuffed out; the hematite skittered across the floor. Incy jolted as if slapped, knocked almost off his feet. He swayed, caught himself, and stared at me, mouth open in shock.

I couldn't believe it myself. I was filled with both exultation and humility.

"You will *never* get my power!" I hissed, my shoulders stretching painfully. As sensation came back into my hands with a tingling burn, I wanted to cry, and my leg muscles screamed as I scrambled to my feet as fast as I could. "You will *never* be strong enough! You're pathetic!"

With a bellow of rage, Incy lunged for me. His hands closed around my neck and I suddenly realized that my power was gone, used up in that one burst. I didn't know enough to sustain it, to come up with something else.

Shit, I thought as I tried to kick him, cursing him out, saying every awful thing I could think of. "You're a murderer, you're crazy, I *hate* you, I will *always* hate you—" But he was stronger and he started to choke me.

"How dare you fight me!" Incy snarled. "How dare you try to be greater than me! Don't you get it? *I'm* the reason you were such a spectacular screwup at the puritans'! I'm the one who made your life turn to sawdust! I wove poison into your existence, to show you how much you didn't belong there, how much you needed me! But you still didn't see it!" He was rattling my head on my shoulders,

360

whipping it back and forth. I felt dizzy and sick and tried to grab his hands, his wrists. In between head snaps, Incy tightened his hands around my throat, squeezing and squeezing. I coughed, trying to suck in air. My lungs started aching and I felt light-headed.

"Screw you!" I got out weakly, then bit my tongue as he shook me. *Crap!* "I hate you! You're a failure! A loser! A poser!"

"*You're* the failure!" he snapped back. "A disgrace! Your parents would be ashamed of you, your weakness! They would have wanted you dead themsel—*aighh!*"

Okay, he might have been stronger than me, but he had one crucial vulnerability, am I right, ladies? Kudos to me for remembering it. In the next second, I brought my knee up into his junk as hard as I could. He froze, then made a strangled sound. His hands fell away from around my neck and he sank to the ground, curling up and dry-heaving. It was like *magick!*

This was my chance. I leaped over him, twisting my still-numb ankle painfully on the awkward landing. I swept up the sword where he'd dropped it, then stood over him. His eyes bugged out and he tried to kick at me, tried to get up, only to stall, wincing and whimpering in pain. Sweat dripped off his brow and he looked ashen.

"I'm going to kill you!" he managed, fury making the veins on his forehead pop out.

"I'm the one holding the sword, genius!" I snarled. He struggled to get to one knee, thrusting his arm out at me. I raised the sword, thinking of what he had done to my life, what he'd done to my life at River's Edge. In the distance I thought I heard thuds and creaks, but every sense was exploded from my magick surge, and I couldn't trust my ears.

"You deserve to die!" I said, feeling mighty and invincible. "After all you've done. You killed Boz and Katy! You almost killed me!"

Incy was still trying to get up, and I made a note of his angle in case I needed to kick him in the balls again.

"Oh, like you could use that sword," he sneered, but I saw fear behind his eyes.

I gave an evil smile, one that I had practiced a lot, years ago, for fun. "You'd be surprised," I said with my best smirk, and saw him hesitate.

Then I stepped backward several feet, in case he tried to lunge, and I lowered the sword, my arms trembling as I made a momentous decision. "I *am* stronger than you. Because I'm...not going to kill your loser ass." I drew in a shuddering breath, wondering how I could disable him long enough to get the hell out of here. "You deserve to die," I said again. "And I *could* kill you right now, and no one on this earth would mourn you. But I'm *better* than that, you *lousy* piece of *horseshit*!" I ended up shouting, enraged all over again. I yanked off the ring he had given me and hurled it over the balcony.

Then the floor shook and I heard another, even louder bellow of rage. Incy looked up, his face changing to shock and anger...

...at the furious northern raider who was thundering down the balcony.

So I *had* died, after all. After all that, as hard as I had tried, Incy had managed to choke me to death. It was over. As if from a distance, I watched Reyn seize Incy by the coat and throw him across the floor. This was what heaven was: watching Reyn beat the crap out of Incy. I would get to do this for eternity, I imagined. It wasn't bad.

Then several things came together for me: I was immortal; I couldn't be choked to death. Heaven would probably smell better and be warmer. I didn't even know if there was a heaven, and it was somewhat unlikely that I would end up there, if there was. Also, River, Asher, Solis, and Anne were running toward me.

It seemed I was still alive, after all, and it was all over.

ot totally over.

"Nastasya!" Asher looked at my face, then carefully took the sword out of my numb hand and examined my wrists, which were bruised, cut, and scraped. River and Solis went to pull Reyn off Incy, who was putting up a fight but had no hopes of winning against someone who had been born and bred to vanquish other people. River said something and drew a sigil in the air, and Incy slumped like a beanbag, eyes staring at the ceiling. Solis took Reyn's arm, pulling him away, as Reyn stood over Incy, breathing hard, clenching his fists.

Now that Incy was no longer a threat, I felt dizzy and ridiculously tired. I realized that Solis and Anne were with Boz and Katy. I heard them murmuring prayers, and I was gruesomely aware that I'd brought this into their lives.

They were here. During my worst moments with Innocencio, I'd longed to see River again, to have another chance of coming to terms with Reyn. Now I was profoundly relieved and grateful but also incredibly depressed that they were witnesses to the complete nadir of my life. I'd thrown the gift of their knowledge back at them, had left them and immediately gotten myself into an unbelievable amount of trouble. These people, whose opinion I actually cared about desperately, were seeing me at my moment of utter defeat. I sank to my knees.

River came and knelt by me. I remembered the first time we'd met; she'd come and knelt by me then, as I wrung frigid ditch water out of my fox stole. Now I didn't want to look into her eyes, but I forced myself. I saw concern, worry, and love. My nose got stuffy the way it did before I started crying. She stroked my flaming magenta hair out of the way with one hand, and we turned to survey the scene. It was so much worse now, seen all at once, when I wasn't under a spell: the warehouse, Boz's desiccated husk, headless Katy, the circle of blood, the chains, the candles used to work evil, loathsome magick. I didn't see how I could ever possibly get over this, and my triumph over Incy, over darkness, evaporated like smoke.

River's clear, light brown eyes met mine. Her hand rubbed my shoulder carefully, and the pain made me want to barf again. She leaned close to my ear and spoke, her words for me alone: "This is very bad. But I've seen worse. You will get over this."

I started to cry. "My face is not that expressive."

My nose was cold. The rest of me was warm. The mattress beneath me was hard. Experimentally, I pushed a hand out and quickly found the edge of the bed. It was narrow. Slowly, holding my breath, I opened my eyes. The first thing I saw was the crack in my ceiling, shaped like Brazil. I let my gaze wander and saw my small wooden wardrobe, the door to my room. The metal bedstead at my feet. My sink. The small table beside my bed. My window.

My room at River's.

That was when I knew I was dreaming. I stayed very still so I wouldn't wake up. I would give anything for this to be true, to be reality. Instead I knew that soon I would really wake up in a fabulous hotel room in Boston, in a thick, cushy bed with down pillows. Someone would come in, talking loudly, ordering room service. I would feel awful until I had four cups of coffee. Then it would be a day of shopping, eating, hanging out, followed by a night at the theater or a snobby new club or an important restaurant. In short, a vapid, purposeless, stupid existence — a nightmare.

I closed my eyes again. But not as much of a nightmare as the dream I'd had about Incy killing Boz and Katy in that warehouse. It had seemed *so real*.... Why did I keep having these dreams, these visions?

I heard a knock on my door and ignored it. It was housekeeping, possibly room service. If I opened my eyes again, I would truly wake up, and the thought of waking up in Boston with Incy filled me with despair.

The door opened. I pretended to be asleep. I smelled... *herbs*?

"I know you're not asleep," said River, and my eyes sprang open.

It was really her. I was actually here. I frowned, thinking back. My last memory was...oh my God, had that all *happened*? The unspeakable atrocity in the warehouse? Had that been *real*? Oh *goddess*.

"Sit up and drink this," said River.

I saw my wrists then, mottled with deep, dark purple bruises, covered with punctures from the splinters of the post. My throat was sore. One hand flew to my neck; someone had wrapped a thin scarf around it. I was touched by this thoughtfulness and felt my eyes fill with tears. I took the mug from River and sipped.

Fresh horror washed over me as I remembered more and more of what had happened. River sat down on my bed. I couldn't look at her, just drank the herbal tisane and let the tears well out of my eyes.

"I'm...so sorry," I whispered, looking down at my comforter.

"I know," River said.

"Innocencio—is he dead?"

"No. Poor Incy will have to endure the healing talents of my aunt Louisette," she answered. "Nell has moved back to England, to another place of recovery. But I think Incy will be with Louisette for quite a while."

"He can't be helped, surely?" I heard the skepticism in my voice.

"I think so, yes," said River.

Good Lord, if Incy could be helped...then I was a freaking *picnic*.

There was another tap on my door, and Anne came in with a tray. The bowl of soup and hunk of bread made me recoil as I remembered the night I had left this place, only a few days ago? Incy's darkness, masquerading as my own, had ruined a meal.

Anne set the tray down on my lap and I edged up against my headboard. "I keep forgetting about your hair," she said drily. "What possessed you?"

I fingered the magenta strands. "Actually—I think

Incy possessed me," I said slowly, trying to recall the words he'd spit at me...when? Last night? "What day is it? How long was I out?"

"About eighteen hours," said River. "What do you mean, Incy possessed you?"

"Last night, when we were fighting, I was saying everything bad I could think of, how much I hated him, how he was horrible and pathetic and I was so much stronger than he was..." I trailed off, embarrassed. I certainly hadn't demonstrated my wondrous ability by doing anything correctly here. I picked up the bread and broke off a piece, dipped it in the deep orange soup. I hadn't expected to ever be able to eat again, after how sickened I was by everything that had happened. But I realized I was starving.

"You *are* so much stronger than he is," River said matter-of-factly. "Then what?"

"He said that I wasn't strong enough to keep him out. He said that he was why everything had started to go wrong for me here. He'd made all the bad stuff happen: my spells blowing up, arguing with people, getting fired. He said it was all him—he was sending bad spells at me and it wrecked everything around me."

River and Anne looked at each other.

"I'll get Solis and Daisuke to do a sweep," Anne said, and left the room.

"If that's true, then there's something here he was using to get to you," River explained. "If there was, they'll find it and destroy it. But I can't believe that Incy would be strong enough to work that kind of magick."

"Not by himself," I said, remembering. I told River everything Incy had said about the mysterious Miss Edna, not that he'd said much. The story of Miss Edna's bar hit me with a new shudder, and I dropped my head into my hands. "I brought all this here," I mumbled, my cheeks heating.

"Yep," said River. She took a piece of my bread and ate it. "But don't flatter yourself that you're the worst, or this is the worst, or that you've set new low records for screwups."

"You're just trying to make me feel better," I said, and ate some soup. It was curried butternut squash, fan-freaking-tastic, the first real food I'd had in days.

River smiled briefly. "Yes. I'm not trying to minimize what happened. It was incredibly bad. Very dark, very evil. Incy is a dangerously dark person and will likely remain so for some time. I'm very sorry for the two deaths he caused. I'm sorry about whatever part you played in this whole fiasco."

Now I felt terrible again. I put down my spoon.

"But you didn't make Incy go dark; you didn't kill those people," River said. "And this, while tragic, is still not as bad as what other people have brought here through the years."

I was dying to know what and who, but figured it would be tacky to ask. "Like what, and who?" I picked up my spoon again.

River gave a small smile. "I won't betray any confidences. But I bet in the coming days, people will feel compelled to share their stories. Some of them will make your hair stand on end. And some of them have had unfortunate, even disastrous, consequences for us here."

Oh, thank God.

You know what I mean.

All the same, I was still ashamed by how badly I had used my time here. And everyone, all the other students, would obviously know what had happened. No, that wouldn't be *at all* embarrassing, to face everyone again. That would be *fabulous*. Ugh.

I ate slowly. River took each of my hands and smoothed some kind of ointiment into the bruises and splinter cuts. It smelled like borage, tea-tree oil, and paraffin and felt immediately soothing. There was still a lot I wanted to know: How had they known I needed help? How had they known where to find me? What happened to Boz's and Katy's bodies? Where was Reyn? Why had he been there?

Suddenly I was exhausted, crushed by the weight of what had happened. Despite what River had said, this was an awful, wretched situation, and I felt tainted.

Except—

"At the end, I had Incy on the ground," I said slowly. "I picked up his sword, the one he'd used to — anyway, I hated him so much, and he'd tried to kill me, and he'd killed my friends, and he'd sent bad stuff at me here. And I wanted to kill him. I pictured myself killing him, pictured him being dead forever."

River sat quietly, listening in that way that made you want to tell her everything. I looked up. "I decided not to kill him. I mean, I wasn't *scared* of killing him. I really wanted him dead right then. But...I had a choice. And I chose not to kill him." I marveled at this for a moment.

I met River's eyes and she nodded, then held up her hand. "Excellent. High five for not killing him." The corners of her mouth widened, and I felt a sudden lightness in my heart. I reached out and patted a high five, for not killing Incy.

I'd been gone a big four days. I'd managed to pack an amazing amount of destruction into that time. But also a lot of understanding and even...growing up, I daresay.

River stood and took the tray. "Go to sleep. I'll see you when you wake up."

She turned off my lamp and left quietly, and for a minute I lay on my bed, trying to start processing everything and failing miserably. And then I slept.

CHAPTER 26

t was almost a week before I manned up
enough to go downstairs. In and ideal
world, I would have stayed in my room
forever, a hermit, and people would have
had to push food into my room through
a slot in the door.

This is not an ideal world. But then you know that.

For days I listened to people passing my door, speaking
quietly. Brynne came to see me and was warmly sympa-
thetic. I was hoping she would tell me about something
truly heinous she had done — besides trying to set someone on fire, which I already knew about — but she just

commiserated and told me to change my hair back, for God's sake.

I realized she was a friend of mine. I hadn't known that before. She spoke the truth to me. She was generous and caring. When I thought back to my old friends, I couldn't remember any of them actually caring about *me*, my feelings, what I was doing, what decisions I was making. Except in how it would affect them. That was the difference. One of the differences.

River and Asher came in one afternoon. "We found what Incy was using," Asher said baldly. "You know the big mirror in the dining room? With the gilt frame? It was spelled. We don't know how he did it. Usually you have to physically touch something to do what he did, but anyway. He was using the mirror as a conduit, and he was sending dark spells aimed at you. We do believe that those spells are why you had such a bad time here the last several weeks."

"The first several weeks were your fault," River said solemnly, and startled me into a smile.

"The mirror has been ritually destroyed," Asher went on. "The room and the house have been smudged and cleansed. Everything should be much better now."

I nodded, hoping he was right.

One day I woke up and there were two suitcases in my room, with some of the clothes I'd bought in Boston.

Later River told me they'd found them in the trunk of Incy's car. He'd brought them with us that night so that if I "disappeared," it would look like I had packed and left on purpose. I went through them and got rid of anything I had worn with Incy and the others. Then I crammed what was left into my wardrobe, next to my flannel shirts and wool sweaters. I wasn't the punk/goth party girl I'd been when I first came here, but I wasn't entirely Hilda the goathered either. I was a little of both.

River fixed my hair with the same spell as last time. I hadn't gotten used to the magenta, even a little bit, and it was a relief to see my white-blond hair again. At least the cut still looked cute, when I remembered to actually comb it while it was still wet.

The bruises and cuts on my wrists healed. The purple finger marks around my throat healed. My emotions were still battered.

It wasn't long before I had the sudden idea to crawl under my bed, pull out the loose piece of molding, and reach inside my hidey-hole. My heart thumped wildly as I felt the scarf, felt the warm metal within. I unwrapped it, looked at it to make sure: It was half of my mother's amulet, my family's tarak-sin. River had put it back, and that made tears start to my eyes again—she trusted me with it. She didn't think I was dark or would use it for dark purposes. And...she'd thought I'd be back to claim it.

Every day I felt Reyn in front of my door, but he never knocked, never asked to come in. I was nowhere near brave enough to actually go over to the door to see him, like a normal person. I longed to talk to him, pictured his face over and over. But I'd been a coward for so long that it was hard to stop.

Finally the powers that be quit bringing me food, to force me to come out. I lasted eight hours. Some bastard started making cookies in the kitchen, and the smell wafted up the stairs and beneath my door. They were probably aiming a fan in my direction to make it worse. I was almost delirious by the time I slunk downstairs to follow the scent.

In the kitchen, Amy and Lorenz were dropping lumps of cookie dough onto baking sheets. Or at least Amy was while Lorenz sat on a stool looking gorgeous.

"Ha!" Amy said to Lorenz when she saw me. "I told you this would work!" She grinned, picked up a still-warm cookie, and tossed it to me. It was Anne's favorite, a cookie made with tofu and almonds and sesame seeds, but it actually tasted really good, and since it was "healthy" I ate about twelve of them for linner.

Lorenz came and kissed both my cheeks, Italian-style.

"Very nice haircut," he said approvingly. "Very chic."

"Thank you." And that was that. These folks were so damn evolved and generous and forgiving, they just took me back into the fold as if I hadn't oh-so-recently been involved in a horrible, deadly, self-induced tragedy. It was hard to bear.

But I couldn't stay here eating cookies forever. In an ideal world, yada yada yada.... So I left the kitchen and saw River in the hallway, in front of the job chart.

"Hi," she said cheerfully. "I'm just adding your name back in. You're up for egg-gathering tomorrow morning!"

"Oh jeezum," I murmured, and she laughed. "Um...do you maybe know where...uh, Reyn is?" I said the last three words really fast, because that would make it totally impossible for her to put two and two together.

"Let's see." River, completely unfazed, checked the accursed chore chart. "He should be in the barn about now."

Yes, because the barn is my favorite freaking place, where I feel the most comfortable, where I'm not tormented by a hundred memories of horses I've loved and lost. Or didn't save.

I sighed.

"Go on," said River.

Reyn was just putting Titus back in his stall. He heard me come in and stood for a second, looking at me. When Titus was in, Reyn murmured something to him, then shut the stall gate. Titus *whuff*ed at him.

"You do have a way with horses," I said, trying to be casual, but my voice cracked and I sounded like a scared little kid, so, crap.

Reyn came closer, looking at me intently as if to make sure I was all right, or real, or something.

"How are you?" he asked.

I almost gave a nervous giggle. Because that's how cool I am. "I'm... actually I don't know," I said. "I'm... glad to be here. But it's hard." I pushed some hair back behind one ear. "It's hard being me. I guess. I know that surprises you."

Reyn nodded—he wasn't even going to pretend to dispute that—then said, "It's no picnic being me, either."

That was number 6,237 of the things that had never occurred to me. "Oh. No, I guess not." I'd never considered how *he* might feel about himself, his past. I guess that goes with the whole "self-absorbed" territory. But yeah, it must be hard to be him, too. Or—*here's a thought*—no doubt everyone has hard times, feels overwhelmed or filled with self-doubt. I'd spent more than four hundred years bemoaning the agony of being immortal, not taking a moment to realize that, immortal or no, life could be a real bitch.

This was a mind-blowing breakthrough that I would examine in greater detail later. For right now, I had questions.

"How did you and River know where I was?"

Reyn pushed open a stall gate to reveal a clean, empty space with several fresh bales of hay in it. The hay reminded me of the night Reyn and I first kissed, up in the hayloft. The night we'd realized our horrible shared history. It seemed a decade ago. Reyn dropped his barn coat on the ground and sat down on the floor. I sat on a bale next to him so I would be taller. A pale shaft of late-afternoon sunlight slanted through the window onto him, throwing his cheekbones into sharper relief, making the lighter streaks in his hair shine. He looked tired. Still a handsome god of a twenty-year-old, maybe twenty-two, but tired.

"We looked for you," he said. "That night. But we felt there was something off, as if you were close by, but we couldn't see you."

"I wasn't actually that far away. I wonder if Incy put a glamour around me or something." It was hard for me to say his name.

Reyn nodded, his jaw tightening with anger at the thought of Incy. "I'm thinking he probably did. Anyway, you were gone, and eventually we couldn't feel you anymore. River and the others, Anne and Solis and Asher, tried scrying spells to find you. With no luck." Reyn let out a deep breath. I regretted *again* that I had put them all through that.

"We tried every day. River contacted people she knew, but no one had seen you, no one had heard anything. Then, finally, a friend of River's called. He'd seen Innocencio in Boston. River had met him, so she knew what he looked like, in general," Reyn explained. Incy had been with me that night in France, in 1929, when I'd met River. "We figured you had to be with him." Reyn had been sounding more and more distant, and now he looked up at me, his eyes cool. "Is he your lover?"

"Incy? No," I said, shaking my head. "Holy moly. Never." *Holy moly* is something cool people say. Along with *jeezum*.

"Is he gay?" Reyn's gaze was very direct, and he just looked so…I don't know—beautiful? He looked like *home* to me. Like my neighbors and friends that I'd known so long ago. I thought about him searching the woods the night I'd left, coming to Boston to find me.

"Not really," I said. "He…plays for both teams. But we've never had that between us." And, everyone? This is an example of the old adage "dodging a bullet." You can see how one might be thankful about dodging this particular bullet.

"You're just friends."

"Yes. Good friends. Best friends." I sighed and felt very old, resting my head on one hand.

"Anyway, so we went to Boston," Reyn went on. "On

the way there—it was already night—we suddenly felt you, felt you very alive. Just...big emotion. River was able to follow that."

That had probably been when I was at Miss Edna's, or maybe right after, when I was arguing with Incy in his car.

"Then you suddenly felt dead." Reyn swallowed and picked at some threads on the worn knee of his jeans. What that man did for a pair of jeans should be bottled and sold. I blinked and focused on what he was saying. "We saw your scarf by the road, soaked with rain. I knew you would never have let it go, not while you were breathing. So we thought the worst. But River said, 'Let's go get her body at least.' So we kept following whatever sense of you we could get."

"You went to all that trouble just for my *body*," I said, amazed and so grateful.

Reyn looked up, irritation on his face. "Yeah. We were going to have you stuffed, as an example to future students."

I grinned. "You could put me on wheels, move me from room to room."

Reyn nodded drily. "We ended up outside that warehouse—we'd driven past it a couple times. River thought it had probably been cloaked in a concealment spell. We finally saw flickering lights in the upstairs windows and started trying to open the loading-dock door.

Then we felt this huge blast of magick, really strong, big power." He shook his head, remembering. "We knew it was you. It felt like you. It was amazing."

My cheeks heated at the wonder and admiration in his voice. I remembered the mingled ecstasy and pain, the lightning-strike feeling of setting my white dove free. I wanted to feel that again. But with more training and less nosebleed.

He shrugged. "And we went in to get you."

I swallowed. Getting the next words out would be like eating nails. "I...appreciate it so much, your coming to find me. To save me, if necessary. Or to retrieve what was left."

Reyn looked at me evenly. "Of course. We had no choice. You were one of River's students."

"Ew," I said, hurt. "That feels great. Thanks."

Reyn pushed his hand through his hair. "That's not what I meant."

"No? Then what did you mean?" I decided to shine a flashlight on this skeleton. "Okay, River had to come after one of her students. Fine. But what about *you*? Why were *you* there? Just because you're big and tough and could take someone out?" There. Pinned him like a bug.

"No," he said, frowning. "Quit being so prickly. I went because what there is between me and you is not finished yet." The honesty that I'd demanded disarmed me. I looked into his eyes, so deeply golden and slightly slanted and so smart, so knowledgeable, so experienced.

I nodded. I didn't have time to pretend I didn't know what he meant. I held my breath; this was where he would sweep me up into his arms and we would make out like crazed high schoolers. I started to feel a delicious Reyn + hay = happiness anticipation.

"Wait here, " he said, and suddenly got up and left the stall. I stared after him. Was he chickening out *now*? But he was back in less than a minute with something in his hands. Something kind of white and larval. He knelt in the hay and showed me: It was the runt puppy from Molly's litter.

"Hmm," I said unenthusiastically.

The puppy moved in his hands, turning over and yawning, stretching its long, straight legs out. I hadn't seen it since the night it had been born, and it was just as uncute and unchunky as before.

"She's mine," Reyn said, and my eyes widened at his look of pride and love. I'd never seen that on him before, and it was incredible to see him seem younger and happier. It was like taking the perfect man and making him inexplicably even perfecter. Fine—*more perfect*. My jaw almost dropped open, and I sat there, mesmerized.

He drew a gentle finger down the puppy's skinny side. It yawned again, opening its small muzzle to show perfect tiny puppy teeth. Then it turned its head and blinked at me.

"Its eyes are open." And its ears were bigger and floppier, I realized.

"It's a she," Reyn corrected mildly. "Her name is Dúfa."

I stared at him.

"Dove," he said helpfully.

"Yes, I speak Old Norse," I said pointedly. I looked down at the puppy again, this ugly white runt that Reyn had adopted and loved and named Dove.

"Huh," I said, marveling at all the weird twists and turns my life had taken, especially in the last three months. "Well, she's . . . quite something."

Reyn smiled at her. "Yes." He extended his glowy smile to me, making me feel a little faint, and then rose to return the puppy to Molly, who had started whining. He was back before I had stopped reeling at the mysteries of life, and he sat down again, closer to me. Slowly he reached out and put his hand over mine. The touch was warm and electric, and I tried not to hyperventilate. "You can share her if you want."

That was what undid me. I didn't want a dog; I never wanted to have another dog as long as I lived. Dúfa was only going to grow old and die, leaving us with yet another scar on our hearts.

It was . . . so terrifying. I mean, not in the same way as

Incy trying to suck my power out and kill me but still terrifying in its own way.

I felt my fingers curl around Reyn's.

"Reyn?" I said.

He looked at me.

"What name were you born with?" Something intensely personal that not a lot of immortals ran around blabbing to each other. I knew he was the son of Erik the Bloodletter. He knew I was the daughter of Úlfur the Wolf. But who had he once been, before he'd been part of my family's destruction?

"Eileif," he said. Ay-liff. "Eileif Eriksson."

It was Old Norse also, which made sense, of course. I recognized the roots of the name: The *Ei* part meant "alone." The *leif* part meant "inheritance" or "legacy." Yeah, that wasn't a burden to hang on some kid. Jeez.

"Eileif," I said, trying to picture this fierce man as a laughing child with sunlit hair and a mischievous look.

"Yeah." He seemed bemused, maybe remembering himself back then as well. "What was your birth name?"

"I . . . my name was Lilja."

"Leel-ya," he repeated. "Lily." He smiled.

I nodded.

"Kiss me, Lilja," he said softly.

"You kiss me, Eileif," I whispered. And then our arms

were around each other and we were kissing as if we'd been apart for centuries. To me he felt as solid as a cliff in Iceland. Before this I would have said I wasn't a very physical person—not snuggly, not demonstrative, not affectionate. Not in centuries. But all I wanted at that moment was to be enveloped in Reyn's warmth.

I squirmed to get closer to him and he fell backward onto the hay, pulling me with him. He rolled, holding me in place with one hand, and then his weight was on me, comforting me, exciting me, welcoming me home. We kissed again and again, unable to get enough of each other, pressing ourselves together as tightly as we could, considering that we were still fully dressed in a relatively public barn. My hands tangled in his hair as he kissed my eyelids, my forehead, my cheeks, my chin, my nose. I laughed because it tickled, and opened my eyes to see him smiling down at me. I pulled his head back to me and found his mouth, remembering how much I had wanted to see him, to talk to him, while I was gone.

This was a choice I was making. I thought it was a good choice. I wasn't letting myself get swept away by what Reyn or anyone else wanted.

"I want this," I murmured against his lips. He drew back, breathing hard, his eyes glittering. "I want you."

"I want you, too," he murmured, kissing me again, pushing one knee between mine. And then my mind whirled with sensations and emotions and the drunk feeling of being completely caught up in him, desperate to be with him, hungry for him, his touch. It was as if I had summoned magick with our kisses—that same intense white light filling my chest, the burst of almost painful joy, the feelings of both power and curiosity. This passion was very strong magick.

Reyn pulled away again. His breathing was fast and shallow, lips red, amber-colored eyes focused like a laser on my face.

"What are you thinking about?" I asked. I felt flushed and heavy, weighted down by desire and emotion. I hadn't thought I would ever feel this way. Hadn't wanted to. But Reyn was obliterating my feelings of caution and reluctance.

"I was thinking that this wasn't going to be easy," he said, wariness coming back into his eyes. He was waiting for me to push him away and change my mind, like I'd always done before. I put the palm of my hand flat against his jaw, memorizing the shape of his face, the way his bones felt, the slight bit of beard that was scratching my cheeks.

"No," I agreed. "Given how impossible you are."

His eyes flared. "Me? You're the one who doesn't—"

I interrupted him. "But I want to try."

Surprise, residual caution, and possibly relief crossed

his face in minuscule alterations of gorgeous Viking land-scape.

"You do?" His voice was rough and made the inside of my chest flutter.

"I do."

He smiled, slowly and beautifully, then became solemn again. He rose up to his knees and reached for his coat, then fished around in one pocket and drew out a crumpled red bandanna.

"I was going to give this to you before you left," he said. "I've been holding it for you. But it's yours."

I looked into his eyes but got no clues. He pushed the wad of cloth into my hand. As soon as I touched it, I frowned. No…surely not. It was impossible.

Slowly I unwrapped the wrinkled bandanna. When I saw what was inside, my mouth opened, but I had no words. With a shaking hand I traced the ancient pattern that I hadn't seen since the night my family had died, 449 years ago. The pattern on the other half of my mother's amulet.

I swallowed, my throat aching. "I thought—wasn't it destroyed?" My voice came out as a reedy whisper.

"No. Everything around it was destroyed. But not it, and not me."

I reached out my other hand and slowly unbuttoned the top buttons of Reyn's flannel shirt, then pushed my fingers inside to touch his skin. On his chest, above his heart, I felt the raised scar that mirrored this half of the amulet.

"It exploded and flew at me, burning through my shirt into my skin," Reyn said. "The cloth was seared right into my flesh—I had to pick it out with a knife."

I winced.

"Everything around me had turned to ash. My father. My two remaining brothers. My father's men. The biggest thing I found was a bit of my father's leg bone. I picked it up, and it crumbled into powder in my hand."

His father had been trying to use magick that wasn't his.

Reyn looked at the amulet. "It wasn't ours to take or use. But afterward I looked for it, and I found it by the side of the peat field. I picked it up—didn't even realize it was broken. I hadn't seen it before. But I kept it. Always kept it with me."

"Why?" It seemed like it would just be a devastating reminder.

Reyn's smile was somewhat bitter. "To remind me— not to want too much."

I breathed in, tracing the symbols again with my fingers, flashing back to being a small child sitting on my mother's lap, playing with her necklace. I would wrap her long blond braid around it, try to look through the moonstone, try to memorize the symbols, which I didn't understand.

"When I realized who you were, I knew I would give it back to you. It shouldn't have been taken from your family in the first place. Somehow I hoped that returning it would help... restore the balance."

I was overwhelmed with this gift, the one thing I would have desired above all else, from the one person I had desired in... forever.

"Of course, first I had to make sure you weren't evil," he said matter-of-factly. "But now—now I know you should have it."

"Because I made out with you?" My voice was shaking.

"Yes. That's why." Reyn rolled his eyes.

Quit hiding, Nastasya. Just—quit. "I can't really believe it."

Reyn looked a bit like he couldn't believe it either.

"It's a princely gift," I said, knowing he would get the archaic reference. Handy that he was as old as I was—I wouldn't have to explain things all the time.

"I give it to you," he said formally.

Plus his heart. He had offered me that as well. I knew he had. And, apparently, part of a puppy.

I cradled the amulet in my hand, hardly able to wait until I could fit it against the half River had returned to me. Then I thought of something. I should have realized it weeks and weeks ago, but then of course I'm fairly blind and stupid sometimes.

I reached into my pants pocket. My moonstone was there, as always. It had helped me fight Incy in that warehouse, and I would never be without it. I pulled it out and held it up to the amulet. It wasn't shaped and had been polished only by my hands. But...it would fit beautifully between the two halves. Just like when my mother had it.

"My family's tarak-sin will be whole again." For the first time in four centuries, I would have both pieces of my shattered life, my broken childhood. And when the amulet was made whole and set with my moonstone, it would enable me to wield incredible power: the power of the House of Úlfur. I would be my mother's daughter, my father's heir. Lilja af Úlfur. Lilja, daughter of Úlfur.

Reyn traced the rune othala on my leg. Birthright.

"Thank you, Eileif," I said. I felt almost unbearably happy, frighteningly happy. But I wasn't going to run from it. Not this time.

Reyn took my hand and kissed my knuckles. "It belongs to you, Lilja. I was only holding it for you."

It was a huge responsibility. I needed help learning what I needed to know, how to use it, how to make magick with it.

I held it in one hand, that hand against my chest.

Reyn clasped my other hand, and we sat close together, leaning against a bale of hay, quiet and full of thoughts and memories.

I was Lilja af Úlfur: the Tähti daughter of Terävä parents. My legacy would be different.

Be sure to read the next
book in the

IMMORTAL
BELOVED

trilogy

available
January 2013